Helen reached  she said to Conr Detective Griersor you have the cop s......

"We can get it."

Helen reached into her pocket and pulled out a gun. "I mean the detective bureau. Ask for Grierson, if not him, see if Wilkerson's around. Tell them where I am and that I went in after a suspect in the Orson slaying."

"If I wait so long, no telling what's going to happen. What if he gets the advantage over you? Why don't you just call them and wait for them there?"

"You want information before the cops start talking to him or not?"

By this time, the man had entered the house, shut the door and turned on a couple of lights. Helen could imagine him cracking open a beer, grabbing some sort of frozen dinner out of the freezer and getting ready to plop himself down to watch a game. If she was lucky, she'd catch him fat, happy, and stupid.

"You going to do anything illegal in there?" Conroy asked.

Helen grinned as she opened the door. "Don't worry, counselor. Nothing that anyone's going to complain about."

She shut the door, put the phone in her pocket and headed across the street.

Other books by Kevin R. Doyle

The Group
When You Have to Go There

And the Devil Walks Away

by

Kevin R. Doyle

And the Devil Walks Away

Cover Art by *Debbie Taylor*

The Wild Rose Press, Inc.
PO Box 708
Adams Basin, NY 14410-0708
Visit us at www.thewildrosepress.com

Publishing History
First Edition, 2021
Trade Paperback ISBN 978-1-5092-3937-5
Digital ISBN 978-1-5092-3938-2

Previously Published: MuseItUp Publishing, 2020
Published in the United States of America

Dedication

To Mike P. Former dean, who did the best he could in the worst of times. All the efforts were appreciated.

PROLOGUE

Thursday, Sept. 19th

A HALF-ROTTED STAIR riser creaked under Helen Lipscomb's foot, nearly snapping in two and sending a crackling sound throughout the stairwell. She paused, holding her breath and straining to listen for any indication someone had heard her. After a minute went by, she began breathing again and, even more carefully this time, resumed creeping upward.

She had no doubt several of the apartments in the building were occupied, but in this part of Kansas City it was probably common for people to sleep until well in the afternoon, in most cases not crawling out of their beds until the sun dipped below the horizon. And anyone who did happen to be awake no doubt followed the dictum that kept most inner-city residents alive: if it's not your business, ignore it.

After several more seconds of cautious treading, Helen made it out of the stairwell and to the door of the targeted apartment. The walls practically sagged with the baked-in smells of overcooked food, human waste, despair and just plain old rot. The front door to 5B looked about as scabby and dented in as most of the others she'd passed. Helen figured the person residing behind the eyesore liked it that way.

Less notice from anyone.

1

Fewer prying eyes.

She paused to wipe sweat off her forehead. Climbing five flights of stairs wasn't the main problem, as she'd always kept herself in good shape. But doing so on a mid-September day, with the old building lacking any modern ventilation, was another matter.

The urge to remove the light cotton jacket was strong, but she kept it on. No sense announcing to anyone who happened to walk by that she was armed.

Helen only hoped the guy was home, that the address she'd found in Toni's house was legit. Or at least it meant what Helen thought it did.

She proceeded cautiously. With no one to observe, Helen crept up to the door, nestling as close as possible, and lightly placed an ear against it. The panel itself was just as grimy and dirt-smeared as all the other doors in this building.

She waited several seconds but could detect nothing. True, the building looked as if it had been built eighty or ninety years ago, and back then doors and walls came with a solidity modern construction lacked, but one could easily imagine that over time various breeds of termites, rats and other burrowing animals had worn away at the structure. Even so, hearing no signs of life, let alone movement, Helen took a small leather bag out of her jacket pocket and began working on the lock, praying the door had never been outfitted with a dead bolt.

Two years earlier, she would have done almost anything rather than illegally enter a suspect's residence. Back then, she'd held almost a reverence for the system, even when it got in the way. That reverence, however, along with several other rock-ribbed principles, had vanished at some point in the last twenty-four months.

After several minutes of effort, not being an expert picklock after all, the door swung open. Pausing again to wipe sweat off her forehead, Helen's hands felt slick, slightly grimy. The first order of business once back at the hotel would be a long, hot shower.

Still not entirely sure the apartment was vacant, Helen eased the door open. She leaned forward and glanced around the edge, holding her breath against any creaking hinges or other slight disturbance.

Her nose crinkled. The various effluvia from the hallway were even stronger here. Maybe because of the shut, bolted windows, or maybe the tenant was a lousier housekeeper than most bachelors. Either way, she frowned at the assaulting stenches mingling in the living room. Then she took another breath, and a much more prevalent odor hit her.

Helen's stomach clenched. Her hands trembled.

The living room contained only one piece of furniture: a ratty, lime green sofa with the springs poking through the bottom. Off to the side of the sofa lay a couple of cotton-ticking mattresses (for overnight guests?) splotched with yellow, green and brown smears. Helen instantly shut her mind off from wondering what the stains came from. A battered, boxwood end table held a TV at least twenty years old.

That lingering odor she'd encountered called out to her.

Helen would have loved to grab a Kleenex, tear it in half and use them to block out the smells. Unfortunately, unsure of exactly what awaited her, she'd left her purse in the trunk of the rental car in a parking garage about five blocks away. Therefore, with no choice but to open her mouth wider and breathe through it, she turned to the right and headed down the apartment's single hallway.

The first door to the right was closed, though not all the way shut. Helen nudged it with a foot, waited a second, then opened the door all the way and walked in, using her elbow to click on the light switch.

A filth-ridden bathroom. The urine-stained toilet seat was up; rust stains marred the porcelain of the curtain-less bathtub; and black, oily smears speckled the sink and faucet.

The room was small enough to see no one was hiding in there. Even the yellow, mildewed shower curtain hung half off its rod, clearly indicating no one hiding in the squalid tub. Helen elbowed the light off, then stepped back in the hall and moved to the door opposite the bathroom.

Going through the same cautious procedure in the next room, she didn't bother with the light switch. As the door creaked open, it was obvious this was the apartment's single bedroom. And even before crossing the threshold, her nose indicated she'd discovered the object of her search.

The stench of voided bowels and kidneys mixed with the smell of flesh, heated in the unventilated room.

It wasn't the fulsome odor it would eventually become, but it was enough for someone like Helen, attuned through years of experience to the sensations of death, to assume she'd reached the end of the line.

Or at least, of this part of it.

She was only half right.

She found what she'd expected to, but not who.

Dim, late morning light filtered its way through the half-opened blinds, providing enough illumination to make out the still, naked form stretched across the cheap, fold-out bed, and enough for Helen, even from the doorway, to recognize it as female.

She knew the truth now, but had to move closer to see for herself. When she did so, Helen struggled not to look away from the body.

She'd been with this woman just a few short hours before, had sat and talked with her, even semi-argued with her. They'd made a deal, practically shook hands on it, but it looked as if the dead woman had tried to renege on that deal.

"Did he make you a better offer?" Helen asked the room. "And why did you even for a minute think he'd honor it?"

The final work had been done with either hands or some sort of strap, the bulging eyes and distended tongue showed that, but there had been a fight here, for sure. The woman's waist was a mess of ugly splotches, black, blue and green. Scratches ran across the face and one arm rested at such an angle as to suggest a break. Even now, only a few hours into the process, the eyes, though filmed over, told a story of struggle, fear, and ultimately, surrender to the inevitable.

Okay, then. Not the intended person she'd come here to question.

Clearly, Helen's job had just become a whole lot more complicated.

Helen hesitated turning on the bedroom light, not wanting to disturb the scene in any way but needing more light if only to check if any life remained in the woman's body. Wasted effort, perhaps, but instructors had drilled into her years ago that you had to make sure.

A slight step sounded behind her. Helen whirled to

glimpse a burly male form hurtling down the hall toward her. Grimacing, she realized the front door was left hanging open, a sure giveaway someone had entered the apartment. Helen dug into her jacket pocket, but the man came on too fast and barreled into her before she could pull out the handgun nestled there.

With his weight pushing forward, the two of them staggered back into a corner, Helen's head cracking against the wall. Glancing down, she caught sight of a glint of silver in the room's weak light. Before any possible reaction, a thin, burning line arced across her abdomen.

Helen gasped at the pain but worked to keep focused on the business at hand. With every ounce of energy left, she pulled her weapon out and swung it in a roundhouse motion against the side of the assailant's head.

The man grunted and shuffled backward. Inhaling a deep breath, curbing pulsating pain, she tried to make out his features: long, greasy, black hair that covered most of his face. With the stranger now framed in the doorway, Helen had the microsecond necessary to level her weapon, but before she could do more he whipped back out of the room and pounded down the hall.

Helen staggered into the hall, ready to pursue, but the now-searing wound changed her mind. She didn't want to take a chance on losing any more blood than necessary and wasn't sure how agile she'd be in a chase anyway.

With the stranger heading down the stairs and out of the building, she turned back to the corpse lying on the bed. After the scuffle with the unknown assailant, Helen figured merely turning on the light wouldn't contaminate the crime scene any more than it already had been, so she used an elbow to flick the switch. The pasty, 25-watt bulb overhead flickering on, provided a good look at the body.

Oh yeah, it was really in the fan now.

Moving out of the room and into the once-again empty apartment, Helen stepped out into the hall and dug her cell phone out of the little holster attached to her belt, kept there so it wouldn't be even momentarily lost in such encounters as she'd just had.

It was a habit left over from former days as a legitimate detective, and for a moment she had to close her eyes, a physical manifestation of shutting out recollections from the past. It had been two years since she'd come upon a dead victim, or fought with a suspect. The flood of memories that suddenly surged through overwhelmed her.

She considered, briefly, whether her employer would approve of what she planned to do next, then decided it didn't much matter. Even though she'd left that former life far behind, Helen still felt some obligation to the brotherhood she'd once been a part of.

Helen walked through the front room, then out of the apartment, before dialing 911.

PART I
NEBRASKA DEATH ROW

CHAPTER 1

Two weeks earlier, Thursday Sept. 5th

THE QUALMS BEGAN as soon as Helen came within sight of the prison. She'd felt fine for most of the trip. Leaving Denver the day before, heading west on I-80 to cross into Nebraska, then a straight shot across nearly the entire state, mile after mile of flat land. For most of the duration, she'd managed to convince herself it was just a job, like any other she'd taken in the last few years. Just another step on her new life path, wherever the hell it may be heading.

For the last hour or so, the smooth motion of the car and lack of distracting sights heading east on Highway 50 had lulled her into a sort of half awareness. But now, a couple of miles off in the distance, a grayish, irregular lump materialized from the plain's horizon. Her chest tightened. Hands clenched the steering wheel harder. Pulling up to the front gates, she wiped both hands on her slacks. While this wasn't the first prison she'd entered, as Helen pulled up to the first of the gates, this experience would be unlike any other.

The hell of it was that she'd expected the long drive to calm her down. When Conroy had first reached out, he'd offered to allow her to fly most of the way. Denver to Omaha, then drive in the rest of the way. Conroy had even mentioned first class, something Helen had never experienced.

Without hesitation, she turned him down flat. Airplanes meant confinement and airports meant crowds, and while Helen didn't consider herself claustrophobic by any means, over the last few years she'd done everything to keep herself cocooned away from other people, squeezed into a self-imposed bubble of reality.

She didn't have any overarching neuroses or anything like that. Quite frequently there would be interaction with society on both a micro and macro level. It was just that she preferred not to be around people if unnecessary.

Thus, while she, somewhat tentatively, accepted Conroy's offer to meet in Nebraska, she came down firmly on the side of driving.

Now here she was, after all that delicious solitude, staring at the facility, her stressors amping up.

From the outside, though, about what she'd expected. More of the flatness she'd just spent hours driving across, tan buildings spread out across the acreage and the standard tall, razorwire-topped fencing. A large, red-brick marker at the front of the institution announced itself as the Redding State Correctional Facility. Yeah, so far it all looked about as expected, but she knew, way deep down, that it wasn't the outward façade that brought about her nervousness.

It was what awaited her inside.

As she pulled the rented Taurus up to the first checkpoint and rolled down the window, an instinctive fight-or-flight response kicked in, flooding her system with adrenaline. In an instant, she wanted to be anywhere else in the world but here, entering through these gates.

On the positive side, this new set of nerves wasn't related to an overall depression but came more from memories of the past.

She'd had similar sensations before, the few times in her former career when she'd had to enter a facility to re-interview prisoners as potential witnesses or even barter for information in some ongoing case, and each time it amazed her how strong the urge to run swept over her.

And just imagine, I can turn around and get out of here at any time. What must it feel like for those who have no hope of leaving?

She drove the car up to the pillbox where a guard waited, the first hurdle for visitors to cross, and rolled the window down as the man leaned out, pale tan uniform shirt stretched tight across a weight-lifter's upper body.

"Helen Lipscomb," she said, holding out her driver's license. "I'm working with Gordon Conroy."

The guard frowned at that, but Helen had expected as much. He peered at her ID, then at her, then back at the card. A thought formed in her mind that any minute he might start moving his lips to read the name on the card.

Cut it out, she scolded herself. Not everyone who wears a uniform is a doofus.

And who are you to judge? At least the man's gainfully employed.

The guard now consulted a computer screen inside his booth. Sliding the glass window shut, he picked up a phone and made a quick call, speaking into the phone and nodding his head a couple of times, occasionally flicking a glance in her direction.

Helen mentally forced herself not to drum her

fingers on the steering wheel.

A minute later he opened the window, reached out and handed her driver's license back.

"Good enough, ma'am," he said, as though they were the best of friends. "When you get through the gates, just follow the road and it will take you to the front entrance. Someone will be there to greet you."

"Has Mr. Conroy arrived yet?" she asked.

The guard gave the car a once over. She was sure he noticed the rental tag on the Taurus, no doubt wondering why someone working for the great Conroy couldn't afford something a tad bit classier.

If he only knew how low her bank account really was, he'd be even more puzzled.

"I can't speak to that, ma'am. Just drive around to the entrance and they'll take care of you."

Helen considered saying something sarcastic, then forced herself to remember back when she wore a uniform. As a young cop, it seemed some days as if everyone she'd met wanted to make a snide comment, throw a rude gesture, or just shoulder past her in a restaurant. She couldn't bring herself to make this young man's life miserable, even for a moment, just because her own was falling apart all around her.

Instead, she thanked him, waited for the gate to rise, then shifted out of neutral and headed in, following his directions. She hoped, but couldn't assume, that Conroy had arrived ahead of her. One of the most sought-after criminal lawyers in the Midwest, the man's arrival could have been delayed for any one of a dozen reasons.

But once coasting past the red brick marker formally announcing the prison, she breathed a sigh of relief. Conroy stood outside waiting for her. She'd never seen him outside of pictures on news sites and brief television interviews, but recognized him right away.

Gordon Conroy was, Helen knew, fifty-eight years old but could have easily passed for ten years younger. Red-haired as a young man, he now sported an even mixture of rust and silver. Just under six feet tall and with a physique that, even in a business suit and jacket, practically screamed daily racquetball and swimming sessions, he stood with an easy, almost swaggering confidence.

Getting out of the Taurus and walking up to the lawyer, Helen's confidence level wavered. Not that she couldn't handle Conroy, or his client as far as that went. More as if she were coming close to crossing a line that, even in the turmoil of her recent life, she'd managed to avoid.

Conroy had called two nights ago, tracking her down after finishing the Denver job, and presented his proposition. Her instinct, to turn him down flat, had mollified somewhat when he mentioned the salary his client had proposed paying her. Even so, she'd been inclined to say no, and attorney that he was, he had a counteroffer ready.

"Come out to meet him," Conroy had urged. "Just show up and listen to what he has to say. Five thousand dollars for a day's travel and an hour of your time. If your answer is still no, I'll write you a check and drive you to the airport myself, throwing in a plane ticket to wherever you want to go in the country. So how about it?"

Wherever she wanted to go? For most people with all the time in the world on their hands, that would have clinched the deal.

But most people have somewhere they want to go,

or at least a direction for their lives. Helen Lipscomb, former cop, former homicide detective and current scapegoat for the powers that be, had nowhere and no one to go to.

Even so, the idea of picking up five thousand dollars, while at the same time avoiding crossing that uncrossable line, proved too tempting. She'd taken Conroy up on his deal.

Now here she was, forty-six hours later, preparing to do something she'd never done in her life.

Enter a prison as a civilian, rather than a cop.

She just hoped she would come out the same way.

CHAPTER 2

DESPITE CONROY ACTING as an attorney visiting his client, or maybe because of that, they had to undergo an intense security screen to get in. The penitentiary was classified as Medium/Maximum security, and the prisoner they needed to see definitely fell on the Maximum end of the spectrum. More than that, this particular facility also held Nebraska's only Death Row, which was why it served as Leo Benson's home.

Even so, the various layers of the screening process merely to get inside, let alone cleared to visit with Benson, seemed a bit much and definitely beyond Helen's previous experience. Her nervousness only increased the farther into the bowels of the building they went.

"You okay?" Conroy asked as they finally sat alone in a small anteroom.

Helen offered a weak smile. "Been a while since I've been around this much officialdom," she said.

"It shows." The lawyer gave her a thorough once over.

If pride existed, Helen would have blushed. As it was, having no clue what the lawyer had been expecting but doubting that it was the ratty jeans, scuffed sneakers and faded Nirvana tee-shirt she was wearing, she let the remark slide. She considered vouching some sort of explanation for her attire, then decided the hell with it. If he and his sleazeball client really wanted to hire her, her wardrobe wouldn't deter them. If it did, so be it.

Conroy gave her a somewhat paternal pat on the leg. "I admit it's a bit much, but you've got to remember the problems they had here a while back."

Helen nodded. A few years back, this same institution had caught the nation's attention, and not in a good way. One night, through some electrical, mechanical or human glitch, several of the cell doors in the maximum-security wing had suddenly buzzed open, and before anyone could do anything, hardened, vicious prisoners were roaming free on their floor. The ensuing riot and fire caused severe damage from which the institution was still recovering.

As they'd gone through the required check-in procedure, an idle comment from one of the guards revealed their visit had been scheduled for a couple of weeks.

"Two weeks ago?" she now asked Conroy.

"'Scuse me?" The lawyer looked up from some papers he'd pulled from his briefcase.

"You've had this appointment arranged for that long? How were you so sure? What would you have done if I'd said no?"

The lawyer took a long, thoughtful look around the room, which looked to have been furnished somewhere around the middle of the twentieth century. They sat at a gunmetal gray table, ringed by six metal chairs with torn green Naugahyde backs, and flanked by four ecru-colored walls. Close inspection of the walls showed numerous cigarette burns at all angles, paralleled by similar burns in the black and white checked floor.

In response to Helen's question, Conroy merely smiled and went back to checking over his documents. A little light went on in her brain.

"I'm not the only person you approached, right? You made the appointment for this meeting between you, Benson, and some third party, the third party to be determined at a later time, right?"

The lawyer gave a slight nod and put the papers back in his case. Snapping the lid shut, he faced Helen directly.

"Correct, Miss Lipscomb. To be truthful, I prepared a list of four people, three of whom came highly recommended, and one who didn't. You were my first choice, but I had the others ready as backups."

"And let me guess, I was the one not highly recommended, right?"

Conroy leaned back in his chair. "You're sharp, lady. Yes. Obviously, I had you thoroughly checked out. Mr. Benson, after all, requires nothing but absolute perfection, as I'm sure you've heard. The reports on you were disheartening, to say the least."

Helen frowned. "So then why me as your main choice? If what you heard was so bad, why go to the expense of paying me so much for my time, even if I turn you down? And by the way, how about we firm up the whole payment thing before this goes any further."

Smiling, the lawyer reached into his jacket pocket and pulled out a sealed, bulging envelope. He slid it across the table to Helen.

"Actually, everything I heard about you confirmed you were the right person for the job. Anyone who can so piss off the members of the power structure is exactly who I need. Even at that, this will be one hell of an uphill battle. Besides, I wasn't the one who made the final choice. That was up to our client."

Helen frowned. "He's not our client yet, Mr. Conroy. I haven't agreed to anything except the sitdown."

"My apologies. I was speaking rather informally."

"Somehow, I doubt you do hardly anything informally, at least while you're on the job."

Conroy glanced around the room, then pulled his sleeve back and glanced at his Omega watch, frowning.

"And I must say," he said, "I don't care much for this kind of petty gamesmanship from the officials here."

Helen, rifling through the envelope, ignored him. There was plenty of material there, and she wondered at it being in paper form. The whole thing could have been sent to her phone much more easily. Glancing up at Conroy, she raised an eyebrow.

"Mr. Benson is suspicious of most technology. Unusual for a man of his wealth, but there you have it."

"You mean he runs his companies like back in the Dark Ages?" Helen asked.

Conroy smiled and removed an invisible piece of line from his pant leg. "Not really. He has more than capable people running things for him, and he can use a laptop with the best of them. But when it comes to—personal—matters, he prefers old-fashioned paper."

"And old-fashioned other things, as well," Helen remarked.

Conroy frowned momentarily, then went back to a blank expression. "You're referring to his killing method, no doubt."

Helen nodded. "Strangling is about as simple and brutal as you can get. But I'm kind of surprised to hear

20

you say it so bluntly."

"Why not?" Another flick of his fingers. "There's nothing to be gained by avoiding the obvious. He was found guilty of murders in two states."

"And suspected of many more," Helen pointed out. "What about appeals? I assume you're working on those."

"Not for what they've already convicted him of. The authorities both here and in Colorado were thorough enough when they prepared their cases. Plus, they had plenty of help from the Justice Department, who also wants a bite out of our boy. Sure, I could come up with half a dozen Hail Mary's, but Mr. Benson has turned down that idea in favor of pursuing a different angle."

Now Helen stared at the attorney, her brain working faster than it had in nearly two years. She replayed Conroy's last words in her head.

"So what are you appealing," she asked, "if not his convictions?"

Conroy glanced at his watch again. "Actually, we're not technically taking anything through the appellate process, though we are trying to work out something of a bargain, so to speak."

Helen nodded, convinced that she was finally on track with what Conroy was saying, if not with her role in it.

"His death sentences," she said. "That's what you're working on."

Conroy smiled. It seemed like his first genuine expression since he and Helen had met.

"Not bad, Miss Lipscomb. Not bad at all. And quite correct. Mr. Benson and I are in the midst of negotiating for a reduction in his sentences."

Helen tensed up. Old cop instincts, dormant since the day she'd walked out on the badge, flared up.

"Then why negotiate? Why not just go the appeal route? Between your reputation and your client's money, you could drag the whole thing out until Benson dies of old age."

"That's precisely why not."

"Huh?" The beginnings of a headache developed as she tried to follow the lawyer's logic.

"Every day that we'd spend in motions, hearings, or actual trial, were we to get so lucky, would be one extra day that Mr. Benson's part of the news. Do you have any idea what the publicity of the last few years has done to his various companies' stock valuations? Not to mention their overall bottom line?"

"I get it," Helen said, leaning back in the chair. "Don't want the entire thing to go down the rabbit hole, right?"

"Exactly."

"You're not going to try to get him out at some point, are you?" she asked.

"I would if I could," Conroy said, "and please don't look so shocked. You know how the game's played as well as anyone. Probably better than most. It's my job to get my client the best deal I can. Even so," he shook his head, "some sort of freedom, any certain number of years, would be too much even for me to pull off. No, Leo Benson, minus all his billions of dollars, is going to spend the rest of his life, however long that may be, in either this prison or one very similar."

"So what you're after is getting rid of the death penalty," Helen said.

Conroy nodded. "Both here and, if it ever gets to

that, in Colorado. And that's where you come in."

"From what I understand, the governor in Colorado has put a stay on the process," Helen said.

"He has," Conroy agreed. "But it would only take one election for that situation to revert. We're going for a complete exception to the entire possibility."

Helen's gut tightened up even more. Palms dampened all over again. The urge to get up and walk away, just leave the prison and keep on driving down the road, swept over her.

But the practical side within kept her in check. After all, where would she go? Precious few funds were left to get anywhere. At the very least, she didn't have much choice but to see this meeting through to the end although she'd already decided that, whatever it entailed, she wouldn't be working for Leo Benson.

"And just how do you intend to get them to commute his sentences," she asked. "Considering the number of victims, it's damned near mandatory."

"As I said, that's what we need you for."

She frowned. "But for what? I'm not a lawyer, and I wouldn't make a good character witness even if I wanted to. What exactly do the two of you expect me to do?"

"I'd rather our client explain that himself," Conroy said. "He's in a much better position to—"

"Uh, uh." Helen placed an extra layer of steel into her voice. She didn't quite employ the same tone she'd used in the past when trying to dominate perps but came pretty close. "Either you give me something concrete right now or I'm heading out the door. And you can keep your damned contingency check."

She was bluffing, but hoped enough of the old

instincts remained to pull it off.

Conroy sighed, glanced down at the table, then back up to Helen. He shrugged, and a look almost of relief swept over his face.

"All our sources weren't kidding when they said you were tough, were they? Okay, Detective…" Helen noted that he didn't use her former title in any derisive way, but with a tone almost of respect. "…here's the lowdown."

But before the lawyer could say anymore, a buzzing came from outside the room, and the green-painted steel door swung partway open. Helen glanced over as Leo Benson, billionaire and convicted murderer of three young women, walked into the room.

CHAPTER 3

THREE CORRECTIONS OFFICERS, two men and a woman, all wearing the slit-eyed, wary look Helen had seen so many times before, escorted the prisoner. The men held onto an elbow on each side and the woman stayed about three paces behind.

A fifth man walked behind the officers. About fifty, wearing a brown suit and an ugly frown, Helen pegged him as Warden Richard Summers. Not idle guesswork on her part. Before taking up Conroy on his offer to drive out here, Helen had gone online and absorbed as much information about the prison as possible.

But she spared barely a glance at the other four before centering her attention on Leo Benson. Somewhere in his mid-fifties, with a badly receding hairline and thin frame, he walked with a bit of a stoop, courtesy of the shackles around his ankles, which accentuated, rather than concealed, a slight, though hard, pot belly. He wore standard blue prison-issue clothing and thick-lensed glasses that gave his eyes a hint of an owlish look.

Barely looking at either Helen or Conroy, the prisoner sat at the one remaining chair at the table, straightened up and placed his arms straight in front of him, at least as straight as he could with handcuffs on.

He looked like an accountant, a clerk in a men's clothing store, or maybe a mid-level bureaucrat in some

Iowa county. Even in dress clothes and walking along the street, Helen couldn't have imagined him as a multi-billionaire who had started his first company, a small hardware supplier, at the age of twenty-one. He then used the hardware business as a side angle into construction, and over the next thirty years built up one of the largest interlocking network of companies in the world.

For a moment, Helen thought of Andrew Sears, the young man who, a few years before, had come to her hometown and begun killing her fellow detectives. Sears had been the youngest son of a wealthy family, and his father had followed much the same path in life as the man sitting before her. That she was even willing to sit and face Benson told her something about how close she was to stepping over that line she'd once thought impossible to even approach.

Once Benson sat, the guards briefly unshackled his handcuffs before attaching them to a support built into the table for that purpose. One of them also bent down and undid the man's ankle restraints, then cuffed those to the table legs on Benson's side, securing him solidly in place. The entire time, the female guard stood back, weapon drawn and trained on the prisoner.

"Twenty minutes," said the warden who hadn't uttered a word up to that point, "then we're coming back in."

"Not a problem," Conroy replied while his client stayed silent. "Just make sure you turn off any listening ports out there, okay?"

The warden scowled at Conroy before he and his men exited the room. Helen wondered if the two had had disputes in the past, or if it were some general animosity.

The door swung silently shut on greased hinges, leaving Helen alone in the room with a defense lawyer and a convicted serial killer.

"Thank you for coming," Benson said, sending a small smile her way. "Considering your background, I'm guessing it was kind of a hard decision for you."

"I haven't made any decision yet. I only came down here to listen."

"And to collect five grand." The smile broadened a bit.

Helen blushed. "Yes," she said, feeling glass grinding in her stomach. "That as well."

"Nothing to feel bad about," Benson told her. "There's nothing shameful about taking money when it's offered."

"Why don't we get to why you asked me here?" Helen said as she silently thought, so I can tell you to go to hell.

"Fair enough." Benson leaned back in his chair, glanced at his lawyer for a moment, then turned his full attention back to Helen. "I called you because I need some expertise in a particular field."

"And that field is?"

"Isn't it obvious?" He spread out his hands as far as the shackles permitted. "Serial murder."

"I'm not exactly what you'd call an expert."

"Don't be so modest, Detective. And yes, I'm going to refer to you in that way, even with the disgraceful actions of your former employers."

"No way," Helen said. "Just call me by my name."

Benson shrugged. "If you insist, though I think you're selling yourself a little short."

"And I don't see why you consider me some sort of

expert. I was just a homicide detective. Not even that by the end."

"Seriously now, Miss Lipscomb. I'm sure you'd concede that I'm something of an authority in the area myself, though not…" He spread his arms out and jangled the chains. "…the most successful of the type. And I'm here to tell you that you can count on one hand the number of law enforcement who have single-handedly brought down one serial killer, let alone two."

"There wasn't anything single-handed in either case," Helen said.

Benson waved his hand to the side, as if brushing away a gnat. "False modesty aside, I figure you have the requisite skills to pursue the investigation I want undertaken. Not to mention that I'll pay you a sizeable amount for the job."

"I don't think so, Mr. Benson. I am kind of low on funds at the moment, but I don't see any amount you could offer that would make me willing to go about working for you. If conventional wisdom is even close to correct, you're on the hook for even more than the three killings they've convicted you of. If for no other reason than that, I just don't see myself working for you. Sorry, but you'll have to find yourself another gopher."

"If your mind was so made up from the beginning, why even come? And why not at least hear me out?"

"I guess I came because I had nothing better to do. I just wrapped up something in Colorado, a state I hear you know well, and was heading back this direction, anyway. As far as hearing you out, let's just say that I've barely been in front of you for five minutes and my skin's already crawling. So why don't we chalk all this up to a mistake and go our separate ways?"

Standing up, Helen turned to Conroy, who'd been silent through the entire conversation. "I assume you'll send me a check for the five thousand. Your office has my address in—"

"Detective Lipscomb," Benson interjected, his voice taking on a sharper tone. Helen paused at the door and turned back to him.

"What?" She wanted to be done with the man and didn't even bother correcting him.

"I think you're working under something of a misconception," Benson said. "You're correct. The authorities suspect me of more slayings than they've convicted me of, though even they can't guess the actual number. But I don't want you to work to prove my innocence. My guilt has been pretty much firmly established, at least in the three cases that have brought me to death row. Considering all the death sentences I currently face, wouldn't you agree that would be pretty much a waste of your time and my money to attempt to prove otherwise?"

Helen frowned and glanced at Conroy, whose face remained impassive, before turning back to Benson.

"Then what do you want out of me?" she asked.

Benson smiled, but the expression had no warmth.

"I want you to prove that I'm guilty," he said in a flat, calm tone. "Guilty of those murders they haven't yet pinned on me."

"Excuse me?" Helen was sure she looked as baffled as she felt.

"I thought that was fairly clear," Benson said. "Someone's out there taking credit for my work, and I want you to put a stop to it. If I have anything to say about it, no one's going to get the credit for my work but me."

PART II
NEBRASKA TO COLORADO
TO KANSAS

CHAPTER 4

Thursday, Sept. 5th

"NINE," HELEN SAID, about an hour later.

They were in Conroy's suite at a Fairfield Inn about thirty miles from the prison. Conroy had Helen follow him in her rental car from the penitentiary until they reached the hotel. She was a little puzzled when they passed a few serviceable motels a lot closer but mentally chalked it up to the attorney having higher standards than her.

"Come here often?" she'd asked the lawyer as he'd taken off his jacket and loosened his tie.

Although technically a suite for vacationers, the area clearly had been turned into the closest thing possible that approximated a working office. Ranged around the main living area, Helen counted no less than four laptops, two fax machines and an assortment of iPads. Yellow legal pads were scattered all over the place and notes covered a portable whiteboard at the far end of the room, next to the bay windows.

"Had to make this my temporary office," Conroy said. "Taking care of Leo's sentencing appeals is nearly a full-time job, but my partners would be overwhelmed if I shoved my other cases off onto them."

"I thought that's why you high-powered types had associates, to do your scut work," Helen said.

"Believe me, they are." Conroy turned her way and made a sweeping gesture with his arm that took in the entire living area of the suite. "All this is just my four most pressing cases, including Leo's."

Helen found herself without words. She'd been around law enforcement enough years to understand just how unglamorous the lives of most attorneys, even successful ones, were. But Gordon Conroy was in a whole other league, nationally known and often appearing as a guest on cable news shows, and even he probably put in seventy-hour weeks.

"That's right, nine. Six he's still under suspicion of, plus the three they convicted him for," Gordon Conroy said.

"All strangled with a leather belt?"

Conroy shrugged. "Or strap of some sort. In eight of the cases, forensics managed to tweeze out microscopic leather fibers from the victims' necks."

"Colors?"

"Black in six of the cases, brown in the others."

Helen tapped the manila folder she held, which Conroy had given her as soon as they entered his suite.

"Nothing more specific than that on the leather?" she asked.

"Beyond the fact that it had been cured and treated to be sold as a fabric, no."

"Girls all the same age?"

"Within a range, late teens to late twenties. All Caucasian. The oldest, at least that he's admitted to me, was twenty-six."

"But he hasn't been officially tagged to most of them yet?"

The lawyer smiled and shook his head.

"But if he's told you, don't you have an obligation to inform the authorities? Or does client privilege even extend to mass murder?" As soon as she asked, Helen realized the words had come out harsher and more bitter than she'd intended.

However, Conroy didn't seem taken aback.

"It's a gray area," he said. "If we go to trial, I'm compelled to turn any sort of confession over to the other side. And if I know in advance of crimes about to be committed, I'm obligated to break confidentiality there. But these murders have already been done, in some cases years ago, and Leo's not yet been indicted for them."

"He just hopes to be," Helen said, still trying to wrap her head around the idea.

"Consider it from his point of view, Miss Lipscomb. If you had the choice between confessing to wrongdoings you'd committed or being executed, which would you pick?"

"Nine murders," Helen repeated.

"Plus possibly several more that he's keeping in reserve, even from me. I learned long ago that most clients lie even to their lawyers. Mr. Benson is a man with a lot of secrets, and I doubt he willingly gives up any more than he absolutely has to. Considering his age, plus the amount of travel he's done over the years overseeing his companies, there's no telling how many victims he may have left in his wake."

Her stomach lurched. "You mean he may be keeping quiet in case he needs even more of his bargaining chips. You don't want to kill me yet, guys, 'cause I can help you clear a lot more cases."

"That's about it."

"Ted Bundy tried the same stunt," Helen pointed

out. "Didn't work out too well for him, though, did it?"

"That was a long time ago," he said. "Beyond ancient history. And considering the instant celebrity/social media culture we live in…"

Conroy bent down over a small computer stand and picked up another manila folder. Walking over, he handed it to Helen.

"Here's the basics I have on the young man in question. Why don't you look it over while I make a few phone calls?"

As he walked away into another room, Helen plopped down in a soft red easy chair and began reading about the life and times of William Gray.

Gray, called Willy by his friends and acquaintances, was a twenty-five-year-old native of Lenexa, a small Kansas town that formed part of the Kansas City Metro area. From his eighteenth year on, he'd bounced from place to place, never staying in any one area, or at any particular job, for more than a year or so. Leaving KC shortly after turning twenty-one, he wandered through Kansas for a few years before, approximately a year ago, winding up in Oklahoma City. He'd worked a variety of jobs there, including bartending, construction and a brief stint as a mechanic, before hitting the road again and eventually making his way to Denver.

In Denver, he followed his usual pattern of bouncing from job to job, working for a while as a janitor at a high school. Upon his arrest, this particular stint raised some concern, but an intensive investigation had yielded no evidence of any aberrant behavior at the school itself.

Helen closed the folder for a moment and leaned back in the chair. Gray didn't sound like the most ambitious of people, but nothing in the file indicated any of the early warning signs of sociopathy. If the man were even a minor-league serial killer, his psychosis seemed to have sprung up out of whole cloth, which basically abrogated nearly forty years of research into such people.

From the other room, Helen could hear the faint murmurings of conversation as Conroy conducted his business. She turned back to the file and continued reading.

Gray had worked as a custodian at the school for approximately three months before one Sunday night, while driving back from Aurora at the end of the long Memorial Day weekend, an astute patrolman noticed a faulty brake light on his ten-year-old Ranger. It was almost a cliché, like something out of a hundred bad movies, that Willy Gray had picked this weekend to hit several bars before heading home, and his obvious intoxication gave the cops, anxious to use the holiday weekend to fill their quota of citations for the month, the excuse to ask Gray to "Step out of the car, please."

Coming out of his vehicle, Gray, twenty-four at the time, had acted, in the words of Officer Sally Briscoe, who had nearly six years on the job, "a little weirded-out."

Of course, "weirded-out" isn't exactly grounds for detention, but Briscoe and her partner, a six-month rookie named Brian Oliver, had wasted little time asking Gray to do a sobriety test. At which point, the young man became belligerent and took a swing at Briscoe.

It took all of five seconds for the two cops to secure the young man, deciding they had probable cause to do at least a cursory search of his vehicle.

On the floorboard behind the passenger seat, they discovered several items of women's clothing, including a yellow halter-top and bright red cotton shorts. Sally Briscoe, ambitious and eager to move up the chain in the Denver force, made an obvious assumption.

And that's when Gray's life fell apart.

"Fun reading?" Conroy asked about ten minutes later as he came back into the suite's main living area. He had changed out of his light blue suit and into a pair of tan woolen slacks and a green golf shirt. He also held a pair of tortoise shell-rimmed reading glasses in his hand.

"Not exactly my thing anymore," Helen replied, "but it seems as if the Denver cops were pretty damned thorough."

"Oh they were, and it didn't hurt that Gray couldn't afford a lawyer, so he was stuck with a public defender."

"Even when things began to pop?" Helen asked

"Even then. His family situation is almost non-existent. Mom died when he was a kid, dad's on either his third or fourth wife now. Actually, Gray's mother was wife number two for his father. There's a couple of half or step-siblings running around, but none of them very close to him."

"So when they pulled him in, he was basically on his own," Helen said, and Conroy nodded.

"Especially after things started going wild."

Helen opened the file again and continued reading while Conroy worked at one of his iPads.

The clothing found in Gray's car matched a girl who'd been missing for about a week. Sami Brayn was fifteen at the time and lived with both parents and a younger sister, a traditional nuclear family, just outside of Denver. Again, the story was almost too stereotypical. An above-average student hoping to graduate early in a few years, she'd been receiving extra tutoring from one of her school's math teachers, preparatory to enrolling in an advanced summer school class.

Tuesday of the third week in May had been one of her tutor days. She'd never returned home. John Freehold, the math teacher, told the police she had left his classroom, as per their routine, at four-thirty on the dot. The last he'd seen of her, Sami had been walking out the door mentioning something about stopping by the library before going home.

According to the school librarian on duty, the girl had never shown up.

By the next day, they had followed the usual pattern: organized searches, tearful pleas from family members for Sami's safe return, and interviews with anyone even remotely within her life. The frantic activity went on for over a week with no clues in sight.

The photo used for publicity purposes showed Sami, a pretty young girl with blonde hair, blue eyes and braces.

According to her mother, she was supposed to get her braces off three days after she went missing.

The second half of the file included information about Gray, containing various motions made on his behalf by his lawyer, as well as public statements from the Denver police and the Colorado Bureau of Investigation.

Helen looked up at Conroy, still working on the iPad. "CBI got pulled into this?" she asked.

Conroy looked up and nodded.

"Why?" Helen asked. "Where's the state connection? And don't tell me Denver just needed the best forensics lab."

Conroy shook his head. "Because of the Brayn girl's age and the circumstances involved, right from the jump they worried that they were maybe dealing with a serial predator."

"Any other crimes in the area lately that fit the general MO?"

"No. They were just playing it safe. With everyone in the country thinking that they're procedural experts now, thanks to all the damned TV shows, they wanted to make sure every stone was unturned. Then, of course, when Gray started confessing to other crimes they were damned glad they'd done so. By the time the FBI got in the mix, everything was up in the air."

Helen grunted and went back to her reading. By the time she'd gotten past the transcripts of the Denver police interview with Gray, she couldn't take it anymore and closed the file without finishing.

"Gray kept wanting to talk to the media," she said. "He seems to think the more famous he becomes the better his chances."

Conroy leaned away from his work and nodded. "He even wanted to let the PD go and be his own counsel when he gets to trial."

"The judge go for that?"

"Not even close. He can't stop the fool from being his own lawyer, but he ordered the PD to stay on as co-counsel."

"Which he must have loved when Gray started confessing to even more killings."

"She. Young go-getter named Marcie Lewis. I've had several conversations with her myself, and I can tell you she hates the whole thing."

"Bad for her career?" Helen asked as she flipped the

folder onto a nearby end table.

"That, plus I think she actually gets the willies being around the guy. After all, he's claiming multiple killings and having a ball dangling the evidence piece by piece in front of the FBI."

Of course. The feds would naturally be involved. One killer working across states, even if only two side by side, was enough to give them an in.

"Who's the main fed in all this?"

"Guy named Sam Powers."

"Task force?"

Conroy shook his head. "Depends on how you define force. At the moment, it's just a small collection of agents, pulled together to look into the possibility that Willy Gray is more than he seemed at first. In the beginning, it was all hearsay, and they assumed Gray was one of those that get off on false confessing. But when he began leading them to bodies…"

Helen glanced at the closed folder resting on the table, knowing that if she ended up taking the job, she'd have to force herself to read through all of it.

"How many others so far?" she asked.

"It's in the file there."

"Humor me, okay? At the moment, I'm still deciding whether or not to take Benson up on his offer. If I decide not to, I really don't want to give myself any additional grist for nightmares."

Conroy sighed. "At the moment, they've unearthed two bodies besides the Brayn girl."

"Bodies that Gray led them to?"

"Correct. One outside Pueblo and the other in Kansas City."

Helen shook her head, already beginning to regret

coming to Nebraska.

"And according to Mr. Benson, these are actually his victims."

Conroy grinned, but the expression didn't have much mirth in it. It actually made his face look almost skeleton-like.

"That's right. Please keep in mind that we need this kept confidential. Whether or not you take the job, you were in the prison today as a representative on my behalf and the privilege Leo enjoys with me extends to you."

Helen grimaced. She wasn't entirely sure that was correct but didn't feel like arguing the point.

And it wasn't exactly like she owed any police force anywhere any sort of loyalty.

"And Benson doesn't understand how someone he says he's never met could know so much about his activities," she said.

"Correct."

Helen stood up. "You mind if I have a drink?"

The attorney gestured toward the wet bar in the corner, and she walked over to make herself something.

"So you going to take the job?" Conroy asked to her turned back.

Helen finished making her Scotch and soda. She turned and leaned with her back against the bar.

"Benson doesn't know Gray at all? Doesn't know of any connection between the two of them?" she asked.

"So he says."

Helen pointed at the file folder on the table. "Yet Gray's somehow able to provide the authorities with accurate information about killings that Benson claims for himself? Accurate enough to have so far led to three bodies?"

"That's about the size of it. And Leo wants you to figure out how he's doing it so we can stop it before all his chips are cashed in, so to speak."

Helen stared down at her drink, her thoughts lost somewhere in the liquid. After a few minutes, she looked back up at Conroy.

"You're smart enough. Tell me you've at least considered the other possibility here."

"Meaning how do I know that it isn't Leo running the scam? That he's just telling me those were his victims when he knows no more about them, or their circumstances than could be read in the papers?"

"Exactly."

"Simple answer, Miss Lipscomb. I don't. But I'm guessing if that's the truth, you could find it out as well. But look at it this way. Where would be the benefit to Leo in pulling such a con?"

"Maybe it's just more of a power trip. He can't dominate women like he used to; he can't feel in control of his companies; so he goes about it this way, by yanking the system around."

Conroy thought it over for a minute. "Could be, but everything I've come across hints that he has a lot more legitimate victims out there, God knows the FBI thinks so, so this seems a little too convoluted, even for someone who likes to see people dance to his tune as much as Benson does."

Helen had to admit to herself that the man had a point. But she still didn't feel comfortable about the whole thing. She turned her back on Conroy and walked over to the window. She looked down into the parking lot below.

A maroon SUV had just pulled up. It sat quiet for a

few minutes before disgorging a family of five: father, mother, two younger kids, and one teenage girl. Even from her vantage point, Helen could see the stock teenager's look of disdain on the girl's face.

Probably thinking of so many more fun things to do than spend time with the fam.

She turned back to face Conroy.

"I think I'm going to pass. The thought of working for a convicted killer just seems too far over the line for me."

"Here's another way of looking at it," Conroy said. "Whether Leo's on the level or not, either about his role in those murders or any connection to Gray, your main job would be looking for the truth, whatever it may be. And in doing so you'd pick up enough money to get you by for a couple of years until you figure out where to go from here."

"And what if the truth I uncover paints your client in a bad light? How much do I collect then?"

Conroy looked as if he wanted to laugh. "How much worse of a light could he be in? He's already facing death row. What does he have to lose?"

Helen nodded, conceding the lawyer his point.

Conroy drummed his fingers on the arm of his chair for a moment, then sat up a little straighter.

"Tell you what. If for any reason, Leo reneges on his deal with you, I'll cover the salary and expenses."

Helen leaned further back, unable to hide her surprise.

"Why would you do that? Or are you just going to pay me off and somehow itemize it on your bill to him?"

Conroy grinned. "You really don't like lawyers, do you?"

"Don't take it personal. These days, I don't care much for anyone in the power structure."

The attorney's face sobered. "Understandable, given your recent history. If you wish, I'll have my office draw up a contract agreeing to what I just offered."

"You still haven't explained. Why?"

"Maybe because I'm not as bad as you think."

"For God's sake, you're defending a serial killer. Someone who spent who knows how many years going around the Midwest butchering women."

"The system entitled him to a defense. And keep in mind that he's asking you to prove him guilty, not innocent, of several more murders. So where's the personal conflict with your principles?"

Helen half-turned. The rest of the family had entered the hotel, but the teenage daughter was hanging around outside, casting glances down the highway.

What was she thinking? What were her dreams, aspirations? If she even had any in her young life. Maybe she was planning nothing more realistic than marrying a rock star or, as a concession to her generation, some famous YouTuber. Did she even consider maturing, getting older, then growing old? Could she even conceive, at her age, of her life falling apart completely as she approached middle age? Like most young people, like Helen herself once upon a time, the kid probably felt immortal, as if nothing bad would ever touch her.

Helen could have told her different.

She could have told the girl about all the bad people and things she'd encountered. Of people she'd met, more than one in fact, who killed others out of some minor slight. Or no slight at all.

There were people right now, all around, who would

have loved to wipe that disgusted look off the young girl's face, only to replace it with one of pain and terror.

Then do it again and again to other innocents whose path they crossed.

Sure, Helen mused, she'd be taking money from the worst of human scum, but anything she came up with would only, at the least, tack even more convictions onto his record. So other than the possibility of leaving Benson with enough leverage to escape death row, which at his age could be drug out with appeals until he died a natural death, from her point of view what was the downside?

And it wasn't exactly as if she had anything else to do at the moment.

"Okay," Helen finally said. "Draw up the papers and get me a copy so I can have someone else look them over. If everything seems kosher, I'll take the job. I assume you have more information for me than just the one file folder?"

"You'd better believe it. Probably more than you'll know what to do with."

CHAPTER 5

Friday Sept. 6th, Evening

"WELL, WHAT DO you want me to say? Sounds like you've already decided."

After leaving Nebraska that morning, Helen had returned home, and now she and George Beacham were sitting in a bar on top of one of the highest buildings in the city with a magnificent view of the river as it snaked its way south. With a clear sky and numerous street lights below them, the slight waves sparkled in the night, unceasingly rolling on their way. Over the course of a few more states and several hundred miles, those ripples would enter the Gulf of Mexico, and Helen wondered if the best thing possible wouldn't be to simply say to hell with it and join them.

"I don't want advice so much," she said, "as validation. Tell me I'm doing the right thing."

"Really?"

Helen sighed and shook her head. Beacham, a dark-haired man of thirty-eight, was just beginning to develop a small potbelly on his lean frame. A detective in the Computer Crimes Division, the two of them had been professional acquaintances for years. When things fell to hell and the brass hung Helen out to dry after the Andrew Sears debacle, Beacham had stepped up to serve as her union delegate. He'd offered to help Helen contest her dismissal and fight to get her job back. In the end, all she'd asked for was that he smooth her transition out of the department as much as possible.

In the few weeks the process took, they struck up a mild friendship. Nothing romantic in any way. Beacham and his wife were in the midst of a separation, with him working as hard as he could for reconciliation, and Helen, while she may have in ordinary circumstances possibly entertained the idea, was still working through the trauma of losing several of her fellow detectives, including her lieutenant and a former partner, to an assassin's gun. Her emotional state was fragile enough that common sense told her not to pursue any sort of relationship, no matter how transitory, until she got herself sorted out.

Now, nearly two years later, she still felt as unsorted as ever, and was wondering if she'd ever feel whole again.

On the bright side, about six months after they'd met, Beacham and his wife had gotten back together, and according to everything he said, they were doing just fine.

"Helen?" Beacham said, and she realized her thoughts had spaced her out again. She snapped back to the here and now.

"Sorry. Been a long couple of days. So tell me honestly what you think."

Beacham straightened up and spread his hands on the table. "I think you have to make one seriously hard decision. Do you want to go on leading an investigatory lifestyle or not? As it is, you're kind of playing it safe. Dipping your toes in the water now and then, enough to keep the lights on and the rent paid, but not so much that you feel like some kind of sellout. The question is, long term, what is it you really want to do?'

"Maybe I don't know."

"Well, don't you think you should go about finding out?"

She didn't have a comeback to that one, so instead took a quick sip of her drink.

"It seems to me," Beacham continued, "that if you want to be an investigator, then do it the right way. Go through the hoops, get your license, and get to work. With your experience, you could easily qualify for the state's minimum requirements. Probably in any state, if you decided not to live here."

"And what do you think would happen when the brass finds out I'm trying to get that private license?"

"You really believe they'd carry their grudge that far?" Beacham asked.

"Don't you?"

He sighed and took a moderate drink of his own.

"No, I don't," he finally said, setting his glass down. "Mainly because it wouldn't get them anywhere, and could potentially boomerang in a big way."

"Yeah?"

"Yeah," he growled, mimicking her tone. "It's a cost/ benefit thing. The reason they hung you out to dry was because they needed a fall guy, or girl as it were, someone to take the blame for our fellow cops being gunned down left and right. They needed someone they could point to and tell the media 'not our fault so many of our detectives bit it. It's this incompetent officer's fault.'"

"Thanks," Helen said, her gaze darkening, "you're making me feel so much better."

Beacham grinned. "What I'm saying is that that was then, and this is now. You served your purpose, from their point of view, and there's no gain, nothing to be had, by going after you again. Actually, if they never heard your name again, they'd probably be pleased as hell."

Helen shook her head, a small tear pushing its way from the corner of her left eye.

"But," Beacham continued, "and I need you to hear me now, Helen. Doing some occasional scut work for lawyers, even defense lawyers, isn't exactly a cardinal sin. But if you do something as major as working for a confirmed serial killer, all bets may be off. It would be a whole 'nother black eye for the department, even if a couple of states removed. If somehow it all fell to hell for you, then everything would come up again, and it would be national news all over."

For a moment, Helen considered breaking confidentiality and explaining to Beacham that she'd be working to prove Benson's guilt, but she abstained. Not only had both Conroy and his client explained she had to keep her work for them as close to confidential as possible, the entire scenario was so goddamned fantastic that few people would actually believe it.

And if Beacham thought she was trying to pull one over on him, that would be one more relationship frayed.

"Maybe I've already decided to take the job," she said, searching for a middle ground. "After all, it's not like I'm rolling in dough lately, and this one job could set me up for a long time. Maybe long enough to decide how I want my life to go."

"Doesn't mean you can't change your mind. I'm not talking about the brass. Hell, their minds were made up on you long ago. But you've still got a lot of support among the rank and file, Helen. Uniforms, detectives, clerical staff. People who know that you're the one who really saved our asses during the Sears fiasco. How do you think they'll feel when they find out your working for a scuzz like Leo Benson?"

Helen swirled her drink a time or two before looking back up at her friend.

"Right now, I can't really worry about what they'll think," she said. "I'm still trying to sort out how I feel about the whole thing."

CHAPTER 6

Monday, Sept. 9th

THE FOLLOWING MONDAY, shortly before noon, Helen, wearing tan slacks and a light-weight blue blazer, walked into a small café/coffee shop on Bannock Street in Denver. She waved away a hostess who approached her with a menu and made her way to a table in the back where a young red-headed woman sat by herself, munching on a salad.

"Marcie Lewis?" Helen asked.

The young woman looked up, nodded and gestured to the chair across from her. "I'm guessing you're Miss Lipscomb?"

Helen nodded in return and sat down.

"Just water, please," Helen said to a waitress who had come up to the table. The girl rolled her eyes, nodded, and headed off. Helen turned back to find Marcie Lewis watching her carefully.

She looked to be no more than thirty years old, with the pale skin and green eyes that went perfectly with her hair color. She wore tan slacks with a light blue blouse and had a navy blazer slung over the back of her chair.

"Thanks for meeting me," Helen said.

Lewis nodded and put her fork down. "Sorry to do it like this, but I'm swamped beyond belief at the office. I've got, at last count, nine different defendants to meet this afternoon, plus three motions to write by tomorrow. So right now is literally the only time I have free."

"I understand," Helen said. "I actually appreciate you giving me the time."

Lewis placed her elbows on the table, folded her hands and rested her chin on them. "Well, when someone calls from out of state and offers to help with one of my clients, it sounds interesting. But I'm not sure I appreciate how vague you were over the phone."

The waitress placed Helen's water on the table, smiled at both of them and walked away.

"Sorry for the vagueness," Helen said, "but, to be truthful, I wasn't sure you'd see me if I gave too much information."

The young public defender's eyes hardened, and she put her fork down. "So you're a private detective?" she asked.

"Not exactly," Helen said, deflecting the question. It had come up several times over the last few years.

"What does that mean? You're not a cop or a lawyer, you would have told me so over the phone. You led me to believe—"

"I'm employed by a lawyer, and I'm doing some investigative work on his behalf."

"Who's the attorney?" Lewis asked.

Helen hesitated. On the way over, she'd considered how to handle the natural questions she assumed would come up. But even though she'd settled on a plan, she found herself reconsidering.

"I'd rather not say."

Marcie Lewis's gaze hardened even more. "Then I'd say this meeting's at an end, wouldn't you?"

"If you could just give me—"

"Not without some basic info. You want to know how many times this year someone's tried to pull one over on me? I'm a public defender, for Chrissakes. You have any idea what sort of clientele that gives me? I could spend all day listing every bullshit story I've gotten over just the last few months. So either you cough something up quick or—"

"Gordon Conroy," Helen said.

The young PD's eyes widened. "Conroy?"

Helen nodded. "Sorry. I should have told you up front, but you can probably see why I hoped to—"

"And he's involved with one of my clients?"

"Not exactly involved, more like interested. And I'm sorry, but I simply can't tell you his client's name. At least not yet."

"In that case, Miss Lipscomb, you'd better state your case quick and make it good. Otherwise, I'll ask you to take off so I can get back to work."

Helen leaned back in her chair and looked the lawyer right in the eye. This next step was a whole lot easier. "Mr. Conroy's interest is in Willy Gray."

"Oh Christ," Lewis said, flopping her arms down at her sides. "What the hell do you want with him? Hasn't he already given you all enough to bury him a dozen times over?"

"What I want is quite the opposite."

"Oh?"

"We think your client's digging an unnecessary hole for himself."

The lawyer's green eyes narrowed. "I don't get you."

"There's reason to believe that he's a false confessor. I don't think he killed those victims the cops

54

uncovered."

"What reason? What sort of information could someone like Conroy have about this?"

"I'm not authorized to get into that."

"Of course you're not. Tell me this. I'm guessing you used to be a cop or something connected with law enforcement. You've definitely got the look for it. Back when you were working my side of the street, would you have put up with such a bullshit explanation as you just gave me?"

Grimacing, Helen had to look away from the woman's righteous anger. She struggled to find an answer, but it turned out Lewis was just getting warmed up.

"I've got some no-account lowlife," the lawyer continued, "who never amounted to anything in his life before going out and abducting, then killing, a young girl. Dude's so incompetent that he even kept the girl's clothes in his car days after disposing of her. Then he doubles down by bragging about all the other women he's killed. Hell, I'm just trying to keep the names straight, and now some hotshot out-of-state counsel pops up wanting to intrude in my case. No thank you."

Helen smiled and took a sip of her water. "You may have just partially answered your own question."

"How's that?" By this point, the young attorney's tone matched her reddish hair.

"According to Gray, he's responsible for the deaths of at least three women, Sami Brayn included, that he's confessed to, right?"

"Yeah, so?"

"And I'm going to guess he's been implying, to anyone who would listen, knowledge of even more victims, more cases for various departments to clear, right?"

"Give me something I don't know."

"Then if he's so incompetent of a killer that he was arrested with the girl's clothing still in his car, how'd he get away with all those other killings? How'd he manage to pull that off?" Helen leaned back in her chair, giving the other woman time to think things through.

After a moment, Lewis slid her salad away from her to the side of the table. "Maybe he got lucky the first handful of times."

"Could be," Helen said.

"Or maybe it was some sort of deep psychology at work. Wouldn't be the first time I had a client who subconsciously worked it out so he'd get caught."

"Did Gray ever present himself to you as that type of a perp?"

Lewis sighed. She reached into her purse, slung on the chair with her blazer, and pulled out her cell phone. She punched in a number, and the person on the other end must have picked up on the first ring.

"Richard? It's Marce. Listen, can you get on my system? I've got a one o'clock with a guy named Thomas Munyon. Right, that guy. Could you get ahold of him and tell him I have to cancel? See if there's any time he can come on Wednesday. Yeah, something came up out of the blue that may take a while. Okay. Thanks, guy."

Lewis turned her phone off, put it back in her purse and turned full attention to Helen.

"Okay," she said. "What've you got?"

CHAPTER 7

"WHAT IT COMES down to," Marcie Lewis said about an hour later, "is that you're really not giving me all that much. Not nearly enough for me to okay you talking to my client."

After thirty minutes, the two of them had moved from the café back to the PD offices. Located in the Denver County court building, Lewis's office was actually a small cubbyhole within a slightly larger cubbyhole within an office suite. Her desk, even in the twenty-first century nearly overloaded with folders, files, and assorted stray scraps of paper, looked exactly like every lower-level bureaucrat's office that Helen had ever seen. Computer age be damned.

All around them were other lawyers, busy talking on the phone, tapping at their computers or immersed in reading files and briefs.

When they'd first arrived, maneuvering around all of her co-workers to get to her cubicle, Lewis had taken one look at the Dumpster fire that served as her desk, said "The hell with it," and ushered Helen into a conference room at the far end of the suite, complete with a large table, a dozen tubular chairs with navy blue cushions, and windows that stretched almost floor to ceiling. The large center table held more folders and papers, almost as if they'd interrupted a meeting in progress.

"Don't worry about it," Lewis said, noting Helen's

look. "This is the first of the week. You ought to see it by Friday."

The two of them sat at adjacent chairs, and Lewis handed over three files that she'd picked up from her desk. "I'm not too thrilled that you've told me so little," she said, "but almost everything in these files is public information anyway, and what isn't I've yanked out. Look them over and tell me why you think Willy is pulling everyone's legs."

Helen had barely glanced at the three files before jerking her gaze back up to Lewis. "You've got files from the other cases?" she asked.

Lewis nodded. "Just the basic info. Obviously, the cops and the CBI have the more extensive files. Technically, the county of Denver is only on the hook to defend him on the Sami Brayn case. But at the moment, he's refusing to talk to any counsel but me."

"Lucky you."

Lewis grimaced. "If you say so. The point is, when he dropped the names on me, I sent them up the line. Once the bodies were found, they allowed me access to the files so I could best counsel him, at least until someone higher up steps in."

Helen frowned, working the intricacies out in her head. "And the feds are okay with this?" she finally asked.

Lewis grinned, though it was a bit strained. "We kept it from them as long as possible, but with the interstate angle, it didn't take long for them to show up. I'm guessing I have about another week or so before they start stepping all over it, and someone with some real clout, maybe your Mr. Conroy, shows up to showboat on Gray's behalf. This damned thing is tailor-made for someone who wants to make a media splash."

"Maybe so," Helen said, "but it won't be Conroy. He's committed to his current client, and it would be about as big of a conflict of interest as there could be."

"You still haven't told me who that client is," Lewis pointed out.

Helen nodded. "And I still can't. I may not be exactly official, but I am working for the man and Conroy's confidentiality extends to me."

Lewis shrugged. "Doesn't matter, really. Once the feds take over, I'll be back to my usual caseload."

"I don't see how they can come into it, other than in an advisory way. Homicide, even serial, is a state crime."

Lewis shook her head. "You're forgetting something. Consider the locations of the other two victims. Powers, that's the man in charge, is contending that Willy crossed state lines in the commission of a crime. As tangled as the KC Metro area is, in some places if you blink you're in the opposite state from where you started. And that's the hook they're using."

Shaking her head at the system she'd left behind, Helen returned to her reading.

What she saw confirmed what Conroy had told her the Friday before in his hotel room. Seeing it all printed out in black and white impacted her more than Conroy's rendition.

When she finished reading, she handed the folders back to Lewis.

"So what you're offering me," said Lewis, who'd been quiet all the way through her reading, "is a chance to prove my client's lying? That he didn't do those murders?"

"Two of them," Helen said. "I'm pretty sure Sami

Brayn was his. But not the ones in Pueblo or KC."

According to Conroy, Leo Benson had vehemently denied that he had anything to do with the murder of Sami Brayn, his main stated reason being her age. Fifteen, the psycho had told Conroy, was a bit too young for his tastes.

The murdered women in Pueblo and Kansas City were twenty-three and twenty-six, respectively.

"Okay. But that would be kind of going against my client's wishes. He's made it clear that he wants credit for the other two. Don't ask me why."

Helen gestured towards the files. "I'm sure you noticed the MO's different between those two and Brayn?"

Lewis nodded. "That's what I hung my hat on originally. Brayn was a savage, out-of-control beating. The two older women were simply strangled. If you can call a strangling simple."

"How's Gray explain that?" Helen asked.

"He doesn't. Just says he did all three and won't go any further."

"So we really have his word only that he did the other killings?"

Lewis nodded. "That plus the fact he led cops to the bodies. Kind of punctuates any speculation, doesn't it?"

A thought crossed Helen's mind, something she should have asked Benson back at the prison, or at the very least Conroy later on. They may not have answered, but she still should have been professional enough to ask.

"Unless he has a partner," she said. "Someone working the murders with him. It's possible he was on his own for the Brayn girl."

Lewis shrugged. "If so, he's given me no indication

of it. And if he did and wasn't giving the guy up, that makes it even less likely he would go back on his story."

"But it would be in his ultimate best interest, wouldn't it? And say for a minute that Mr. Conroy and I are right, that he's not guilty of the other two women's deaths—"

"Then the actual murderer hasn't been caught yet," Lewis finished her thought.

Helen sat back and waited as Lewis spent a few seconds mulling the idea over.

"Okay," she finally said. "But if Gray's only guilty of the one, and note I'm not yet asking you how you know that, doesn't his knowledge predicate at least some involvement? How else would he be able to lead the cops to their locations?"

"That's part of what I'm trying to dig out," Helen said. "But I need your help."

"You realize that, even though Gray's a major case, he's one of only a couple of dozen I'm juggling at the moment. And I hate to say it, but judicial zeal only goes so far when it smacks up against reality."

"Trust me," Helen said, "I get that entirely. What I'm wondering is, can you get me in to see him?"

Lewis frowned and drummed her fingers on the conference table. She stared off into space for a minute before turning back to Helen. "You realize what you're asking, lady? They're keeping this guy under lock and key like you wouldn't believe. And that was even before the feds started butting in. What's the reaction going to be when I bring in some outside civilian and expect to waltz in with her?"

"I understand, but…"

"Hell," Lewis continued, "the last few days I

practically have to get a court order any time I want to see him."

Helen looked down at the table, furious with herself. Had she really been out of it that long? How could she have forgotten how the maze of officialdom could wrap itself around someone?

"On the other hand," Lewis said.

Helen looked back up. "Yeah?"

"Don't get your hopes up," Lewis said, "but there is someone you may want to look up."

CHAPTER 8

Tuesday, Sept. 10th

THE NEXT MORNING, Helen walked into the main building of Denver's District One police station and paused just inside the door. When it came right down to it, a police station was a police station. It may be in Denver or Los Angeles; it may have only one story or six; and it may reside in the midst of an inner-city or the outlying areas of the farthest suburb. The walls may be painted green, blue or tan, the lights fluorescent or LED, and the sergeant behind the front desk may be a fifty-year-old white guy or a thirtyish Asian lady.

Didn't matter.

A cop shop was a cop shop, pure and simple.

Helen had never been in this building before. Even so, she felt as if she could close her eyes and move to directly where she needed to go. And as she stood there, she found herself, not for the first time and probably not for the last, regretting the decision she'd made to pack it in and abandon her career.

Shrugging off her qualms, she walked over to the large, central desk and stood behind a couple of uniforms who were handing paperwork to their sergeant. As the two moved on, allowing Helen to move up in front of the desk, the sergeant glanced her way.

"Yes, ma'am?" the sergeant asked. A smooth-toned

black man, somewhere in his mid-thirties, with a full head of hair just beginning to gray at the temples.

"I'm here to see John Carstairs."

The sergeant reached to his side and picked up a clipboard stuffed with various papers and memos. Despite his obvious youth, Helen got the idea he didn't care much for the computer at his right elbow.

"Is he expecting you, Miss —"

"Lipscomb, Helen Lipscomb." She tensed, waiting for some sort of reaction, then chided herself for being silly. What did she expect? That sirens would go off and the doors and windows automatically slam shut? She was two states away from her home city. And while her name had been in the national news for all of a day or two, that was years ago and nary a peep about her since.

So no, she didn't realistically expect the sarge to recognize her name. Detective Carstairs may be another matter. Marcie Lewis had called Helen the evening before and told her it was set, that the detective could squeeze her in around ten in the morning, but she hadn't said anything about Carstairs recognizing her name.

According to Lewis, by their agreement, she had only described Helen as an investigator working for a lawyer who had some questions about Willy Gray. She hadn't indicated any consternation on the detective's part, and Helen could only take her at her word.

Still, when you got right down to it, the whole thing constituted quite a risk. According to standard procedure, either the public defender or the detective should boot Helen out from the get-go. And Lord knew what the feds' reaction would be if she ever crossed paths with them.

The desk sergeant held up a finger in a "please wait"

gesture and picked up a phone. He mumbled into it for a few minutes, then hung up.

"Stairs to the right," he said. "Third floor up and hang the first right you can. Carstairs will be waiting for you."

Helen nodded her thanks and headed to the stairwell. As she did so, she glanced around for an elevator but didn't see a sign of one. Shrugging, she headed up the stairs, by the third riser stepping aside for a plainclothes woman shoving ahead of her a Hispanic man who must have weighed three hundred pounds, his wrists in cuffs behind him and wearing dirty brown chinos and an oil-stained tank top, the type of shirt usually called a "wife-beater."

The female detective rolled her eyes at Helen as she hustled her prisoner past.

Shaking her head, Helen continued on her way until she made it to the first right turn on the third floor. She found herself on the threshold of a squad room that, just as the station itself, looked almost like the ones she'd worked in. She figured that all detective squad rooms around the country, or even the world, bore the same unmistakable stamp and layout.

Tiled floor, bank of metal filing cabinets off ranging along one wall, glass-enclosed lieutenant's office on the far side and a small, thigh-level hinged gate separating all of that from the corridor beyond.

A short man, barely topping five seven and with fiery red hair, waited on the other side of the gate.

"Miss Lipscomb?" he asked as Helen approached. She nodded, and the short man swung the gate open, holding out his hand to her at the same time.

"I'm John Carstairs," he said as they shook. "Over

this way." He gestured toward an empty desk against the west wall. Helen sat in a wooden chair in front of the desk, as the young detective plopped himself behind it.

"So you're looking into the Sami Brayn case?"

Helen shook her head. "Not quite. I'm actually focusing on the other two murders he's confessed to."

"Not Brayn?"

"No."

Carstairs frowned. "I don't quite follow."

Helen wondered again how much Marcie Lewis had shared with him.

"I have no reason to believe that Gray didn't kill the Brayn girl. But I also believe he's falsely confessing to the other two."

Carstairs frowned for a moment.

"And why is that?"

Here came the delicate balance. "I can't tell you right now. It's a confidentiality thing."

Carstairs gave her a hard look, his initial friendliness slipping away.

"Mind if I see your license?"

Helen leaned back in her chair. "I've got a bit of a confession to make, detective. I'm not a licensed P.I. I don't know how much Miss Lewis told you, but—"

The red-haired cop grinned and leaned forward, his forearms on his desk.

"So if you're not an actual P.I., what are you? What exactly is your game? And no, Marcie didn't tell me much beyond I should give you a hearing."

Helen reached into her jacket pocket. She brought out a sheaf of three pages stapled together, a letter on Gordon Conroy's professional letterhead, and handed it to Carstairs.

Raising his eyebrows, the cop took the papers and looked them over. After a moment, he handed them back.

"Not exactly SOP," he said.

"That's actually the second time in two days I've heard that."

Carstairs nodded. "I'm sure you wouldn't mind if I check this out?"

"Of course not. Feel free to call Conroy himself if you want."

"But you think Gray did the Brayn girl?"

Helen nodded. "For now. I'm guessing you took his confessions?"

"I did on Sami Brayn. We were starting on Mary Parker, I figured that'd be the easiest one to check, when the feds popped in and began taking over."

"I'm not out to sabotage your case, detective."

Carstairs leaned back in his chair and stared at the ceiling for a minute. "Never said you were, but if you're looking to blow his confessions—"

"Not blow," Helen said, "augment."

Carstairs leaned forward now, placing his forearms on his desk. "You saying Gray didn't act alone?"

Helen hesitated. If anything, among all the players in this case, her natural sympathy went to Carstairs. She'd done the man's job for years and knew how much clearing such a case could weigh on someone. Because of that, she couldn't bring herself to lie to the man, not even a little.

"I'm saying that there may be more to this than seems to be on the surface."

Carstairs stared at her for a minute. Around them, the thrum and hum of the squad room went on. Computer keyboards clacked, phones buzzed, and the small hinged gate at the front of the room creaked back and forth. A young man, looking more like a football player in his prime than a plainclothes cop, walked past them with a sheaf of files in his hand and went up to an old-fashioned filing cabinet in the corner. Faintly, from somewhere unseen, Helen could smell coffee brewing.

"You have any solid reason to think Gray's innocent of the other two?" Carstairs finally asked.

"You mean beyond everything in his record? Beyond the fact that he's an itinerant day laborer who barely makes enough to feed himself?"

"Doesn't mean he can't be a killer."

"No, but it does mean he can't be a very smart one. How many more bodies has he claimed to have left behind?"

Carstairs's eyes flashed. "What makes you think— "

"Call it a gut instinct," Helen said.

"I'd say more like a cop instinct."

"So you did check me out ahead of time."

"Hell, yes. Wouldn't you have?"

Helen grinned. "That'd be first thing up."

Carstairs stared at her for a minute, seemingly weighing the situation in his head. Helen let him weigh, hoping he would follow the same course she would have in his position.

"Tell you what, Lipscomb," he finally said, "seeing as how you used to be one of us, why don't we go grab a drink and figure out just what to do here."

Helen shrugged and rose from her chair.

****

"You don't believe it either, do you?" Helen asked about fifteen minutes later. "Probably haven't believed it for a while now."

She and Carstairs were sitting in the front booth of a small burger joint called The Pit. Helen wondered if all Denverites, or just the legal system types, preferred doing business away from their offices.

About ten minutes walking distance from headquarters, the outside of the establishment looked about as plain and ordinary as could be. It could have been anything from a small burger joint to a postage depot, and judging from the plain white exterior no one would know the difference. The only noticeable oddity was, on the overhead outdoor sign, a moderate-sized gap between the words "The" and "Pit." Helen wondered why anyone would name a food establishment with such a label. She saw Carstairs looking at her.

"Up till about a year ago it was a BBQ joint," he said, pointing at the sign. "Used to be called The Pig Pit. When the new owner bought it and wanted to make it a bar, he figured that with his location so close to a cop shop having the word 'Pig' in the name would be a license for trouble."

"Why didn't he just come up with an entirely new name and put up a new sign?" Helen asked.

"Damned if I know."

Helen gave Carstairs a quizzical look. "Are we eating or just getting away from prying ears?"

The cop waved a young waitress over their way. "The latter, actually, but we might as well get something to drink to make it look good at least."

After both of them had ordered iced teas, they got down to it.

"So explain to me," Carstairs began, "why an out of towner is coming in here and telling me that my open-

and-shut murder case isn't so open and shut."

Helen stared at him for a moment, processing her thoughts, then decided to go for the direct approach.

"I don't think I have to explain. Something tells me you've thought so as well."

The Denver cop sighed and shook his head. "I'll bet you were good at your job back when. Yeah, I've had serious doubts myself."

"About Sami Brayn?"

"No, not that. We've got forensics all over the place on that. For Chrissakes, he was stupid enough not to get rid of the girl's clothing. Plus, when we found the body, his own DNA was all over it."

"Semen?" Helen asked.

Carstairs shook his head. "No, but skin cells, some hair, even a little of his blood where she scratched him and it fell on her. The supposition is that he tried to do something with her but couldn't, umm, consummate the deal. All of this, uh, isn't for public consumption just yet, you know."

Helen nodded, understanding only too well. In these days of social media and a glut of procedural TV shows, even a confession wasn't considered good enough evidence. The Denver PD was probably sitting in fear that some hot shot lawyer, say someone like Conroy, would come along and screw up their slam dunk case. Considering that she'd shown up and was nosing around, it wasn't an unrealistic assumption.

Which made it even more curious that Carstairs was talking to her.

"You didn't seem all that concerned when I showed you the paperwork from Conroy's office. Aren't you worried he's going to take Gray's case and try to get him off?"

"Not really," Carstairs said. "I mean, sure that's a general concern, but the way you went about setting this up doesn't seem how a good lawyer would go about things."

"So the Brayn case was sloppy?" Helen asked.

"Beyond sloppy. Almost like a teenage kid pulling off a crime of passion."

"Strangled, though."

"Uh huh."

"And no intercourse. Same as the other two. So why don't you like him for them as well?" Helen asked.

"Geography, for one thing."

"Meaning?"

"The Garcia woman, from Lenexa, I can understand. Gray's bopped in and out of the Kansas City area his whole life. But Mary Parker—"

"The woman he's claiming he killed in Pueblo."

Carstairs nodded. "Right. We don't have any actual validation that he ever was in that area."

"But he did live in Oklahoma City for a while, before he came up here. Pueblo's not exactly out of the way."

"True, but it still feels off."

"Carstairs, if you're any kind of decent cop, there's something more."

The detective shook his head, then took a long drink of his tea. Putting his thoughts together, Helen thought.

"Tell you what," the Denver cop said. "Let me pull some strings, if I can, and get you in to see him. Then you tell me what you think."

"Will the feds allow that?"

"They're just hanging around the periphery, waiting

for the hard work to be done so they can take it away from us. For now, Willy Gray is still in Denver's custody."

It was what Helen had come to the city for, a chance to meet with Willy Gray one on one and see if she could determine just how the kid knew the details of two of Benson's killings.

"You sure you can get me in?" she asked.

"Hell, no. But I'll give it a try. If I do, though, it will only be to see him, to get a feel for the guy. You can't question him, or even say a word. I can't even take you in the room with me. Sorry, but if a new lawyer does come along and this ever gets to trial…"

He didn't have to finish the thought. Helen would have felt the same way in his position. She took another minute to think it over, even though she really didn't need to.

"Set it up."

CHAPTER 9

Wednesday Sept. 11th

THE NEXT MORNING, Carstairs picked Helen up outside the Marriott, and drove out to the Denver County Jail. The night before she'd spent searching on her laptop, mainly for images, to get some idea of what she'd be getting into. On the internet, the place looked clean, spacious and well-maintained, but she had a hunch most of those pictures had been taken shortly after the building had finished construction.

All in all, it didn't look too bad, even on the outside, but Helen couldn't help but compare it with the prison up in Nebraska where she'd met Conroy and Benson. Both places had the same overall ambiance, that of crushed dreams and shredded hopes, but at least the jail looked transitory, as if there were still hope that when you entered you'd come out okay on the other end.

Most who entered wouldn't, of course, but the fleeting sense of possibility was still in the air.

Marcie Lewis had to be there, of course, as by this point she would in no way allow her client to be questioned without her presence. Confession to one murder was bad enough, but three went over the top, so to make sure that Willy Gray didn't do anything equally stupid, she insisted on her presence.

Helen mentally shook her head, wondering just how

the woman managed to remain so committed in her job. Most PD's she'd known would have shuttled this guy off long ago.

After passing through the various levels of security, made a tad easier by the badges both Carstairs and Lewis flashed, they ended up in a small anteroom adjacent to a fairly standard-looking interrogation room. Glancing through the requisite one-way mirror, Helen saw Willy Gray already ensconced within, ankle and waist chains draped around him and two guards hovering in the background.

She wasn't yet sure what pretext Carstairs was going to use to question the man, but she did notice someone missing.

"If you're questioning him, shouldn't there be someone from the prosecutor's office here?"

Carstairs grinned. "I'm going to write this up as a mundane follow up. Dotting i's and crossing t's. If anything comes up of significance, I'll call them in."

Although it sounded a little unorthodox to Helen with a prisoner as far into the system as Gray, she didn't see much point in arguing. Her own position was about as unorthodox as it could get, so who was she to make waves?

Lewis and Carstairs locked gazes, nodded slightly to each other, then turned and entered the interrogation room, leaving Helen in the outer anteroom. She took a few steps closer to the mirror and looked long and hard at Willy Gray, the supposed murderer of three women and, if his insinuations were to be believed, many more.

What she saw didn't add up.

According to Gray, he'd strangled his three victims. According to forensic analysis, Sami Brayn had been strangled manually while indications from the other two bodies, granted a bit dicey because of much longer decomposition periods, indicated their killer had used some sort of leather belt or strap.

One point in Leo Benson's favor, she mused.

Sitting down, Gray looked to be no more than five-nine, if that. The table he sat at shielded his lower body, but what Helen could see didn't look all that powerful. She guessed his weight at around one sixty or so, with skinny arms and an almost concave chest. At twenty-five, his stringy blond hair was already thinning, and his face looked shadowed, indrawn, the pale blue eyes presenting a haunted appearance.

When Carstairs and Lewis entered the room, Gray barely looked up. His eyes seemed to flicker a bit as they rested on Lewis, but other than that he showed no emotion, either positive or negative, at their appearance. When the two sat down at the table, Carstairs opposite him and Marcie Lewis by his side, he continued staring down at the scratched, weathered tabletop.

As Carstairs began talking, asking a few routine questions that they'd probably gone over several times before, Gray continued to sit hunched over and stare at the table. While Helen watched, Marcie Lewis occasionally interrupted Carstairs to redirect his questioning.

"Okay, Willy," Carstairs said at one point, "let's talk about Mary Parker."

As the cop mentioned the woman killed in Pueblo, Gray began showing signs of life, his eyes dancing back and forth, and he actually shrank further back into his chair. After Carstairs asked some random questions, Gray began to stutter and stammer. Finally, with his answers becoming almost incoherent, Lewis called a halt to it.

Didn't matter. Helen had what she needed.

A one-off killer of a young girl. Maybe done in heat of the moment.

Yeah, Helen could see that.

But a long-term, successful serial killer?

No way did Willy Gray fit that bill.

So how did this itinerant kid sitting in a Colorado jail cell know Leo Benson's secrets?

CHAPTER 10

Wednesday, Sept. 11, Evening

"DID YOU GET to talk to him?" Gordon Conroy asked her that night.

Helen switched her phone from her right hand to her left. She then reached across the hotel room's desk she was sitting at and snagged the complimentary folder which held, among other things, the room service menu.

"Come on, Gordon," she said while flipping through the folder, "you know better than that."

"It would have been nice if—"

"Those two were probably breaking a couple of dozen regulations just to let me stand in the next room and listen in. Can you imagine the hell that would fall on them if it gets found out they let a civilian, let alone a disgraced former cop, question the prime suspect in three murders?"

"Nice reasoning, Lipscomb. If you ever want to go to law school, feel free to put me down as a reference. But I'm not quite sure how the last few days has advanced anything. Please tell me you're doing more than having fun on Mr. Benson's expense account."

Helen used her index finger to begin tracing down the entrée column of the menu.

"Think about it. You really think I'm going to try to cheat someone like Leo Benson? Even if he is in prison for the rest of his life?"

On the other end of the phone, the lawyer chuckled. "So what was your feel for Gray?"

"You want the brutal, honest truth?"

"Sure."

"He's a loser," Helen said. "A complete failure at twenty-five. And I think Detective Carstairs is pretty sharp. He just doesn't see Gray as a cunning serial killer."

"Serials are usually loners and losers," Conroy pointed out.

"True. But they also usually possess some sort of dynamism, some particular quality that makes them distinct. Gray's just — blah."

"Maybe whatever he has can't be seen sitting in a prison cell. Or maybe he's just hiding it, trying to throw them off the scent."

"What throwing off?" Helen asked. "He's admitted to three killings so far. Does that sound like someone trying to hide?"

"Well…"

"And according to Carstairs," Helen continued, "he's alluded to more, maybe as many as half a dozen. If he were willing to fess up like that, why play a double game?"

"But so far, using his information, only two have been discovered, correct?"

"That's what the official file says."

"The Parker woman from Colorado and Garcia from Lenexa, Kansas."

"Right."

"Both of them around four years ago," Conroy said.

Helen's finger hovered over a chicken parmigiana.

She wasn't sure if she was hungry enough for something so rich, but the little thumbnail picture next to the description looked enticing. She paused, though, wondering if her hips could stand it.

Then again, lately, there wasn't anyone in her life to appreciate her hips, so what the hell?

"You caught that, huh?" she asked the lawyer. "Both of them from roughly the same time frame, separated by quite a few miles, made me wonder."

"And the cop?"

"Carstairs? Yeah, he'd caught on to that a while back, one of the reasons he's been yelling to his superiors that there's something off about Gray's 'confessions'."

A slight chuckle came over the phone. "And I'm guessing those superiors don't want to hear about it. Why look the gift horse in the mouth, right?"

"You'd be right," Helen said. "The way he tells it, they're about to kick him out of the station over it."

"Has he run his theory by the feds?"

"Uh huh. With even less success than with his own band. But at the moment, those guys are kind of hovering in the wings."

"You must have seemed like a saving grace to him."

Helen sighed, got up from the desk and angled over to the king-sized bed. She stretched out all the way and stared up at the ceiling fan above her. Early September a mile above sea level wasn't exactly the same as early September back home, so she'd kept the ceiling fan off.

"Something we need to go over Conroy," she said.

"Okay."

"Two things, actually. One, are you sure you've gone through the records on all of Benson's companies?'

"Absolutely. We did the fine-toothed comb

routine."

"And there's no record—"

"None. As far as can be determined, Gray never worked for any of Leo's concerns. Period. Not even on a part-time or seasonal basis."

"And Leo still insists he doesn't know the man?"

"I double-checked with him this morning, and that's what he claims. Did you ask the detective to float out Benson's name to Gray and see what he said?"

"No," Helen said. "I thought about it, but decided not to."

"Because?"

"Because, to be honest, Conroy, I'm not convinced that your client's being square with us. And if he's not, I saw absolutely no reason to muddy the waters for these guys. They're under enough pressure as it is."

The silence which followed went on so long that Helen almost wondered if Conroy had disconnected.

"That's your call, of course," the lawyer said. "At some point, if you continue investigating, someone will make the connection. If nothing else, Leo swears to me that the other two women were, in fact, his victims, and somewhere down the line, he may want to stop keeping it a secret."

"But has he given you any chapter and verse on the killings?"

"Not yet. I don't think the man really trusts anyone, and if he's done everything he claims, who could blame him? I only know that when the news got out about Willy Gray confessing to the Parker and Garcia murders, he hit the roof."

"And that leads to the second question I had for you."

"Yes?"

"Benson's worth how much money, more or less. A couple of billion?"

In which case, Helen wondered, why am I debating on the room service?

"More or less."

"And I assume he still, to some extent, has control over his finances, even in prison?"

"Of course. How else could he fund his defense? What's the point, Helen?"

"Well…" She sat up on the side of the bed and looked out her open window as the sun began dipping behind the Rockies. "…if he has so many resources, why didn't he hire the best? There's tons of actual, legitimate investigative agencies out there, the kind who could devote thirty or forty operatives and a host of resources to his problem."

"That's true."

"As far as that goes, you probably have a couple of experienced pros either on your staff or on retainer, correct?"

"True again."

"Yet Benson decided to reach out to an unofficial part-timer whose bank balance is a couple of decimal points away from the negative zone? Surely you questioned him on this point."

"I did."

"And?"

A long pause, and when he spoke again the hotshot celebrity lawyer sounded almost embarrassed. "He wouldn't clarify. Said this was how he wanted to do it and not to question him. As I said, he doesn't tell me everything."

Now it was Helen's turn to stay silent as she digested that.

"Let me get this straight," she finally spoke up. "He didn't necessarily want a single operative. He wanted me specifically? All the song and dance about interviewing other people was just a front?"

"That's correct."

"Okay, so I'll add that to my list. Once I've figured out how Gray synchs up with Benson, if I can, I'm for damned sure going to find out what's so special about me in his eyes."

A moment of silence stretched between them before Conroy spoke up. "What's the next step?"

"I've got to backtrack Gray's life. There has to be some connection between him and Benson, and if Benson doesn't know it, assuming he's telling the truth, then I have to find it."

Hanging up, Helen flipped over and snagged the room phone from a nightstand. She dialed the front desk and ordered the chicken parm, with a glass of beer.

After thinking for a minute, she also ordered a brownie for dessert.

What the hell, she thought, might as well live a little at a serial killer's expense.

CHAPTER 11

Thursday, Sept. 12

THE NEXT DAY, Carstairs picked her up from the hotel in an undercover car. Within two blocks, he turned away from the downtown area and headed into the suburbs.

"Where we going?" Helen asked.

"To Sami Brayn's house."

Helen frowned but didn't say anything.

About thirty minutes later, they pulled up to an unmarked intersection in Littleton. Pulling into the curb, Carstairs shifted into park and pointed to a double-story, light red house halfway down the block on the north side of the street.

"The Brayn house?" Helen asked.

The Denver cop nodded. He stared for a moment, drumming his fingers on the console, before turning to Helen.

"They're damned near an anachronism nowadays. Nuclear family, first marriage for both parents. Three kids and a family dog. Dad's a factory foreman, mom stayed home till the youngest kid was in middle school, then got a part-time job at the local library. Dad goes hunting with his buddies a couple of times a year and mom, believe it or not, belongs to an honest-to-God book club."

"John," Helen began.

"There was two years age difference between the big brother and Sami, the middle kid. A year between her and her younger sister. She was into soccer, gymnastics, and cheerleading. Her brother was QB for the high school team since his sophomore year."

He paused for a second, but Helen wasn't sure if he was speaking to her or to himself.

"So tell me, can you get any more white bread, middle America than that?"

Helen, still silent, shook her head.

Something seemed to snap behind Carstairs's eyes, and he sat a little straighter in his seat.

"See that balcony-type window on the second floor," he said as he pointed it out.

"Yeah."

"That's her bedroom, top of the stairs on the right. You have to go right by the parents' room to get to Sami's. Matilda, the German Shepherd, was basically Sami's dog and always spent the night in her room. The dog's full-grown by the way. She'd usually take the dog with her whenever she went out with friends or just walking around. The way everyone tells it, whenever Matilda was apart from Sami, she'd whine for a while, just loved that kid."

"But obviously, the dog didn't go to and from school with her," Helen said.

Carstairs nodded. "That's right. Some kind of irony there. The one time she needed the dog, they weren't together."

"What's your point?" Helen asked.

"My point is Sami Brayn was a bright, athletic, and active teenager. Willie Gray is a wasted-out schizo who weighs about a hundred and forty the day after a good Thanksgiving meal. He tops out at five-nine, if he's on tiptoes, and wears a size 29 pant."

Carstairs paused and took a breath, wiping his forehead as he did so. "Sorry. Like I said, this one's kind of gotten to me."

"What you're saying is you don't think he could have physically done the deed," Helen said.

"He could have. We both know that determined killing takes more than physicality. But it just doesn't sound right to me."

"Has he talked much about how he abducted her?"

Carstairs shook his head. "After he took us to where he buried her body, he stopped talking about her. He's not saying anything about the Brayn girl, just bragging about the other two. We haven't been able yet to determine for sure where their paths crossed. If he was handsome, charming, or had money, I could see a dozen different ways he could have gotten close to the girl. But knowing what I do about him, I just don't see Gray pulling it off."

"At least not alone," Helen said.

Carstairs nodded. "That's right. I'm not saying he's not connected in some way. But I've run through it a hundred different ways in my mind, and for me it just doesn't add up."

A slight chill ran down Helen's spine as she got an inkling of where the conversation was heading. "And what do the DA and your bosses think of that?"

The Denver cop grimaced, confirming Helen's gut feeling.

"They consider the case closed. Gray confessed, took us to the spot and that's that."

"So you think he had an accomplice?"

"Nope," Carstairs said, and his eyes had taken on a new look, an almost furious look. "I don't think he had an accomplice. I think he had a boss. Willie Gray is, at most, somebody's gopher."

Helen didn't respond. Carstairs's entire demeanor changed. His face had drawn tight, the skin contracting until his face looked like a death's head. His shoulders had tightened under his JCPenney sport coat and his hands, gripping the wheel, turned white at the knuckles.

"Willy was nothing but hired help, and piss poor help at that," the cop continued. "But he's confessing like crazy, and the DA's in a couple of states are loving it. But I don't want the gopher. I want the man in charge."

Now he leaned forward and, if anything, his voice became even tighter.

"So why don't you tell me, former homicide cop Lipscomb, just who the top guy is?"

CHAPTER 12

Monday Sept. 16th

HELEN STAYED MOST of the weekend in Denver, speaking by phone several times with both Lewis and Carstairs and spending a large chunk of the rest of the time on her laptop. Conroy's office had sent her a PDF that contained everything they could find online concerning Willy Gray. It wasn't a whole hell of a lot.

At least according to official sources, the guy simply had done little with his two-and-a-half decades of life. According to Gray himself, in his conversations with both Carstairs and other law enforcement officers, he'd spent a fair amount of time roaming the middle part of the country strangling women. Speaking with Carstairs, Helen got the impression that Gray had spoken boastfully of his exploits. She had a hard time reconciling that with the wizened, withdrawn man she'd seen down at the jail, but put it down as a possibility that Gray had some sort of disorder that could cause wild mood swings.

It wasn't that much of a stretch, she realized. Even if he'd only killed the Brayn girl, something definitely was not right in the guy's psyche.

On the other hand, assuming for even a fraction of a second that he was telling the truth about his activities, his life story so far held little in the way of the usual telltale signs.

At that, it wasn't much of a life to begin with.

Early Friday evening, Helen had figured, what the hell, and sounded Carstairs out about setting up her own interrogation with Gray, or at least one where she was in the room. The answer she received in return was about what she'd expected. So far, Carstairs had managed to keep his lieutenant unaware of her presence, and he wasn't about to jeopardize the status of the investigation just so she could get a shot at Gray. Helen understood with no hard feelings.

Hell, in her former life she doubted that she would have been even as helpful as Carstairs had been up to this point. He had definitely veered over the line of official protocol, and she could only theorize that the Brayn case had managed to burrow its way into his soul.

Between the phone conversations, reading over the PDF, and digging around online, by early Sunday evening Helen's brain felt like it was ready to fall out of her skull. She had a quick glass of wine from room service, took a long shower, pulled the drapes against the same Rocky Mountain sunset and clambered into bed.

By seven, she was out solid.

She woke to almost complete darkness, blinked her eyes a few times in the nightstand's direction, and saw the red digits 1:30 staring back at her. Rolling out of bed, she stretched her arms over her head and took several deep breaths. Even though she'd only slept about six hours, she felt completely awake.

She took a few minutes to make two phone calls, one to Lewis and the other to Carstairs, leaving messages to update them about her current plans.

Then, dressing and packing her one suitcase as quickly as she could, by two she was downstairs checking out, preparing to drive east.

In her time, Helen had interacted with several law-enforcement colleagues from both Kansas and Colorado, and she'd often heard the refrain that nighttime was the best time to drive across western Kansas. To get to KC, she could have flown, but between arriving early at Denver International Airport, plus the hassle of debarking at Kansas City and finding a car, it seemed easier, and not too much longer, to make the drive, with a straight shot on the Interstate only taking a little over eight hours.

Quite a lot of time, but what else did she have to spend it on?

Besides, she had a fair amount of thinking to do, and a long, dark drive with no distractions seemed the perfect way to do it.

CHAPTER 13

Tuesday, Sept. 17th

"WE SHOULD START selling tickets," Deputy Louisa Reynolds told Helen the next day.

The two of them were sitting on a bench outside of the Wyandotte County Sheriff's building. Headquartered in downtown Kansas City, Kansas, the sheriff and his staff served as principal law enforcement for the city as well as the surrounding county.

"Tickets?" Helen asked as she took a closer look at Reynolds. The young woman didn't appear more than thirty years old, and her dark skin offset a pair of startling black eyes. Her hair was done up in a bun so tight Helen wondered it didn't cause frown lines on her face. She had no doubt that the sheriff's office had some sort of stricture on length and style of hair, but doubted it was quite so severe as the deputy made it appear.

"Yep," Reynolds replied, "tickets. Ever since Gray started shooting his mouth off, we're getting more people snooping around than we can accommodate. Journalists, feds, you name it." The deputy gave Helen a closer look. "None like you, though. John Carstairs called me to smooth your way."

"You two know each other?"

Reynolds shrugged. "We've had some dealings. He says you're not quite the traditional private eye."

Helen smiled and shook her head. "I'm not any kind of one, traditional or otherwise. Just a hired hand doing some legal work."

"Then you've got no license or official standing in any state?"

"'Fraid not."

Reynolds nodded her head. "At least you're honest about it."

Helen sat silent for a minute, rolling the thought around in her head. "Back in my old life," she finally said, "I probably wouldn't have spoken to you at all."

Reynolds laughed. "Guess that puts me one up on you, huh?"

"So what can you tell me about Gray?" Helen asked. She could have just gone with all the documentation Conroy's office had dug up, but figured it was helpful to get the locals' feel for the guy.

"Young William Gray? At the moment, I'm just glad he's Colorado's problem instead of ours."

"He's got history here?"

Another shrug from the deputy. "Minor stuff. A few assault collars, which just turned out to be teenage guys fighting. One or two girls who claim he got a little rough in high school. In his old neighborhood he was known to vandalize cars now and then, especially the richer types."

Helen perked up at that. "Richer types?"

Reynolds held up her hand and wagged it back and forth. "Comparatively speaking. You're talking a guy who barely graduated then shuffled between minimum wage jobs. Not that unusual in his neighborhood."

"Okay."

"And, at least while he lived around here, he barely made it out of that neighborhood. But every now and then he'd get a job at a fast food joint or such, and word is he'd have problems when guys came in with sharp cars. At least, sharp by his standards."

"Resentful?"

"Oh, no doubt. We see it all the time, though. You take a guy who can't do better for himself than some thousand-dollar clunker off a used lot, if that, and some asswipe comes along with a 'Vette or Mustang, there's going to be resentment. Seeing as Johnson County, one of the richest in the country, is right next door, that kind of stuff happens all the time."

"And?"

"And every now and then, so the story goes, Willy would go overboard showing his resentment."

"Smashed windows? That kind of thing?"

"More like keying. Have you seen Willy yet?"

"I watched him for a while from another room."

"Then there you go. That's not a guy who's going to actually confront anyone straight up."

"So he's been in the system?"

"In and out," Reynolds said. "More out than in. Honestly, he's just a small-time punk, like you see in any city. Or at least he was."

"You've got his official history down pat," Helen pointed out.

Reynolds grinned. "Like I said, Little Willy's turning himself into a bit of a celebrity. But tell me, what's your interest? Who's your client?"

"'Fraid I can't get into that."

"Uh huh. According to Carstairs, you don't think Willy did the Garcia woman, right?"

"Right. What's your gut tell you? Is he up to it?"

"Look, Lipscomb, the kid's a fuckup, pardon my

language. You've got to understand. KCK isn't nearly as big or diverse as our big sister across the state line, but that doesn't mean we don't have our fair share of losers. And ole' Willy is one of them."

"I'm looking for a handle. If he's not this big, bad killer, why's he confessing?"

"And even more, how's he managing to confess, right?"

"Yeah, there is that, too."

Reynolds cocked her head at Helen, regarded her for a moment, then gave a short nod.

"How about we take a trip?" she said.

CHAPTER 14

FIFTEEN MINUTES AFTER climbing into Reynolds's department-issued, 2009 Focus, they pulled up outside of a small bar just to the east of KCK's small industrial section. The building, comprised of dirty red bricks and blackened out windows, with one lonely Paulie Girl sign hanging in the middle window, squatted in the middle of the block, spaced equally between a lot, cordoned off with chain link fencing, that held about two dozen rusted-out cars and a small bakery. At this hour of the day, the bakery's windows were shuttered.

Ryans, the sign in front of the bar read.

"The owner named Ryan?" Helen asked.

Reynolds nodded.

"And he doesn't know about apostrophes?" Helen gawked at the sign.

"Ryan's not much for reading and writing," Reynolds responded. She looked sideways at Helen. "I know the answer to this but got to ask before we go in there. Are you carrying?"

Helen shook her head. "I'm strictly on a fact-finding mission."

The deputy nodded. "Good enough. Just wanted to make sure you weren't going to pull some idiotic stunt on me."

Helen climbed out and adjusted her suit jacket. "This your usual MO?" she asked. "Carrying civilians along on an investigation?"

"Ordinarily, no," Reynolds said as they walked up to the bar's front door. "But I figure you know how to keep quiet."

"Uh huh."

"Besides," the deputy said as she grasped the oversized, tubular door handle, "I owe John for a few favors, and I know he's about to throw a fit back in Denver."

Helen frowned. The deputy's description didn't match the calm, collected detective that she'd met back west. "Meaning?"

Reynolds, her hand still on the door handle, turned and gave Helen a deep look. "I don't know if he showed it when you were there, but from what I get he's about to buck his bosses to get the truth about Willy. This thing is starting out small, but there's the potential for a lot of showboating to go around, and the brass out there are all itching for their moment of glory. There's not much any of his friends can do to help, but I figure someone unofficial may have a shot."

"You all seem to be a lot more connected than I would have guessed," Helen said.

Reynolds shrugged. "Not really. After all, Gray doesn't even fall under our jurisdiction. As far as current investigations go, he's Denver's problem. From what I hear, Lenexa's next in line after that. But if there's any chance Gray was up to something before he moved away from here, I want to know about it. So why don't we go in and meet the proprietor of this fine establishment. Oh, and one other thing. Ryan may not show it, but he's going to hate a couple of women coming into his place."

Helen puzzled over that one as the deputy flung the

door open and they went inside.

The main thing that impressed itself on her senses as she walked into the place was—darkness.

Even with the blacked-out windows, Helen hadn't expected it to be so gloomy inside. At a quick glance, she counted a grand total of six lights hanging from the ceiling, and they all looked to be no more than sixty watts. A small light behind the door and next to the cash register would barely allow the bartender to count the money.

At that point in the day, ten customers ranged around the place. All men, and all looking over fifty. They bore, as much as Helen could tell in the gloom, the rough, weathered look of working-class Midwestern men, the type of guys who'd seen life pass them by and never could quite understand why.

The man behind the bar was a slightly younger version of his customers. He turned their way as the two women entered. Even in the dark and from a distance of several feet, Helen could see the man's posture, with his shoulders hunched down, and how he kept his arms close to his sides.

The bartender had done some amount of time somewhere down the line.

As the two of them approached, he pulled a wet mug out from under the tap and began wiping it dry.

"Christ, sheriff. What now?" he asked, his voice moderated.

"Come on, Brown. You know I'm not the sheriff. At least call me by my actual title, huh?" Reynolds turned to Helen. "This here is Ryan Brown. Local stumblebum and, among other things, childhood friend of your guy Gray."

At the mention of Gray's name, Helen thought she saw several of the customers scowl, though it was hard to tell in the lack of light. She could clearly see that Brown didn't like the reference.

"A creep like that's no friend of mine," the barkeep muttered.

"Come on, Ryan," Reynolds said. "You guys grew up together. Went to school together, at least as far as you went, and even got busted together a few times for keying up cars. Why be shy now?"

"I never hung out with no murderer."

Reynolds sighed and made a brushing motion with her hand. "Whatever you say, Ryan."

"So whadda ya want?"

The deputy jerked her thumb in Helen's direction. "This here is Miss Lipscomb, and she's got a few questions for you."

"She a cop?" he asked without even looking at Helen.

Reynolds sighed. "No, she's not a cop. Just an interested party with some questions." Reynolds paused and looked around the bar, all the patrons staring down at their tables and barely drinking. "It's not like you've got a ton of work to do right now, is it?"

The bartender finally stopped wiping the mug he'd toyed with the whole time and put it top down on the bar. Considering how greasy and stained the bar top looked, Helen figured he'd just wasted all that washing.

"Doesn't matter how much I've got to do. Don't like talking to no cops."

"She said I'm not a cop," Helen, tiring of the whole exchange, finally spoke up. "But if you've got a few minutes to talk I could make it worth your while."

97

"Oh yeah?" Ryan's face perked up and he squinted at her. "How's that?" Reynolds was giving Helen a sideways look.

"I need some information about Gray," Helen said. "About his early life. Stuff I can't find in police reports or on the news. If you can give it to me, I'd be willing to pay for your time."

Now the bartender took a step backwards, as if trying to hide in the murk behind him.

"I don't know nothing about any dead girls," he said, his eyes shifting back and forth.

"No one said you did. But you know Willy, right? Grew up with him?"

"What if I did? Lots of guys grew up around here. Didn't turn us all into goddamned killers."

Before Helen could frame a reply, an elderly man, his gray and black beard matted and tangled, looked up from his table. He had two beer mugs, both half full, in front of him, and his eyes, even in the bar's dimness, looked even shiftier than Brown's.

"Brown," the old man croaked. "Don't tell those bitches anything. Except maybe to come on over here and give me some entertainment."

The bartender began squirming as both Reynolds and Helen turned and looked the old man's direction. He stared back at them, half hunched over his table, and stuck his tongue out, wiggling it back and forth.

"Come on over, gals. Let's see how much of it I can take."

"Don't mind him," Ryan said, his tone almost pleading. "Old Harv gets this way every day about this time. He don't mean nothing by it."

"The hell I don't, kid! You think you know me so

goddamned much, why don't you tell them who really killed that girl in Denver. Sure as hell wasn't stupid old Willy. Huh? Come on, deputy woman. I'm the one you want. Why don't you step over and slap your cuffs on me?"

The geezer sat up straighter and flapped back and forth the front of the faded old army coat he wore. Louisa Reynolds walked over to the man, gave him the cop stare for about half a heartbeat, then shifted her hand half under her suit coat. At the same time, she leaned over and whispered something in the old man's ear.

The drunkard lurched backwards, his eyes widening, before catching himself and trying to right his chair. His mouth twitched, and as Reynolds walked back over to the bar, Helen couldn't help but compare herself with the smooth, confident deputy.

As a cop, Helen never quite had the swagger that Reynolds displayed, but she had developed the ability to dominate, some would say intimidate, other people, sometimes more than one at a time, with her confidence. She'd never, at least from her perspective, abused that power, but it had always been nice to know it was there if needed.

The day she took off the badge for good, she'd felt all that power, all that ability, drain away, never to return. Seeing Deputy Reynolds standing up straight, her back turned to the sketchy old guy at the table, Helen became fully aware, maybe for the first time, of exactly all that she'd lost two years before.

"You were saying," she said as Reynolds stood silent and drilled the bartender with her gaze, "that not all of you turned out to be girl killers?"

"Uh, yeah, that's what I meant," Ryan said. "Don't

go trying to throw anything Gray's done on the rest of the neighborhood."

"Even so, I'm guessing that not all of you have exactly walked a righteous path in your lives?"

Reynolds barked out a short laugh, shaking her head, before Ryan could even respond.

"I don't think I want to talk about this anymore," the man said as he began to turn away.

"You have something to hide?" Helen said to his back.

The bartender stopped, his fists tensing. Through his thin white shirt, Helen could see the muscles rippling in his back. Three or four of the bar's patrons, minus the one Reynolds had silenced, leaned forward to watch the action.

Eventually, Brown turned back to face the two women. "I've got nothing to hide where that punk's concerned."

"So prove it," Helen said. Deputy Reynolds had taken a few steps back, letting Helen run the play. "Give me ten minutes of your time, max, and I'll be on my way."

A whole spectrum of emotions played across the man's face. Another old timer, sitting about halfway down the bar, raised his empty mug, and Brown shushed him.

"Ten minutes?" he said.

"That's right. Then I'm gone. We're both gone."

"And this one," he pointed at Reynolds, "doesn't come around hassling me anymore?"

"It's not a lifetime guarantee, Ryan," Reynolds spoke up. "But if I don't have good reason I'll always have something better to do."

Helen wanted to smile her appreciation but didn't want any change in demeanor to change Ryan's mind.

"Okay," he said. "Let's grab a booth in the back. You girls want anything to drink?"

Two years ago, Helen would have gone off on the guy for calling her a girl. Now, she just shook her head and followed him as he raised the barflap and headed to the back.

CHAPTER 15

"SO WHERE'S THE money?" Brown asked as the three of them sat in a back booth, the bartender on one side and Helen and Deputy Reynolds on the other.

"In a minute."

Although Helen had enough disposable funds on hand, courtesy of Gordon Conroy's office, to pay anything reasonable, she knew that if she showed the money too soon she'd get minimal info, if that. She was the buyer, and the dominance had to flow from her.

"Do you know this man?" she asked as she pulled out her phone and brought up a picture of Leo Benson.

Brown took the phone from her hand and peered at it, a bluish cast showing on his face.

After a moment, he slid the phone back to her. "Looks kinda familiar, but I couldn't say from where."

Helen drummed her fingers on the table. She doubted that Brown was the kind to keep up with national news, but Benson's face had been plastered, off and on, across cable TV for the last few years. There would be months of nothing about the man, then some new development came along and the networks hauled out their stables of legal experts to dissect, resect, and discuss the event ad nauseam.

"What I'm wondering is does he look familiar from around here? Have you ever seen him with Willy?"

"Willy hasn't lived around here for a while," Brown

said. "At least a couple of years."

Helen repressed a sigh, and she could feel Reynolds, sitting next to her, rolling her eyes.

"I realize that, Mr. Brown. I know it's been some time since you've seen Willy. What I mean is, back in the day, could this guy have been one of his associates?"

As she inadvertently slipped into cop-speak, she saw Brown's eyes glaze over.

"His what?"

"Friends, acquaintances," Helen said. "Could they have hung out at all?"

Brown reached out for the phone again, and once more Helen slid it across to him. He picked it up, peered at it even longer and harder than last time, then put it down, barely missing plopping it into a small puddle of leftover beer.

"Don't think so," Brown said, leaning back in the booth and crossing his arms. "After all, that dude's kind of old to be with someone Willy's age, wouldn't you say?"

Helen stared at him for a moment, pondering her next move. Was he lying or not? She had no solid reason to believe he was. According to Benson's own account, he had no clue who Willy Gray was before the youth popped up on the news taking credit for some of Benson's killings. If he was telling the truth, absolutely no reason existed why any of Gray's former homies should recognize the man's face.

"Does that man," Brown pointed toward the phone, "have something to do with Willy claiming he killed all those girls?"

"He's only admitting to three women," Helen said.

"Yeah, but we keep hearing how he's claiming he

did a whole bunch. I got to tell you, almost all of us thought that was bullshit as soon as we heard it."

Helen leaned closer to Ryan, and she saw Deputy Reynolds perk up too.

"Why's that?" she asked.

"'Cause unless he's changed a whole lot in a few years, the Willy most of us remember wouldn't have the balls for something like that."

Helen frowned as she looked around the bar. Except for the older guy that Reynolds had put down when they first entered, the various men scattered around the place weren't even trying to look disinterested. From tables and barstools, they all had glued in on the action going on in that back booth.

"Gray's got a record," she said as she turned back to the bartender. "Assaults and such . Why do you say the idea of him stepping up to killing is bullshit?"

Brown snorted and shook his head, relaxing more than he had at any moment since the two women had entered his business.

"'Cause Willy's rep is just that, a rep. He would always go into some club, pool hall or whatever, always with some friends of his, stir something up, usually by coming on to some dude's girl, then when things started flying he'd step back, get the hell out of Dodge, and leave his buddies to finish things up."

"You know this for a fact?" Helen asked.

"Sure. He roped me in on more than one occasion. Got more than my share of bruises and cuts because of that little punk."

Helen frowned, and beside her Reynolds shook her head.

"So why keep helping him out?" Reynolds asked.

104

The bartender shrugged and looked down at the table. "The dude's a bud. Besides, it wasn't that bad, especially if his older brother was around. Now that guy could kick ass when he wanted to."

"Brother?" Helen asked.

"Yeah, Phil. A serious badass. But he couldn't stand his folks. Took off a long time ago, back when we were still in school."

Helen studied the man for a minute. Brown may think he had some sort of hot intel, but none of it indicated that Gray couldn't have started killing, Maybe he was a wimp in his youth who managed to grow into a monster.

"Besides," Ryan said, looking back up at them. "The guy was scared of blood."

"Phil?"

"No. Willy. Guy was a wuss when it came to the real thing."

"Yeah?"

"Oh, yeah. I've seen him puke when someone had a nosebleed. One time, back in school, I got smacked in the mouth playing basketball in gym. Damned near took out a couple of teeth and had me bleeding out the mouth. Willy was about six or seven feet away, and most of us thought he was going to faint he looked so sick."

"Did he?" Helen asked.

"Did he what?"

"Faint."

"Naw, but he did end up puking on the gym floor. I'm telling you, whoever killed that girl out in Denver, and those others, it sure as hell wasn't Willy Gray."

Helen sighed, and reached into her pocket to pay the bartender, beginning to realize that she'd spent the afternoon chasing a wild goose.

"On the other hand," Ryan looked up, and a light appeared in his eyes that hadn't been there before, "if you really want to know everything about Willy, there's someone better you can talk to."

CHAPTER 16

ACCORDING TO RYAN Brown, the person Helen should really talk to was a young woman named Toni Orson. Brown provided her address, as of a few years back, and a topless bar on the Missouri side of the area, where she used to work as a waitress. She was without a steady boyfriend or husband, at least as far as Brown knew.

"Your crowd really keeps in touch, don't you?" Helen asked Brown.

The bartender only shrugged and looked down at the table, hunching his shoulders a bit more as he did so.

Even though she had no reason, other than general police instincts, to doubt the info, she wanted to make sure she left things clearly understood.

"Thanks for your help," she said as she pulled a couple of hundred-dollar bills from her wallet. She slid the money across the table as Brown broke out of his hunch and reached for it.

But when his fingers grasped the paper, Helen didn't let go. The bartender looked up at her, confusion in his eyes.

"I'm willing to pay what I agreed," Helen said, "but let's be clear about something. When I go to talk to this woman, I'm not going to find out she's your girlfriend, or your dealer, or your cousin and this is a quick scam to get my money, right?"

Brown shook his head, and Helen gave him the dough.

****

"So what do you think?" Reynolds asked as she and Helen walked out of the bar.

Helen shrugged, her mind still going back over the last several minutes. "It seems like a stretch, almost the first thing that came to his mind to get paid."

"I agree. An old girlfriend? Who they used to party with? What's she going to tell you that he couldn't?"

"You know how this works," Helen said as the two of them climbed into the Focus. "You take a strand, pull on it till something else pops up, then pull on that and keep going down the line."

"In other words," Reynolds said.

Helen grinned. "In other words, it's probably a waste of time, but I can't let any possibility go by without checking it out."

As Reynolds pulled the Focus out of the parking lot and pointed it back in the direction of the station, both women went silent, each consumed with their own thoughts.

"That bit about him being scared of blood could just be so much crap," Reynolds finally said.

Helen nodded without looking the deputy's way. "Or maybe he actually was that way, but something happened somewhere along the line to snap him out of it."

Reynolds hung a sudden right and powered the Focus into a convenience store parking lot. Shifting into Park, she turned to face her passenger.

"You don't believe that," she said.

"No," Helen said. "I really don't."

"Then what the hell is it all about? Is the kid just a glory hog trying to be somebody big for fifteen minutes?"

"Could be, but I actually think it's a lot more than that."

"You interested in sharing some of your info? Friendly cooperation only goes so far."

"I'm working for a lawyer," Helen said.

Reynolds grimaced. "Which means you got an obligation not to reveal stuff. Just tell me this. Have you come across knowledge of any crimes in Wyandotte County?"

"No," Helen said, glad she could be truthful with the young deputy. "As of now, everything connected to Gray happened after he left here and headed out on the road."

"Except for the Garcia killing."

"Right. And even that took place after he'd originally left. Nothing else on the radar before then."

"That you know of."

"That I know of," Helen conceded. "But I'll tell you, confidentiality or no, if I come across anything, I'll get it right to you."

Reynolds nodded and shifted the car back into gear.

"I can't go with you to check out the girlfriend," Reynolds said. "It's across the state line, and I wouldn't have any official pull."

"How many jurisdictions you have butting up against each other out here?"

"More than you'd care to count. But if you want, I can give you someone's name."

Helen mulled that over for a while as mid-day traffic streamed by them. "I don't think so," she said after a few minutes. "Thanks for the offer, but I think I can take it from here."

"Okay, but if you feel you need some backup, or if the address the pop star back there gave doesn't pan out, let me know and I'll see what I can do."

Helen smiled and leaned back in the seat as Reynolds turned the car around and headed out of the parking lot.

CHAPTER 17

HELEN FIGURED TONI Orson would hold until the next day. As a bar waitress, if in fact she wasn't a flat-out stripper, she no doubt would be working well into the night. Helen had the home address, and it would be easier, and less of a hassle, to accost the girl at home.

Provided the address was correct.

And that she actually did work nights.

And hadn't brought someone home with her.

Sighing, Helen kicked her heels off the moment she entered the hotel room. A DoubleTree this time, nice enough for the comforts of home, but not so extravagant that she'd feel like a member of the idle rich.

Flopping on the bed, she turned over on her side and stared at the wall. A watercolor adorned the center of the far wall, a depiction of some old-time naval battle, with the warship that served as the focus of the painting taking a hell of a beating from an assortment of other ships. Although the area of battle was lit up by a bright sun, marred only a little by swirls of cannon smoke, dark storm clouds gathered in the background, ominously signaling that the beleaguered ship was experiencing its last moments.

"I know how you feel," Helen said to the artwork, instantly wondering if talking to herself was the first sign that she'd finally begun to crack up.

Twisting away from the picture, she stared up at the

ceiling, running through the events of the last few days in her head, trying to put the whole thing together into some sort of pattern that made sense.

The cops in Denver were convinced, for good reason, that Willy Gray was guilty in the murder of Sami Brayn, primarily because Gray was doing everything possible to convince them that he was a bad son of a bitch. While going through the legal song and dance in Colorado, Gray had begun copping to other murders, leading authorities to other crime scenes than just the one he was on the hook for.

So okay, first item that didn't make any sense. Wouldn't any halfway competent person, even a bottom scraper like Gray seemed to be, do everything possible to keep himself out of legal trouble? Who would willingly, with no offers on the table, go out of his way to pin even more murders on himself? Murders that, until he started talking, the authorities had absolutely no inkling he was connected to?

Which led to item number two. Helen's sort-of client, Leo Benson. Benson was foaming at the mouth, more or less, because those murders Gray was confessing to were actually committed by himself. Or so he said. And Benson had been keeping those crimes in his back pocket, so to speak, hole cards he was planning to use to try to finagle himself out of a death sentence. And Benson, at least as far as he insisted to Helen, had absolutely no connection to Gray. Had never even heard of the guy until he started splashing himself all over the news.

So how could Gray possibly know the specific details, even down to names and body locations, of murders committed by someone he'd never met?

She puzzled that one over for a while, not moving and barely breathing, until an obvious possible solution popped into her head. She glanced at her watch. Still early enough that the man would probably be in his office. She got up, went across the room and dug her phone out of her bag. An instant later, she was back on the bed, this time sitting at the head, her back propped against the pillows, and listening to her phone ring.

Almost simultaneously with the third ring, the person picked up.

"Yes?"

"Got a question for you," Helen said. "It just came to me."

"Are you making any progress?" Conroy asked.

"Not that I know of, though it's a little too soon to tell. But I do have something I want to bounce off of you."

Conroy sighed. "I'm currently working on the fourth appeal for one of our clients, accused of assault and battery on a cop. He swears he didn't do it and refuses to do a simple plea. He's already been found guilty and had three appeals denied. You catch the irony?"

"Not really," Helen said, "but what I need—"

"The irony is, if he'd just pled out and gone to prison like a good little boy, he would have been out by now. This damned thing's dragged on for nearly four years. Four years out of his life when he could have gotten it over and—"

"Conroy," Helen interrupted. "I really didn't call you to hear you bleed out over someone who attacked a cop."

A heartbeat, two, then the lawyer answered. "Sorry about that, Lipscomb. I'm so annoyed with this guy I forgot your history for a minute. Started talking to you like you were one of our associates. So what is it you needed?"

"Want to run something by you, but I want your word that you won't pass it on to Benson."

Another pause, longer this time. "I'm not sure I can do that. Leo's my client, after all, which technically means he's your client, as well. It'd be hard for me to justify keeping information from him. I'd need a damned good reason to even consider something like that."

"It's not information. Nothing concrete. I just have an idea I want to bounce. Okay?"

"Well, then, I guess. Throw it at me."

"A whole new angle on this thing came to me that could change everything."

"Okay." Conroy's voice sounded slower, lower, as if doubting that a simple ex-cop could come up with any ideas he hadn't already thought of. "What is it?"

"The way Benson laid it out is that this Gray kid had somehow gotten hold of intelligence about some of Benson's kills. Ones that no one else knew about, right?"

"That's the gist of it. But you already know that. So what?"

"But it seems impossible. If this kid knows nothing about Benson, how could he have successfully copped to those killings?"

"As I recall, that's what Mr. Benson's hired you to do. Figure out how Gray is pulling off the impossible so I can put a stop to it."

Helen took a deep breath, her phone almost slipping from her sweaty hand.

"That's correct, counselor. But if you think about it for a minute, there's another angle, another way of looking at this, that makes a whole lot more sense."

Conroy stayed silent for a minute, and Helen thought that in the background she could hear the sound of him tapping a pencil.

"And what would that other angle be?" he finally asked.

"What if," Helen said, "just consider. What if we've got it backwards?"

"Backwards?"

"Right. What if it's Benson who's somehow trying to take credit for Gray's killings?"

CHAPTER 18

Wednesday, Sept. 18th

TONI ORSON'S RESIDENCE turned out to be about what Helen had expected. Almost a lean-to, the house, complete with peeling yellow paint, sat in the middle of a neighborhood almost too bedraggled to be classed as rundown. Five houses, with Orson's in the middle, occupied the north side of the block with four homes on the south side. On the southeast corner sat a convenience store with four gas pumps and a boarded-up window.

Three houses on the block had "For Rent" signs posted in their front yard, and Helen would have bet that all the other homes were rentals as well. Up and down the block, in both driveways and doorless garages, rested a collection of rusted pickups, decades-old muscle cars with shocks so worn their fenderwells scraped the ground, and assorted foreign compacts that hailed back to at least the eighties, most with duct tape securing windows.

The cracked, oil-stained driveway in front of Orson's house held a fifteen-year-old Subaru, complete with primered fenders and a catalytic converter hanging loose. The front curtains were pulled shut at nine in the morning.

A chain-link fence that encircled the house had a

standard "Beware of Dog" sign, but Helen had sat in her car for nearly twenty minutes and seen no sign of an animal. The yard and house were both small enough that even a near-comatose animal would have made some movement. Plus, from the front and side angles, Helen couldn't see any doghouse or food and water bowls.

Didn't mean there wasn't a dog inside, but sometimes you had to go with half a loaf.

She hadn't detected any sort of noise or movement from within the house, that in itself not that unusual. If Toni worked regular bar hours, she'd probably make a habit of sleeping till noon.

Which was exactly Helen's hope. It was often better and easier to get people off guard if they were half asleep.

Helen exited her rental car and headed up the cantilevered sidewalk to the house. The chain link fence enclosed the front yard, but there was no chain or padlock around the gate handle, allowing her easy access to the porch. The porch steps had once been painted a rather putrid green, but as with so much of the paint in this neighborhood, most of the green had scabbed off, exposing the bare concrete beneath.

The boards that made up the porch were so warped and watersogged that crossing the few feet to the front door in heels would have been an ordeal. Helen was glad she ordinarily wore flats during field work

In the future, if I ever get depressed about how shitty my life's turned out, I can always think back to this day and feel better.

She saw no doorbell and doubted that it would have worked if there were one, so she opened up the screen door and gave a couple of quick raps.

A second went by, a few more, and after a full two minutes, Helen knocked again. Lowering her hand, she heard a faint shuffling behind the door. Then another few seconds with nothing, before the door opened. Only an inch or so, enough for Helen to make out an eye and see that the door either didn't have a chain or it hadn't been secured.

"Yeah?" The voice, though young, already seemed coarsened by either too many cigarettes or too much alcohol. Or maybe something even more potent.

"Toni Orson?"

The single eye scanned up and down, sizing Helen up.

"Yeah? Who are you?"

Helen kept the screen door open with her shoulder.

"My name's Helen Lipscomb. I was wondering if we could talk for a few minutes."

Orson's eye did that scanning thing again before moving back to center and locking with Helen's gaze.

"About what?"

Now came the make or break moment. Helen had no clue how the woman currently felt about Willy Gray, but considering her lifestyle, there was a better than even chance that saying Gray's name would get the door slammed in her face.

Of course, on a practical level, if that happened Helen was sure she could either kick or bull her way in anyway. Being a private citizen made that a little less problematic than when she'd been a cop.

But only a little.

"About William Gray," Helen said.

Through the door crack, the woman's face seemed to shrink in a bit.

"Willy?"

Helen nodded. "Yes, William Gray. I believe you used to know him?"

The girl shook her head, but not in a very forceful way. "I don't know what you mean."

Helen was getting tired of standing there propping open the screen door.

"You're Toni Orson, right?"

"Who sent you here?" the girl asked.

"No one sent me, but I was talking yesterday with Ryan Brown."

Even through the narrow crack, Helen could see the face the girl made. "Ugh. Ryan's nothing but a—"

"Look, Miss Orson, I'm sorry if I woke you up, or am bothering you in some way. But I just need a few minutes of your time to ask a couple of questions about Gray then I'm gone. So what do you say? I'll pay you for the time."

The girl moved back a step or two, and the door opened another inch.

"You're a cop," she said.

"No."

"You look like a cop."

Helen sighed, wondering how many times she'd have to go through this scenario.

"I was a cop, a long time ago," she said. "I'm not now. Would a cop offer you money for information?"

The Orson woman made another of those faces. "Some of the ones I've known..." she faltered and left the thought unsaid. "So why you interested in Willy?" she said after a minute. "What've you got to do with him?"

Helen guessed that she hadn't heard about Gray's

recent legal troubles, which indicated that she really didn't stay in touch with her old crowd.

"Let's just say I'm running an investigation, okay? Now, you going to let me in or not?"

Helen had put an extra timbre in her voice, her tone close to how she used to interrogate suspects. By her own admission, this wasn't Orson's first go-round with law enforcement, and if she felt backed into a corner she may revert to old habits.

The girl stared through the slightly-wider crack for another moment or two, then sighed and swung the door all the way open. "Come on in."

The living room was about what Helen had expected, looking as if a cross between a tornado and a hurricane had taken up residence. A panoply of smells assaulted her as soon as she crossed the threshold, causing her to wrinkle her nose and begin breathing through her mouth.

Orson, dressed in cut-offs, flip flops and a once-white tank top with the faded-out name of some obscure rock band etched across the front, shuffled over to a yellowish, spring-deprived cloth couch and plopped into it, slouching about half of her length down the front.

"You're the first," she said, "but I'll bet you won't be the last."

"Come again?" Helen said as she gazed around the room, looking for some place safe to sit. The only other furniture, besides the couch, were two lawn chairs with half their plastic straps frayed. Shrugging, she stayed standing.

"Not the last," Toni repeated. "Once other people start digging around Willy's past, it's going to be like a subway station through here."

Okay, so she had kept up with her old boyfriend's troubles.

Orson waved around the gracious expanse of her domicile.

"Uh huh," Helen said.

"You think I'll be able to make something?" the girl asked.

"Make something?"

"Yeah, like tell my story to a TV station or something? Maybe one of those cable networks that run all those legal shows?"

Helen peered at the woman for a moment, trying to remember if she herself had ever been so visibly desperate in her life. Not that she could remember. Then again, she thought as she glanced around the squalid apartment, I've never sunk quite so low as this.

At least, not so far.

"Possibly," she said, "but you've got to be careful."

"Careful?"

"Sure. Start blabbing about criminal stuff and the cops may start looking at you."

"Me? I split from Willy long before he got into this killin' stuff."

"Then you may be okay. But just to make sure, why don't we talk it over?"

Orson flopped a hand in the direction of the lawn chairs and, sighing, Helen eased herself into the one with fewer frayed straps.

"And anyway," Toni continued, "I got something that will be valuable to the cops when they find out. Something that will convince them I got nothing to do with any of his stuff."

"And what would that be?" Helen asked.

A sly, somewhat shifty look came into the girl's eyes. "I can give them Willy's partner."

Helen felt her breath catch for a minute. "Partner? You mean he worked with someone in Colorado?"

"No. Geez, don't you guys know anything? I mean a guy he grew up with back here. A guy who Willy would do whatever he wanted. I mean, this guy would say shit and Willy would squat down and ask what color."

Helen took a moment to mull that over. "You're not talking about Ryan Brown?" she finally asked.

Toni puffed in exasperation, causing her bangs to flop against her forehead. "Ryan's a dweeb. Always has been. Most of those guys Willy hung around with were dweebs. Always strutting around like they were something tough. Truth is, if most of them came across actual, real tough guys, they'd piss their pants."

"So you're talking about—"

"I'm talking about the guy who ran all those guys. Had them jumping through whatever hoops he wanted. If you're looking for a killer, you're looking for this guy. Not Willy, for Chrissakes."

"I talked with Ryan yesterday. He didn't say anything about this bogeyman of yours."

Another puff, and Toni slunk deeper into the soiled couch. "Like I told you. All those guys Willy used to run with are scared to death of him. There's no way any of them would dare give you his name. If you can make it worth my while, the dude's yours."

Helen stared at the girl, weighing her options. Could it be that she was actually onto something here? She remembered Carstairs' doubt back in Denver that Gray himself could have pulled off the Brayn killing, let alone the other two.

"What about you?" she asked after a minute. "If he's so big and bad, aren't you worried about giving him up?"

Toni Orson swiveled her head back and forth, encompassing the entire ratty room in which the two of them sat.

"Yeah, right," she said. "Like I've really got anything to lose."

CHAPTER 19

"WHO IS HE?" Helen asked.

Toni grinned, stood up from her chair and went into what passed for a kitchen. She opened the refrigerator door and looked over the top.

"You want some iced tea?" she asked.

Helen, wanting to keep the woman talking, nodded. A minute later, Toni came back into the living room and handed a jelly jar full of a rather mawkish-looking tea to Helen. She pantomimed taking a quick sip and put the glass down.

"Who is this guy?" she repeated.

Toni downed half of her glass before replying, the whole time she drank her eyes staying fixedly on Helen.

"Why?" she finally asked. "You want to question him, too?"

The simple answer was yes. By now the mystery of Willy Gray had gotten inside of her. But there was a much more practical reason she wanted to find this mystery man of Toni's and talk to him.

"Of course," she said. "I'm investigating and anything I can turn up, anyone I can talk to, could be helpful."

"Uh huh." Toni went back to silence as she finished drinking her tea. She set the glass down, wiped her mouth with the back of her hand, and leaned back on the couch.

"And what about me?" she asked.

"Excuse me?"

"What do I get out of it?"

The two of them studied each other for a minute as Helen framed her reply.

"Willy's on the hook for a murder, possibly three or more. If there's a chance he didn't do it…"

"If he didn't do them, he's done plenty of other shitty stuff. And I haven't seen him in years, so why do I care?"

Okay, so morality didn't work.

"What is it you want?" Helen asked the younger woman.

Toni did a slow swivel with her head, taking in the entire living room. She had a look on her face as if she were seeing the house for the first time, and not thinking much of what she saw.

"Who are you working for?" she asked.

"I can't tell you that," Helen said. "It's a legal thing."

Toni nodded. "Whoever it is, they must have bucks. You're here, you were in Colorado. You look like you're doing okay for yourself."

Helen glanced down at her outfit. She was wearing tan slacks, a white blouse, and a gray blazer. The entire outfit, including her gray pumps, were strictly Kohl's. She didn't see it herself, but to someone from Toni Orson's background, she possibly looked highly fashionable.

But she didn't want to come off as out of the other woman's class if she could help it. For all she knew, Toni was the type to resent those better off than her.

"I've missed my share of meals," she said,

"especially lately."

"Yeah, well, you don't look it."

"Ms. Orson, how about we get back to—"

"How much?"

"Excuse me?"

"You want information on this other guy. Okay, that's fair. But what am I getting for it? Especially if he has something to do with this trouble Willy's in, shouldn't I get something for it?"

Good God, Helen thought. A shakedown. What's in it for me.

"How much would you think is fair?" she asked.

"Uh uh," Toni replied. "You tell me what you think is right, and I'll tell you whether or not you're even close to the ballpark."

Helen thought quickly. It wasn't a matter of available funds, of course. Benson had more than a thousand Toni Orsons could spend in their lifetime. At the same time, she didn't want to become a walking ATM for anyone who knew any little fragment about Willy Gray.

"How's a thousand sound?" she asked.

The other woman mulled that one for a minute then looked around her living room again. "Not bad," she said, "but five thousand sounds a whole lot better."

To a man of Benson's resources, the difference between the two sums would be unnoticeable, but Helen wasn't sure if Gordon Conroy would feel the same, and of course, any funds would have to be funneled through the lawyer.

"Are you sure you've got something for me?" Helen asked. "If you are, I can probably get more. But I have to know for sure I'm getting something of value."

Toni grinned, showing a couple of tobacco-stained teeth. "You come by tomorrow at this time," she said, "and I'll give you something of value."

CHAPTER 20

Thursday, Sept. 19th

HELEN CALLED CONROY that night and filled him in on Toni Orson's story, and while the lawyer hemmed and hawed a bit at the amount of money, he ended up okaying the deal.

"Provided," he stressed, "that she actually gives us something of value."

"Don't worry. I'll check it out from each direction before I hand over a penny."

The next morning, she left her hotel room and headed back to Toni Orson's neighborhood. As she turned the corner that led to Toni's block, everything looked pretty much as it had the day before.

The first intimation of trouble came when Helen knocked on the door and got no answer. She glanced over and saw the VW sitting in the driveway, seemingly in the exact space it had been the day before.

Helen knocked again and waited an adequate amount of time but received no answer.

Toni could have been gone for all sorts of reasons, the most obvious that she'd changed her mind about cooperating. But that VW perched in the driveway like an omen, almost daring Helen to think the worst.

She glanced to both sides, then turned around and surveyed the entire neighborhood. No one was around, not a single soul to be seen. While kids in the area should be in school, this didn't seem the type of neighborhood where one could automatically make such an assumption. Even so, any minute now a car could turn a corner or someone could walk out of their house, so if Helen was going to do anything, it had to be now.

The front door lock didn't present much of a challenge, though she noticed right off that a safety chain wasn't affixed to the door. When she'd left yesterday, she'd noticed the chain, so the fact that it hung loose made her breathe a bit easier. More of an indication that Toni left on her own power and less of a chance to find something bad inside.

Of course, something bad could have come and gone via the back door, but Helen wanted to grasp at any positive indicator.

Once inside, she shut the door and stood still for a minute, listening intently. She heard nothing beyond the usual ambient noise of an empty house, slight whistles of a breeze through poorly constructed windows, an occasional creak, and the hum of electrical appliances.

Even as she moved forward, Helen knew Toni wasn't there. Where the woman had gone, and by whose conveyance, assuming the VW was hers, wasn't clear. Hoping to find an answer, she began at the small dining room table, looking for any scrap of paper on which Toni might have scrawled something. True, these days most people kept any sort of contact or appointment information in their phones, but since Helen obviously didn't have access to Toni's phone, she was going for the next best thing.

The dining table, though, turned out a bust. It held only a random handful of playing cards; a half-drunk can of Coors Light; an ashtray with about a dozen half-smoked cigs smashed out, and an envelope from a credit card company, the bill placed on top that showed Toni owed over five hundred dollars on her MasterCard.

Helen next went around the corner and down a short hall to what she assumed to be Toni's bedroom. That room also contained the same jumbled miscellany that the rest of the house held, even more scattered. Although she despaired of finding anything in the accumulated mess of clothes, hosiery and shoes that dotted the bedroom floor, she spotted right off what she was looking for.

On the nightstand next to the unmade double bed sat an honest-to-goodness landline telephone. Whether working or not she didn't know, but there was also a small notepad, the kind comprised of varying layers of pastel-colored pages, and a red Bic next to the phone.

Toni was still on the first layer of the pad, pink, and the page on top was blank. However, squinting in the morning sunlight that filtered through the unshaded window, she made out some scratches on that pad.

She glanced around the bedroom, didn't see what she needed, then headed back out to the front part of the house. In the age of cellphones, the odds were long that most people, let alone someone like Toni, would have one handy, but lo-and-behold, on the coffee table in the living room Helen spotted what she needed.

A pencil. Next to a worn copy of Cosmopolitan.

Shrugging, she took the pencil and did the old-fashioned light tracing technique, darkening that top pink sheet in an attempt to pull up whatever had been on the sheet above it.

And damned if it didn't work.

Helen could make out what looked like an apartment address. She wasn't all that familiar with KC, at least not as much as a native. And even the natives didn't know every street name in the metro area, but for some reason, she had the feeling the address belonged in one of the grungier downtown sections.

Oh well, that's what Google Maps was for.

She didn't know for sure she'd find Toni there, but at the moment it was the best guess to make.

PART III
Kansas City to Nebraska

CHAPTER 21

Thursday, Sept. 19th

THE TALL BLACK cop, wearing a pale gray suit with dark blue shirt and black tie, handed Helen's wallet back to her, then sat down beside her on the ambulance's bumper.

"They taking you in?" he asked, jerking his head at the two paramedics standing off to the side.

"As soon as you guys clear me from the scene. You think you could see your way to doing that?"

The plainclothesman, who had identified himself as Raymond Grierson upon arriving on the scene, grinned at her. "Looks to me like you're not that hurt. You're managing to sit up straight and everything."

Silently, Helen agreed with him. What had seemed a shocking wound during the heat of action had subsided to a dull ache. When the paramedics had looked her over, they'd both agreed the cut wasn't too deep, but they wanted a doctor to examine anyway. Helen had been all for that, but so far the police, in the form of Detective Second Grade Raymond Grierson, hadn't allowed them to move on.

"So how do you know Louisa Reynolds?" he asked.

"Oh, we go way back," Helen replied.

"Uh huh." Grierson looked dubious. Still, the man's posture was relaxed, his shoulders slumped a bit and his hands dangled by his sides. He was about the loosest-looking cop Helen could ever remember seeing around a murder scene, herself included.

"You ever work with her?" Helen asked.

Grierson held his hand up in a flat plane and wagged it. "More or less. We're on different sides of the state line, of course, but around here we look at jurisdictional lines a lot looser than some places do."

"Did you call her?" she asked.

Grierson shrugged. "She's at a crime scene and not available. Kind of like me right now. So I guess for the moment it's up to you to be square with me and tell me what you were doing in that building and who the murdered woman is."

"Her name's Toni Orson. She's a local. I've got her address in my purse, if you want it."

"That's okay. We can get it off the net. How do you know Miss Orson?"

"She's a potential source in a case I'm working on."

"So why did you come here looking for her instead of going to her home?"

Helen paused, unsure of how much to share with the mellowed-out detective. On the one hand, she wanted to share as much as possible, mainly because there was a stone-cold killer running loose. On the other hand, she had no way of knowing if giving out too much information would be detrimental to her own investigation.

"Miss Lipscomb?" Grierson prodded.

"I was supposed to meet with her today to follow up on an interview. She didn't show up, so I went looking for her."

"Meet with her where?"

"At her house."

"And she wasn't there?"

"No."

"And knew to find her here? Did she leave a message or anything?"

Helen paused again while Grierson gave her a searching look.

Of course, the guy was suspicious. Were their roles reversed, Helen would have known right off the story was, at the least, incomplete.

"You're looking at me as if I'm the malefactor. I'm not the one who killed that woman."

"Doesn't mean you're not involved somehow," he said.

"You want me to lift my shirt so you can see the knife wound again, detective?"

"No need. Got a look at it once, and I'm sure it hurts like hell. But it's far from being a mortal wound, if you get my drift."

Helen gritted her teeth for a moment to work her anger down. Unloading on the locals was never a good idea, even if you once belonged to a branch of the club yourself.

On the other hand, as soon as they went to search Toni's house and talked to her neighbors, who knew what they'd find.

"I went inside," she said.

"Broke in?"

Helen shrugged. Attempting to curb her irritation, she looked away from Grierson and scanned the crowd, seeing the motley assortment usually found hanging out at recent crime scenes. Senior citizens shaking their heads at what their neighborhood had come to, young people skipping school and treating the whole thing as a lark, and shop owners pulling their hair out at what all the official attention was doing to their business.

"Lipscomb," Grierson almost snapped at her.

"Look, Detective," Helen said, turning back his way, "I went inside and looked around. Something tells me she's not going to worry about pressing charges for that. I saw an address on a notepad and figured it was worth a shot to check it out."

"You mean like she called someone up and asked where so and so lived?" Grierson asked.

Helen nodded. "But since she knew who she wanted to find, she obviously didn't bother writing the name down as well. So all I had was the address, and here we are."

"And when you came out here found the Orson woman dead. And practically bumped into some guy who you assume is the killer."

Now it was Helen's turn to scowl. "I'd tell you everything if I could, but I don't know that much. Maybe if we pool our information together and—" She cut herself off as the black cop started shaking his head.

"You should know better, Detective. It doesn't work that way." The cop nodded as Helen's eyes flared. "That's right. Of course, I recognized your name. Would have come to me eventually, anyway. Few years back, I followed your story as closely as I could, especially the way the higher-ups hung you out to dry."

Helen stared at the man, searching for an answer to that. She wondered if he'd caught on to her story as a cautionary note, an example of what could happen to a minority if they bucked the power structure too fiercely.

"Plus, it sounds like you're working private in some

way, but my instincts are telling me not quite as officially as some of us would want? Mind telling me what sort of game it is you're running?"

"I'm working for an attorney, out of state."

"Of course," Grierson said, a look of disgust crossing his face. "You know the man you saw running away?"

"Not by sight, no."

Grierson scowled even more. "Know a name?"

"No. Orson was supposed to give me that today. I gave Officer Paulson over there…" She pointed towards a young uniformed officer standing close to the building's entrance. "…a description of him. Or as much as I could."

"Yeah." Grierson opened up a small notebook. "White guy, you're pretty sure. Average height or a little more. Heavyset and long, dirty black hair. How far away you say you were from him?"

"I was kind of concentrating on the knife in his hands."

"So you say. 'Course, so far it doesn't look as if he used a blade on the woman."

Helen shrugged. "Set me up with a sketch artist," she said. "If you've got someone good we may be able to put something together for you."

"We'll do that. Can I trust you to come by the station as soon as the docs are done checking you out?"

Helen nodded. "Sure thing. And as long as I'm annoying you, how about answering a question? Have you checked with the property manager yet to get the identity of that apartment's tenant?"

"No, I hadn't. I figured I'd wait about a week or two, maybe go through the phone book and call everyone in the greater KC area to ask them if they live there, and if that didn't work I'd call my aunt down in New Iberia who dabbles in voodoo and ask her to—"

"Okay, okay." Helen held up her hands in a placating gesture, grimacing as she did so with the pain the movement caused on her belly.

"Far as that goes," he continued. "That's where it gets interesting. Turns out that apartment's been vacant for the last month or so."

Helen scrunched away from Grierson, giving her some space to look him more fully in the eye.

"You sure about that?"

"It's what the man said. And we verified the apartment number just to make sure."

"Grierson, that place is inhabited. Hell, you were up there. You saw the furniture and everything. The place is definitely being used by someone."

"Sure it is. And that someone is paying the manager, or maybe a maintenance man or two, under the table to let him stay there off the books. Which is why a pair of uniforms is currently escorting said manager down to the station for a little talk."

Helen decided to relent. "Okay, Grierson," she said with a smile, "you know your job, so I'll back off."

"Mighty kind of you."

"You got a partner around somewhere, or are you one of those hot shot solo types?"

Grierson grinned and hooked his thumb behind him and to the left. "See the short guy back there? Blue suit, blond hair? That's Phil Wilkerson, my better half."

Helen almost laughed, but even that slight stretching of her abdomen caused her to grimace. She motioned to the paramedics.

"So you want to tell me what a former homicide cop from the other side of the state working for a lawyer somewhere else is doing in a neighborhood like this? Or do Phil and I have to start getting rough?"

The paramedic, a young Korean woman, had come alongside of them. "Sorry, Detective. But we need to get her going."

Grierson sighed and rolled his eyes. "Which hospital?"

"Truman. We'll be there inside of twenty minutes if you want to follow us."

"Tell admissions that she's not to leave until either myself or Wilkerson talk to her again. I'm assuming you'll be amenable to that?" he asked, his remark directed Helen's way.

"As much as I can within the purview of—"

"Yeah, yeah. Sounds like the same old crap. I figured an ex-cop would do better. Get her the hell out of here."

"Keep in mind, if it wasn't for this ex-cop you wouldn't know about that dead woman up there."

"Sure, we would," Grierson said with a somewhat grim look on his face. "You notice how she was already smelling after just a few hours? In this heat, how long would it have taken for even the people who live in that building to catch on?"

As the ambulance doors slammed shut and an attendant eased his way past Helen and into the passenger's seat up front, she saw Grierson turning his head away and muttering something to a uniformed officer off to the side. Naturally, she couldn't hear, but she could easily imagine the tone of disgust in his voice, whatever he was saying.

"We going to do the whole lights and siren thing?" she asked the two paramedics up front as the engine thrummed to life.

The guy in the passenger seat turned back, and out of the corner of her eye Helen caught a faint grin. "Sorry, ma'am. You're not really that important."

"Yeah, right," she mumbled to herself, thinking as she did so that the attendant was probably more correct than he realized.

CHAPTER 22

IT ONLY TOOK a couple of hours for Helen to get a clean bill of health, or at least as clean as possible with a thin knife slice across her abdomen.

She was buttoning up her blouse, and doing so in a fairly gentle manner, while a young woman in business clothes sat on a stool getting information from her. Helen had already offered to write a check for her treatment, courtesy of Gordon Conroy's office funds, but even so, they wanted a complete record.

"Well, I think that's about it," the clerk said after eliciting enough personal info to practically write Helen's biography. She stood up and rolled the stool back into a corner. "If you'll just stop by the admitting desk downstairs, they should get you all set up."

"I was supposed to wait for one of the detectives to come get me," Helen said.

The clerk smiled, nodded in a rather confused manner, and left the room.

Helen stood up, stretched her arms over her head, groaned a bit and thought, good enough. She wasn't an action figure or some kind of female Rambo, but she had to make sure she could move at least nominally for the next few days.

She walked over to the mirror and fluffed her hair a bit, checked to make sure there wasn't any visible grime from the encounter with Toni Orson's killer, then raised her gaze up as, in the mirror, she saw Gordon Conroy enter the room.

He was wearing a black suit with a thin red pinstripe, white shirt, and maroon tie, and he looked as if he'd just come out of court. But as he moved closer she could see, even in reflection, his eyes a little bloodshot and a slight puffiness of his face.

"You okay?" were his first words to her.

Helen turned, gave him a bit of a smile and sat back down on the exam table.

"I've been better, but at least I'm still in one piece."

Conroy glanced into the hall outside the room, then reached over and closed the door.

"What the hell happened? All your phone message said was, I need help."

"Yeah, well, I think I may have overreacted a bit. Being set on by a knife-wielding maniac will do that to you." She took a deep breath and laid out the entire story for him, up to and including the questioning she received from Detective Grierson. Conroy frowned through most of it, and frowned even harder when she'd finished.

"You know what this means?" he said after she'd wrapped up.

"What?" Actually, she had a pretty good idea what was on the lawyer's mind, probably the same thing on hers, but she wanted to let him spell it out.

"This is our first possible avenue of investigation."

"Really? How do you see that?"

Conroy shook his head, giving her a "tsk tsk" look with his eyes. "Come on, Lipscomb. Let's assume for a second that Leo's being honest with us."

"You mean about not knowing Gray in any way?"

"Correct. So if he's being truthful there, there has to

be some other link, some middle ground connection between the two."

"Makes sense," Helen said, unsure if she kept the gleam from her eyes.

Conroy caught her look, not for nothing was he an ace courtroom advocate, and looked like he wanted to groan.

"You already sorted that out, didn't you?" he asked.

Helen nodded. "Given what we know at this point, it made sense. Again, seems like it's taking a lot on faith that Benson is being straight with us, but if we start with the assumption he is, then it leads to a fairly straightforward conclusion."

Conroy nodded. "If there's no connection, no matter how faint, between the two men, then there's no way that Gray could know any details of Benson's killings."

"And if that's true, then there has to be someone who's connected to both, and it's somehow through them that Gray got the information he's been giving the cops."

"And now we have a violent person connected to Gray."

"Which still doesn't hook up with Benson," Helen pointed out.

"Of course not. But it does show that Gray isn't necessarily a dead end, and it gives you your first real angle to investigate."

"It's slim," Helen said.

"Slim. But it's something."

"Be nice if we could hook my attacker, whoever he was, up with one of the other two bodies."

"Three," Conroy said.

Helen blinked. "Come again?"

"I was going to call you later tonight anyway. The

news just bubbled up out of Denver about an hour ago. Gray's led the authorities to the remains of another body, a woman outside of Boulder, dead about three years."

"Damnit. Strangled? No signs of sexual assault?"

"Too soon to tell. She hasn't even been identified yet. According to Gray, he never knew her name, just dragged her off the street. They're going through their records now, looking for any missing women who would fit within the time frame. I'm assuming an autopsy will jump the line on this one."

"Where'd they find her exactly?"

"Buried in a fairly deep grave out in the woods."

Helen ran it through her head, looking for some rhyme or reason to the pattern.

"Have you checked with Leo yet?"

Conroy flushed a bit. "You mean as to whether it's his or not?"

"Right," Helen said, feeling slightly sordid as she did so.

"Not yet. It's not the kind of thing I wanted to go into over the phone, when you have no idea who else is listening. I'm planning on heading out tonight so I can see him personally first thing in the morning."

"I assume he has access to all standard news media?" Helen asked. "TV?"

"Of course."

"So he'll probably have already heard by the time you get there."

"Yes?"

Helen shrugged. "It's just too bad. It would have been nice for you to spring the news on him. Less time to prepare a reaction."

"You mean in case he's playing us somehow?"

Conroy asked.

Helen nodded.

The lawyer sighed, reached out and hooked the stool the hospital clerk had been using earlier and parked himself on it. For a moment, he stared down at his hands before looking back up at her.

"Miss Lipscomb, when this is all over, no matter how it ends up, I'd like you to consider permanent employment with my firm. We can help you get your license, and be there in case your former employers try to make waves, though I doubt they would."

"I don't—" Helen began.

"At least think about it," he said. "But first, we have to clear this all up."

Helen nodded and got to her feet. "I have to swing by the copshop and give a statement to Detective Grierson about this afternoon. And they'll probably hook me up with a sketch artist as well, try to ID the guy who attacked me."

"Any chance you could get a copy of that sketch for your own use?"

Helen gave him a level stare, and after a second the lawyer broke eye contact. "No, that doesn't sound very practical, does it? By the way, did you happen to tell them about—"

"Relax, counselor. I'm respecting Benson's confidentiality, at least for now. But I'm sure you realize how legally shaky my ground is, and understand that whenever it gets to the point where I have real evidence to provide, all bets are off."

"You're forgetting the bigger picture, Lipscomb. Any real evidence you come up with I'd insist you hand it over right away. That is, after all, what you were hired for."

Helen grimaced and shook her head. It was such an odd feeling to be working for a confessed criminal that she was having a little trouble keeping her bearings.

"Fair enough."

"Do you want me to come with you?" Conroy asked. "If they try to make it rough I could—"

She waved away the suggestion. "Let me try it on my own. I actually didn't do anything wrong except for the whole breaking and entering thing, and I don't think they're going to push that. Showing up with a lawyer would just make them think the worse of me."

"Didn't you actually illegally enter twice?" Conroy asked.

Helen, suddenly tiring of the conversation, merely shrugged.

Conroy pursed his lips in thought for a second, then reached into his pocket and brought out a rather thick wallet. He sorted through it for a few minutes before pulling out a card and handing it over.

"That's a firm we reciprocate with here in KC. I'll give one of the partners a buzz and let them know you may be calling and to help you out if you do."

Shrugging, Helen put the card in her pants pocket. "One other thing," she said. "Sooner or later, I need to head down to Oklahoma."

"Oh?"

"Yeah. Gray spent some time down there before he made his way to Denver, so whatever caught him up in all of this may have happened down there. It's at least worth checking out."

"Makes sense."

"But before that, I need another meeting with Leo."

Conroy arched an eyebrow. "Why?"

Helen paused, unsure of just how much she wanted to reveal. "Let's just say it's time he and I had a slight meeting of the minds."

CHAPTER 23

ANOTHER SQUAD ROOM. Another reminder of herself as the outsider.

The central KC station was several stories tall, with the Homicide unit all the way up on the seventh floor. The building's floor plan was organized in its own unique way, yet Helen got to her destination almost by instinct.

She'd followed the familiar routine of checking in downstairs, informing them that Detective Grierson was expecting her, then following the directions up to the seventh floor.

She considered it a good deed for the day. Neither of the two detectives was waiting at the hospital, as Grierson had said they would be, and she could have just bolted and been gone. But she had no way of knowing where the search would lead her, and it was never a good idea to leave pissed-off cops in your wake.

Standing inside the doorway, she queried a plainclothes woman passing by, who directed her to Grierson's desk. It was empty at the moment, and there were no chairs next to it. She leaned against the wall and waited.

The desk looked about as scattered and messy as most detectives' desks, even in the time of modern electronics. Almost as messy as Helen's had been in the various postings she held in her previous life.

Leaning there, waiting for Grierson to show up, it occurred to her for the first time that her time as a cop was completely, irrevocably over. She suddenly realized that for the last two years she'd held onto the hope, far deep inside, that someday, she'd be a cop again. Not in her hometown, of course. But somewhere, maybe in some other part of the country.

Then a second, just as powerful, thought crashed into her. In her mind's eye, she had a vision of herself, twenty-five to thirty years in the future, in the same position as she now found herself. Working for law firms, insurance companies and other assorted enterprises, treading the line between legitimacy and illegitimacy, little in the way of assets or savings, lurching from one temporary job to another.

And she wondered if, along the way, she would gradually erode whatever standards and ethics she still held. If she was willing at this moment to take money from a confessed killer, how much further would she eventually sink? How flimsier would the justifications become?

"Lipscomb," Grierson's voice sounded behind her, "thanks for coming by. Sorry we didn't hook up at the hospital, but things got kind of hectic."

Helen nodded in greeting, but said nothing.

He sat behind his desk and looked her over. Helen took a deep breath, pulling thoughts completely to the here and now, focusing on the man and situation in front of her.

"So," the cop said, lacing his hands behind his head and leaning back in his chair, "you ready to clarify anything you told me earlier today?"

Without answering, Helen decided the hell with it

and grabbed an empty chair next to another desk, slid it over to Grierson's, then sat down.

"By all means," the black cop said, "make yourself at home."

"Where's your partner?" she asked. "Did he take off early and leave you with the graveyard work?"

The cop smiled and pushed himself away from his desk, leaning back in his chair as he did so. "Phil's down at the morgue, waiting on the PM for your murder victim."

Helen frowned. "So quick? Back when I'd usually have to wait a week or so for an autopsy. I'm not that familiar with KC, but I know your murder rate's not so low around here that you can get a cut in just a few hours."

"You got that right," Grierson replied. "But every now and then, there's a special case. Tell me, a couple of years back, did you guys have to wait at the end of the line when cops were being killed in your town?"

Helen blinked for a minute, then settled back in her chair. Simultaneously, Grierson's smile vanished.

"Sorry. That came out rather harsh. Didn't mean it that way."

Helen took a deep breath. "It's okay. It's a valid question, and you're right. That was seen as a special circumstance, and they put everything on hold for us. Your point?"

Grierson spread his hands. "At first, what we've got here looks like a regular, everyday inner city killing. But considering that, thanks to you, we know there's some connection between the dead woman and Willy Gray, who's currently making headlines one state over, the higher ups figured it wouldn't hurt to bump the PM to the front of the line."

"That connection's a little sparse," Helen pointed out.

Grierson nodded. "True, which is why I'm hoping you can shed some more light for me."

"I'll do what I can."

He reached into his top desk drawer and pulled out a legal pad. As he shut the drawer, the phone on his desk rang.

He picked it up and turned half away from Helen. A one-sided conversation went about a minute, with Grierson throwing in an occasional "uh huh."

"Okay, Phil. I'll let the boss know. I think he's still around here somewhere." Another few seconds as the person on the other end spoke before Grierson replied. "Yeah, just about to get to it. She's sitting right here as a matter of fact." A few more seconds of silence went by on Grierson's end, then he hung up.

"Autopsy?" Helen asked.

"Yeah. Nothing too surprising. Lots of blunt force trauma to the head and chest, but you probably figured that by the bruises."

"Actual cause of death?"

"Well, you nailed that one this afternoon," Grierson said. "Asphyxiation."

"Belt or something leather?"

"Nope. Best the ME can come up with is manual. A few of those bruises around her neck were finger impressions. Also, clear indication of sexual activity."

Helen frowned.

"Thing we still can't figure out," Grierson said, "is what the Orson woman was doing in that apartment."

"Have you managed to trace down who was living

153

there?"

Grierson slammed the legal pad he'd been holding down on his desk. Not an angry slam, more like to let Helen know he was peeved. "Look, lady, I've been willing to cut you an awful lot of slack, considering your history and all. My partner's not quite seeing it that way, which is the main reason he went down to the morgue and I stayed here to meet you. And I can tell you that when I write this up my boss really isn't going to be as understanding. So why don't you take a quick minute and remember who actually is the cop here and who's the civilian, okay?"

Helen slumped, feeling as if her cord had been cut. She hadn't yet given herself time to process that she'd witnessed a woman dead, a woman she'd been conversing with barely twenty-four hours before. The fact that she herself more than likely had something to do with Toni Orson's death made it even worse.

"Fair enough," she finally said. "You're the cop and I'm the civilian. So let me tell you what I know, and if you want to you can give me something in return."

"Good enough." Grierson picked up the pad and positioned it on his desk. "So talk."

Helen laid it out for him, everything she'd done since arriving from Denver. The only thing she deliberately left out was Benson and Conroy's names.

She included enough previous info that it would make sense why she was interrogating Toni, and that it all led back to Willy Gray. She made it sound like she was doing more of a background search than anything else, but at the sudden glint in Grierson's eyes, she wasn't sure the KC detective believed her. Then, she retraced for him how she'd managed to track down where Toni had ended up, though she'd gone through that at the initial crime scene.

"You were willing to give this woman a thousand dollars?" Grierson asked when she'd finished.

"If her info was on the level, sure."

"I'm guessing whoever hired you has quite a few bucks at his disposal."

Helen only shrugged at that one.

"Still doesn't answer my base question, though," Grierson said. "How do you think she ended up in that dump of a place?"

"Come on, Grierson, that should be kind of obvious."

"Why don't you go ahead and explain it then for the big, dumb cop who's not smart enough to chase the big bucks by going private."

"I think she decided to play both ends against each other."

"You mean take your thousand dollars but see what she could get out of the guy she was selling out as well?"

Helen nodded. "That's what I'd guess happened."

"Sounds kind of dumb and foolish to me."

Helen shrugged, silently agreeing with him.

"What'd the dude look like? I know you told the officers at the scene, but you've had some time to think now. Why don't you give me as complete a description as possible."

Helen paused, furrowing her brow. "Like I said before," she said after a moment, "he seemed to be about medium height. Five eight or nine."

She stared off into space, concentrating, as in her peripheral vision Grierson continued making notes on the pad.

"The main thing I remember is the hair, really dark and greasy. He was wearing faded jeans, I think, and one of those old green Army coats."

Grierson looked up. "In this heat?"

Helen nodded and continued, talking slower now as she drew on as much memory as possible.

Had she been a true civilian, she no doubt would have asked Grierson when she would see the sketch artist. But she knew that, television notwithstanding, hardly any departments used sketch artists or even Identi-Kits any more. These days, there was so much visual surveillance around that they usually found it much easier to find some sort of video footage of suspects, and the cost/benefits of police artists just didn't add up.

"I think he was really pale," she said, "but with all that hair in the way it was hard to tell. And I remember a distinctly sour body odor as if he hadn't bathed for some time."

"That could have just been the apartment," Grierson said, "the whole place was pretty rank. What about eyes, nose, anything distinguishing?"

Helen concentrated even harder, but after a few moments leaned back and let out a sigh. "Sorry, that's all I've got."

Grierson finished scratching out his notes, then drummed his fingers on his desk for a second as he stared off into space.

"Could be something else," he said after a few seconds. "I mean about what the Orson girl was up to. Could be that she was all giddy at the thought of the money she would get from you that she shot her mouth off to friends and such. Could be that word got back to our guy somehow, and he managed to snatch her to shut her up. Which would make me wonder just what was so important about this guy, whoever he was."

With that last line, he angled his gaze back to Helen, as if inviting her to fill in the blanks.

"Could be," she said, keeping her face as expressionless as possible.

Sighing in about as theatrical a manner as possible, Grierson literally threw his hands up in the air.

"Okay, Miss Lipscomb. It's not much, but it's better than what we had before. That number you gave me earlier for your cell phone?"

"Yes."

"Be sure you keep it on you, huh?"

He was clearly done with her, but Helen decided to take at least one shot at getting something out of him.

"Did you manage to get a name out of the manager?" she asked.

"Name?" Grierson at that moment looked as open faced and naïve as possible

"Yes. Name. Of who was staying in that apartment?"

"Well, now. I think that would be filed under police business."

Helen nodded, accepted the rebuke, and headed out of there before the man changed his mind.

CHAPTER 24

Friday, Sept. 20th

SHORTLY AFTER NOON the next day, Helen paid a second visit to Ryan Brown's establishment. Stepping into the gloomy interior, the place looked almost exactly as it had on her previous visit with Deputy Reynolds, even down to what appeared to be the same customers sitting in the same positions as before.

She paused inside the door, the tableau causing mild disorientation. It looked like a set piece for a movie, grungy bar inhabited by broken-down old men, merely transferred from one motion picture to another.

Brown stood behind the bar, once again polishing mugs, the only difference this time a young blonde woman in the murk looking barely old enough to be in such a place, helping him.

In the instant that Helen stopped to evaluate the scene, Brown looked toward the door. Even from the distance she could see his shoulders slump.

One or two of the patrons turned her way as well, but if any of them recognized her from the other day, they showed no sign. Ignoring them, she strode up to the bar and planted herself in front of Brown.

"What?" he said, trying but failing for a snide tone.

"I'd like to talk for a minute," Helen said.

"I ain't giving you your money back," he said as the

blonde girl gave both of them an odd look.

"Not interested in getting it back, but you owe me a little bit of an explanation, don't you think?"

"Explanation for what?" He placed the rag and mug down and propped his hands on the bar edge.

Helen wondered if he did so to keep his hands from trembling.

"I'm guessing you don't watch a lot of news," she said. "But I'm also willing to bet that one way or another you heard about what happened to Toni yesterday, right?"

"That girl who got killed," the blonde girl spat out, her voice high and kind of squeaky. "Did you have something to do with that, Ryan?"

"Christ no, Melissa. This broad's just trying to cause trouble for me 'cause of some people I knew back in the day."

"Ryan." Helen leaned over and placed her face within about six inches of his. "I know you're probably a bit put out at seeing me again, but call me a broad one more time and you won't be able to pick up a glass for a month."

The young man snickered and cast a look at his helper. But the snicker didn't quite have much oomph behind it, and the girl backed away another step.

"Ryan." Helen snapped her fingers to get his attention back on her. "Five minutes. No more. Then I'm out of your hair for good. How about it?"

Brown's face paled. "You're the one I heard about, the woman who found her."

"That's right, and I'd bet you already guessed that, seeing as how you pointed me in her direction. But in case you're not certain, I could show you the cut on my stomach your buddy's knife left."

"Hey, whoa." Brown raised up his hands.

"So you're going to talk to me," Helen said.

"And what about the cops coming right behind you?"

"No cops. At least not called by me. Five minutes, then I'm gone."

Brown shrugged, his face resigned, and turned to the girl next to him. "Watch the bar, okay? I got to talk to this woman."

Melissa nodded, her expression about as bored as it could be as the two of them walked to the back part of the building and slid into the same booth they'd occupied two days before.

"You heard about Toni," Helen said to start off.

Brown nodded while simultaneously shrugging. "Everyone heard about it. Kind of a bummer, though. She wasn't all that cool, but she didn't deserve what she got."

"Then let's make it right. Give me the man's name."

"What man?" Brown asked, his eyes downcast to the stained wooden table.

Helen slammed her hand down on the table as hard as she could. Brown's gaze jerked up, while about half of the customers in the front part of the building turned their way.

"Don't bullshit me, Ryan. Toni was telling me about one of your running buddies. Someone who basically ruled your pack back in the day. Where I screwed up was I should have forced her to give up the name right away instead of letting her put me off."

"You offer her money?" Brown asked.

Helen nodded.

"How much?"

"That's not really important, is it?"

"Maybe," Brown said. "She may have thought she could do better from the guy she was going to sell out to you. You know, going for the highest bidder?"

"That's kind of what I thought. So who is he?"

"What's in it for me?" Brown asked.

"Are you freaking kidding me? He killed your friend, and who knows what the hell else he's up to. What sort of loyalty do you have, guy?"

Brown leaned back on his side of the booth, squared up his shoulders and lifted his chin. "Loyalty to myself, lady. The way you're digging into this, I figure you've got someone pretty special paying your bills. Whatever you offered Toni for the information, I figure I should get about double, right?"

Helen sighed, leaned across the table and, before Brown could react, snared his right wrist with her hand. Her thumb found a certain spot and bore down, causing Brown to jump about half a foot out of his seat. As he opened his mouth to yell, she pressed even harder on the spot, and he snapped his jaw shut, tears welling in his eyes.

"Sit back down," she hissed.

Leaning across the table had irritated the cut on her abdomen, causing it to sting, but Helen kept her composure so Brown wouldn't notice her discomfort.

He slid back into the seat, angling his body, no doubt in an attempt to alleviate the pain coursing through the right side of his body.

Helen was pleased. She'd learned the trick at the academy, a lifetime or two ago, as a young recruit. She'd never actually used it and was surprised that it came back so instinctively when the need arose. The physical combat instructors had assured the recruits that the training regimen would instill the techniques in their instincts, never to be lost, and it seemed they'd been correct.

"Here's how it's going to go," Helen hissed, spearing Brown with a harsh gaze. "I've spent the last couple of days mucking around with you people, and I'm about done. The real cops are going to be coming by any time now. I'm sure they're going to want to talk to everyone who knew Toni. But before they do, you're going to give me the man's name, the bastard who used to run your bunch of low rents. And you're going to tell me where to find him. Got it?"

She gave one more extra hard squeeze then relented, letting go of Brown's wrist.

He yanked his arm off the table and nestled it in his lap, his eyes still welling with pain.

"His name's Jake," he said after a minute. "Jake Brounton. But whatever you do, don't tell him that I sicced you on him, okay?"

"Fair enough. But I need more. Where's he live? That rat nest of an apartment just looked like it was something he used, not a place to live. So where do I find him?"

"You got some paper?" Brown hissed, his expression showing that the pain was beginning to subside.

Helen reached into her slack's pocket and pulled out a small notebook and pen. She tossed the items to Brown, who crouched over and began writing.

"You better be packing when you go after Jake, lady. Don't judge him by me or Willy Gray. He's one

162

serious badass."

"You don't have to tell me," Helen said as he slid the notebook back in her direction. "I've seen his work."

She got up from the booth and headed out, scanning the address Brown had written as she did so. She didn't know for sure if she'd find Brounton there, but an even more pressing question was uppermost in her mind.

Was Brounton somehow connected with her client?

CHAPTER 25

Friday, Sept. 20th

IT WAS NEARLY midnight when Helen pulled up
outside of an abandoned house in roughly the same
neighborhood as Toni Orson's home, though removed
by a few miles. The house almost a copy of Toni's place.
Same run-down appearance, peeling paint, and sagging
chain-link fence and cracked, oil-stained driveway.

The one difference being that this late at night, with
only a single streetlamp down at the corner serving for
the entire block, it looked even more rundown than
Toni's neighborhood.

Helen had specifically waited until late at night for
two reasons, both the fact that the gloom would help hide
her activities and that she had been waiting on Conroy's
office to gain information about Jake Brounton. As she
shut off the car's engine, she had her phone up to one ear,
with Conroy on the other end.

"Mr. Brounton is twenty-six years old," the lawyer
said. "Been in and out of trouble most of his life,
including a stint in Maryville for rape."

"Connection to Gray?" Helen asked.

"Like your source said, the two of them went to
school together. They were both pinched a few times for
vandalism, once for a pool hall fight. Lots of suspicion
of other things, but nothing concrete enough to indict

on."

Helen stared at the darkened house as she tried to sort it all out.

"Rapes and assaults, right?" she asked.

"More or less."

"Sounds like your typical loser."

"Actually, kind of sounds like Gray, wouldn't you say?" Conroy asked.

Helen stared at the house for a minute. "Judging by his place, he's in the same social class as Toni was," she said.

"Sounds about right."

"Also," Helen said, "no car. No vehicle around."

"Which probably means he isn't there, wouldn't you say?"

"Not necessarily. For all we know, he doesn't have a car of his own."

"Or maybe he sold it to get some meth."

"There is that," Helen said.

Several minutes went by just staring at the house.

"Assuming he's involved in all this," Conroy finally spoke up, "what's the chance that I can get the entire story out of you?"

Helen mused that one over before Conroy spoke up again. "Far as that goes, we tried everything possible but could find no trace of a link between this Brounton character and Leo. Are you sure he's involved?"

Helen started to answer, but stayed silent as a lone man came walking down the street. It was hard to tell in the gloom, but his posture and manner of walking reminded her strongly of her brief encounter with the killer in the apartment.

There was no question in her mind that he was

carrying a weapon. It wasn't out and, in the dark, not visibly obvious at all, but Helen knew her instinct was correct. People, especially men, carrying guns moved differently, walking in a particular way that, to someone who'd spent their life around such people, fairly screamed "gun." Experts and professionals were trained not to give themselves away by how they moved, but Brounton was clearly neither trained nor professional.

Still, he'd managed to elude Helen the day before.

"I may have someone," she told Conroy.

"Brounton?"

"Pretty sure," Helen said. "I'll know for sure if he turns…"

Almost as she said the words, the man slowed down and turned to go up the driveway of the house she'd been watching.

Helen reached for the door latch. "I'm hanging up," she said to Conroy. "Wait fifteen minutes, then call Detective Grierson of the KC Department. I'm guessing you have the cop shop's number?"

"We can get it."

Helen reached into her pocket and pulled out a gun. "I mean the detective bureau. Ask for Grierson, if not him, see if Wilkerson's around. Tell them where I am and that I went in after a suspect in the Orson slaying."

"If I wait so long, no telling what's going to happen. What if he gets the advantage over you? Why don't you just call them and wait for them there?"

"You want information before the cops start talking to him or not?"

By this time, the man had entered the house, shut the door and turned on a couple of lights. Helen could imagine him cracking open a beer, grabbing some sort of frozen dinner out of the freezer and getting ready to plop himself down to watch a game. If she was lucky, she'd catch him fat, happy, and stupid.

"You going to do anything illegal in there?" Conroy asked.

Helen grinned as she opened the door. "Don't worry, counselor. Nothing that anyone's going to complain about."

She shut the door, put the phone in her pocket and headed across the street.

CHAPTER 26

HELEN GINGERLY LIFTED the metal gate latch and, cautious of rusted or squeaking hinges, eased the gate open. The precaution proved unnecessary as the old gate swung open soundlessly. Stepping into the backyard, she paused for a moment to adjust to the darkness.

Illumination from the one working streetlight at the end of the block didn't even begin to reach back there, and there were no back porch or window lights showing. On top of that, as she'd noticed earlier, none of the adjoining houses, either to the sides or behind, showed any signs of life. After rounding the corner, even the faint beams coming out of the front window drapes had dissipated, leaving her only the dim rays of a quarter moon as a guide.

Standing behind the house, Helen paused to listen, alert for any indications of a dog. Though there had been no signs on the fence, and from what she knew, Brounton didn't quite seem the pet-loving type, anyway. But who this house belonged to or what surprises may lie ahead were worrisome concerns.

After a few seconds of detecting nothing, Helen turned toward the back door. Using a small flashlight attached to her keychain, she grasped the knob and gave it a twist.

Locked, as she'd expected. Brounton was being

risky enough staying in the same city. If most people had had to run from the cops after attacking a bystander and leaving a woman's corpse in their apartment, they would have been halfway across the country by now. But she had learned early in her police career that predators often, despite the best logic, stayed in the same general area. Sure they were easier to apprehend there, but it was also for many the only geography they knew. Thus, it was entirely possible that Brounton had never even considered leaving the KC area.

However, if that turned out to be the case, what did it say about any possible connection to Leo Benson's crimes?

Thoughts strayed to Willy Gray. He'd left his native stomping grounds, seemingly for good. True, bouncing between Missouri, Oklahoma, and Colorado wasn't exactly the same as jetting off to Tahiti, but it at least counted as a move of some sort.

And with the departure from his hometown came the change in temperament that seemed to have turned him into a killer. Even discounting the now three other women he claimed to have murdered, what could have changed so drastically in his life that he'd ended up at such an extreme?

Hopefully, some of those questions would be answered in the next few minutes.

The house was old enough, and the original construction rickety enough, that the backdoor lock didn't present all that much of an obstacle. She made it inside in a little under two minutes, stepping into what once may have been a fairly nice, homey little kitchen. The only illumination came from the backglow of a living room light, the same one she'd seen from outside.

There was no doubt that in full light the kitchen would have looked as dilapidated and used up as the outside of the house.

Problem. The crinkling of old, curled up linoleum echoed underneath her feet. She paused, thought briefly about taking off her shoes, but that wouldn't really help in this case, then mentally shrugged it off and continued on.

Brounton would know of her presence soon enough anyway and Helen hoped she could keep the element of surprise for as long as necessary.

Helen was well aware all actions so far technically constituted illegality. She'd already broken and entered a private domicile, and it was quite possible that the next few minutes would see some degree of assault upon a person who, had she left it alone, posed no threat to her or, at the moment, anyone else. But as she'd told Conroy upon leaving the car, she doubted that Brounton would raise too much of a stink about it.

And if anyone did, if some glory-hound lawyer tried to make a case for the scuz's rights being violated, at the same time the entire KC force was probably out looking for the guy, she was sure the prosecutor could make a case for what the lawyers called inevitable discovery and call it a wrap.

She couldn't hear anything in the house, other than the occasional creak or groan of the old woodwork, but could sense Brounton's presence. She assumed no one else was present. Two people moving around such a small area would make some sort of noise, unless they were both asleep. But she couldn't imagine Brounton sleeping after what had gone down just a few hours before. If anything, he should be hyped up, on edge, practically climbing the walls as he tried to figure out how to get out of his jam.

Or, and this thought crossed her mind while approaching the kitchen doorway, he could have taken something, either snorted, injected or drunk, in order to calm his nerves and escape the danger of his situation.

It turned out, upon crossing the threshold from the kitchen to the small living room, that something entirely different was the case.

The man in question lay slantwise on a yellow couch that had begun to turn brown from years of non-cleaning. Two medium-sized throw pillows behind his upper back propped him up as he stared fixedly at the front door. Helen paused in the kitchen doorway for a second, watching him, but even though in plain view, her quarry didn't even glance in her direction.

He did, however, have his hands wrapped around a heavy, silver automatic, gripping the weapon so tightly that the veins corded in his arms.

He was dressed in faded Levi's and a stained wifebeater, and the patchy hair on his shoulders had matted with sweat. The living room held a stench, something apart from Brounton's body odor, that Helen recognized instantly.

It was a smell that most civilians had never experienced, and one which, in fact, the majority of people wouldn't believe actually existed. But Helen Lipscomb had been a cop for a large number of years, and she could testify that that particular odor did in fact exist.

The small living room, and Brounton in particular, smelled of fear.

With his gaze riveted to the front window, even with

the drapes closed, Helen could tell that Brounton had pretty much given up and was just waiting for the cops to arrive. Not sure how long it had taken to circle the backyard, then come into and cross the kitchen, she didn't really expect Conroy to wait the agreed-upon fifteen minutes before calling Grierson.

Whatever she wanted to do, had to be done quickly.

The first step was getting Brounton's attention. She'd already drawn her own weapon and was holding it about halfway down her thigh, low enough to bring it up in a flash but not all the way extended in the most threatening way possible. With no backup, Helen planned to take him down without any violence, but he looked desperate. She had one chance to pacify him and get the necessary information.

But hope wavered when she realized Brounton was already aware of her presence.

"How many of you are there?" he asked, still not taking his gaze away from the window. Helen assumed he expected to see flashing red and blue lights at any moment.

"I know you're there," he continued when she didn't answer. "Heard you walking around in the kitchen. That fuckin' linoleum. You notice I'm not unloading on you, right?"

"Right," Helen said, pitching her voice a shade above a whisper.

"Doesn't mean I'm going to just let you take me in."

"That's actually not my intention," Helen said.

Brounton's eyes darted her way for a fraction of a second, then focused back on the window. If anything, the cords in his arms tightened up even more.

"What kind of cop doesn't want to arrest someone?"

he asked.

"The kind that's not a cop," Helen said, something she seemed to be pointing out quite a lot lately.

He looked her way again, slightly longer this time, before returning to the window.

"Don't think so. You sure look like a cop."

"I'm working private," she said. "And I'm alone." A bit of a white lie, seeing as she didn't hope to be on her own much longer.

Another dart of the eyes. "Step out into the light, so I can see you better."

You mean make myself a better target. But if she wanted to get him talking, it wouldn't do to start off by being obstinate. She stepped into the living room, and Brounton's eyes widened.

"You're the gal from earlier, the one who tried to take me back in the apartment. The one who got me into this mess."

"You would have been in it anyway," Helen said. "You couldn't have kept her body in there for very long without all the neighbors noticing, and how were you planning on getting it out of there?"

Brounton's lips twitched. "So maybe I didn't have it planned out too far. But who are you and why did you come to my place?"

Helen wanted to look at her watch, try to guesstimate how much time she had before the troops showed up. She'd had enough experience with standoffs to know it was hard to gauge the passage of time while in the midst of them.

"I was looking for you," she said.

"Kind of figured that, seeing as how you came to my place. But why? I know you from somewhere?"

She shook her head. "I tracked you down. I'm looking for someone you know."

Brounton started to talk, but went silent as a car rolled down the street. Helen could clearly hear the whine of an engine and tires passing by.

The house must have been even more shoddily constructed than it looked.

A moment after the vehicle passed, both of them began breathing again.

"Figured that was it," the man said. "So who you want to talk about?"

"Willy Gray."

"Seriously? Willy? I haven't seen him for a couple of years."

Helen didn't have the time or inclination to go into the whole story, and she didn't think Brounton would really care very much.

"He got into some trouble in Denver," Helen said. "I'm trying to get him out of it."

"Yeah, I heard about that. He never was good for much."

Again, Helen resisted looking at her watch.

"If you help me out, maybe I can help you."

Brounton coughed and winced as a lance of pain seemed to go through him. It was only then, looking closer, that Helen saw a bloody, sloppily-made bandage arrayed along the left side of his face. It took her a second to catch on.

In his apartment, when he'd attacked her and she'd smacked him in the head with the pistol. It must have done more damage than in the turmoil, not to mention the pain of her own wound, she'd realized.

He coughed again, then pressed one hand on the

couch cushion, as if to steady himself. Helen wondered if the man didn't have a concussion, or something even more serious.

"Don't see how anyone can help. Once the cops get here, I'm done for. They are coming, aren't they?"

Helen nodded.

Brounton smirked but didn't lower his gun even a fraction.

"What you want to know about Willy? How he was such a major league fuckup when we were kids? Fucked up nearly everything he touched? You have any idea how many times I had to drag his skinny ass out of trouble?"

"That's pretty much it," Helen said. "But even more, what happened to change him?"

"Change him? How do you see him changed? Isn't his ass sitting in jail, just like mine's about to be?"

Helen started to protest, but Brounton used his gun to wave her objection aside. "Don't insult me, lady. I may not be a genius, but I'm smart enough to know that you didn't waltz in here without any sort of backup. I'm guessing they've got the place surrounded, or at least are on their way. Right?"

"I told you I'm not a—"

"Yeah, yeah, I know. But you sure do stink like one. And after I sliced you up yesterday, you're not stupid enough to try to take me down on your own. So I figure one way or another my ass is cooked. Right?"

"Probably."

"So what the hell. Ask your questions. But do it quick, 'cause sooner or later either the real cops are gonna show or I'm gonna get tired of holding this piece up. And who knows what's going to happen then."

CHAPTER 27

THE POLICE ARRIVED about ten minutes later. Not wanting to look away from Brounton, Helen didn't put it together until later that Conroy had not only waited the required fifteen minutes, but a few minutes past that. By the time they arrived, with Grierson and Wilkerson leading the way, she not only had about as much information as she expected to get, but the man himself was almost passed out from the effects of his head wound.

Hence, as soon as the sound of vehicles approached, she felt fairly safe in going to open the front door.

Seven regular patrol cars and one SWAT van, called The Bear, were arrayed in front of the old house, but none of them had their lights flashing, no doubt in an attempt to approach as stealthily as possible. Helen placed her gun down on the floor next to the door and raised her hands, calling out at the same time that she was unarmed and Brounton was no danger.

As she would have done, back in the day, they didn't take her word for it. Grierson and Wilkerson knew her, of course, but none of the others did, and for all the cops knew Brounton could have been standing to the side, holding a gun on her while she invited them to come on in.

One of the SWAT guys, replete with sealed faceplate and body armor, stepped a little away from their vehicle and commanded Helen to lie on the ground. She did so, locking fingers behind her head.

"There's one weapon just inside the doorway," she called out. "It's mine. Brounton's passed out on the sofa, just as you enter to the right."

Two more tactical men, or they could have been women for all Helen could tell through their faceplates, stepped out and joined the first as they proceeded towards the house. As they approached, Helen gazed down to the ground, hoping to appear as non-threatening as possible.

The three moved past her, their weapons up and out, and behind them came two uniformed officers, a black man and woman, who stepped over Helen.

"Who are you, miss?" the woman asked.

"My name's Lipscomb. Helen Lipscomb. Detective Grierson knows me." She wondered why Grierson hadn't stepped forward yet to vouch for her and considered that he may be playing some half-assed version of a pissing contest.

Before she could think about it too much, though, one of the SWAT stepped out of the house.

"Bring the ambulance up," he hollered. "This guy's in pretty bad shape."

Simultaneously, the two officers had moved both arms down behind her back and snapped handcuffs on her. She thought of protesting but, easily placing herself in their shoes, decided against it.

No reason in raising the stakes any more. As soon as they got downtown it could all be sorted out.

And maybe even before that.

"Let her go," Grierson's voice sounded somewhere to her right.

"She's okay, detective?" the black woman uniform asked.

"Don't know if I'd go so far as to say okay, but I'm pretty sure she's not a threat to anyone, at least not an immediate one."

Helen felt a slight tugging at the wrists, and the cuffs fell away. She sat up on the grass, rubbing her wrists while Grierson stood right above her. He started to say something but stopped when the paramedics came out of the house, carting Brounton away on a stretcher.

"He going to make it?" Grierson asked as they walked by.

One of the paramedics looked up. "Probably. Far as we can tell it's not quite as bad as it looks, but his head's kind of busted up. Have to wait for a doc to tell for sure."

"Where you taking him to?"

"North KC. You want to follow us? We should have him processed in twenty minutes or so."

"I'll be along in a bit," Grierson said as he cast a mean eye Helen's way. "Got something to take care of first."

The paramedics nodded and left. A flurry of people headed into the house to secure the scene, and Grierson grasped Helen by the arm, yanking her towards an old yellow Charger parked about half a block down.

"Where are we going?" Helen asked, though she had a pretty good idea.

"Where do you think? We're heading back to the station, and this time you're going to give me some answers."

"Maybe," Helen said as they approached Grierson's car, "but there's something else I'm going to do first."

"Oh, yeah?" The anger, frustration and confusion

practically rolled off the cop in waves. "And what would that be?

"Call my lawyer," Helen replied.

"Great," Grierson replied.

CHAPTER 28

AS SOON AS she mentioned her attorney, Grierson had followed correct procedure and quit trying to talk to her. They took a long and silent ride across the KC Metro area, which wasn't all bad. The trek offered time to think, a little bit of stretch in which she could organize in her head the information Brounton had given her right before the troops arrived.

On the way in, she asked Grierson to call in for an update on Brounton's condition, Although he'd managed to give her some pointers as to the next direction to take, having the man himself alive and talking would help a lot.

"Uh uh," the cop replied. "You ain't talking to me, so I ain't helping you."

And that was that. Helen considered arguing the point with him, but decided it best to keep her powder dry until she could talk to Conroy.

Arriving at the station, they allowed her to use her cell phone for about five minutes, in which time she managed to contact the lawyer's office. Her first call, to his personal cell, had gone to voicemail, so just to be sure she called his office.

Naturally, someone was there, and Helen began to wonder if Conroy imposed the old post office motto on his staff. She left word as to where she was and the current situation, asking that word be passed along to the man himself who, last she'd known, was somewhere around the Kansas City area.

Then she sat back and waited for developments.

Back in her cop days, Helen had spent a fair share of time in interrogation rooms, jail cells, and courthouses. From the handful of times as a rookie in uniform she'd had to testify in trial proceedings, up to the numerous instances as a detective that she'd sweated a suspect or even gone to state prisons for follow-up interviews. So yes, Helen was very familiar with the confines of such official places.

However, she'd never found herself in any such location against her will, as the powerless one facing off against the overwhelming force of the State. She didn't really count the handful of occurrences when she'd been on the receiving end of some official proceeding, including a couple of instances where she'd had to square off against Internal Affairs. Even then, she'd still held the badge, still had some amount of control over her actions.

Now, for the first time in her life, such was not the case.

Grierson asked one of the uniforms to take her to the interrogation rooms at the rear end of the detectives squad room and make her as comfortable as possible, promising to be in to talk in a few minutes.

The room was standard issue, much like detective squad rooms carbon copied all across the country. Single ratty old table with three chairs, two on one side and one facing those. Common instinct would urge someone to sit at the single chair because who wants to have an empty chair next to them? And Helen would have bet her entire payment from this job that that individual chair had one leg shaved slightly lower than the other three, so that it would wobble anytime someone sat in it.

In the old days, the plain gray walls would have been decorated with cigarette marks, and no clock or any other decoration at all.

She also assumed there was a camera somewhere around, if not people on the other end of the large mirror that took up nearly one entire wall. Without looking to either side, she walked over to the table and swiped the lone chair for one of the two on the other side, then sat down comfortably.

She wasn't sure, but suspected they'd locked the door on her.

Settling into the seat, Helen didn't for a minute believe the detective would be right in. It was a standard tactic, one she'd often used in the past, to make a suspect sweat for a long time, sometimes hours on end, in order to begin the process of wearing them down.

But was she actually a suspect? Helen didn't know for sure, and other than interfering with an investigation didn't see what they had on her. It was possible that some enterprising ADA could make a case for obstruction of justice, but why even bother with that when she'd just handed them a killer?

The door opened, and a young woman in uniform poked her head in. "You want anything?" she asked. "Coffee? Pop?"

Helen smiled and shook her head, and the young cop nodded and left. This time, Helen could definitely hear the click of the door lock.

Her heart fluttered a bit, but she tamped it down. Could be they wanted to do some serious questioning. Or it could be that Grierson just wanted to play games for a while. Either way, as soon as Conroy, or one of his associates, showed up they could get it sorted out.

In the meantime, she had a little downtime to continue sorting through what Brounton had said back at his hideaway.

She really could have used a phone, or at least a pencil and some paper, but didn't want to take the chance of the cops saying no. So far, they were treating her halfway decent. If she began making demands, no matter how slight, that could change.

Not that she would blame them at all. In the past, she probably would have handled a similar situation the same way.

Maybe even worse. It had been years now, but she still held vivid memories of when she had, full of procedure and official zeal, hounded an innocent man, chasing after him in a case of multiple killings. The fact that no one, even in hindsight, had found any fault in procedure, at least not officially, did nothing to mitigate the personal guilt.

Unofficially, the powers that be had made her life miserable for some time after until she finally said to hell with it and pulled the pin. So, no, Helen completely understood the cops' actions, but also, with the benefit of hindsight, wondered if this were the best way to handle things.

At least they'd offered her something to drink, and hadn't cuffed her to the table or anything, so maybe things weren't quite as bad as they may have seemed to a civilian.

About an hour and a half later or so, the door opened and Grierson and another man, older and with a thick mane of gray hair, entered the room.

Helen's insides clenched up as she recognized a command grade officer.

"This is Captain Denslow," Grierson said as he closed the door behind him. "He's got a few questions for you."

"I don't think so," Helen said. "Not without my attorney present."

The two men looked at each other, sighed and, almost in unison, snagged the two other chairs in the room and sat down.

"Miss Lipscomb," Denslow said in a gravelly voice. "We'd like to know what you and Mr. Brounton talked about before my officers arrived."

Helen glanced from one to the other of the two men seated opposite her.

Taking a deep breath, she placed both palms flat on the table. "Assuming he and I discussed anything, I wouldn't mind telling as long as we can have an understanding."

Denslow glowered and leaned in towards her. "Miss Lipscomb, right at the moment we don't have much we intend to charge you with, and we may let you off entirely. But if you continue in this vein—"

"You shouldn't intend to charge me with anything. If memory serves right, I made you aware of a young woman murdered in your city and led your force to her killer. So exactly what sort of offences did I commit that you're thinking of charging me with?"

"You know damned good and well," Grierson interjected. "Sure, you found the dead woman, but we would have had a lot easier time of tracking him down if you hadn't been so incompetent as to let him get away in the first place."

"Maybe, but—"

"Far as that goes," he continued, "I'd say there's a good likelihood that the Orson girl wouldn't have died if you hadn't butted into her life."

Helen's breath came quick, and the injury from earlier began burning across her belly.

"If that's what you really think," she said, "then we'll just let it lie until my counsel shows up and we can—"

"Miss Lipscomb," Capt. Denslow cut her off. "I'm familiar with your—attitude—towards authority and your somewhat, shall we say, lackadaisical approach to police work. But what transpired here today is a bit much even for someone of your reputation."

Helen glared at the man, working as hard as possible to keep from lashing out any more than she already had. The smart thing would be to wait for Conroy, or whoever he sent to help her out, but she wasn't sure how much more frustration she could take without blowing completely.

Last she'd known, Conroy was here in KC, so where the hell was he?

All in all, it was starting to get a little out of control.

"You really don't know anything about me, Captain. And I wish you wouldn't act as if you do. But like I said, I'm just going to sit here quietly and wait for my…"

She didn't manage to finish the sentence because the door opened, and Gordon Conroy himself walked in the room. Even at the tail end of a day he looked fresh and well-groomed, as if moments away from stepping into a courtroom.

"Gentlemen," Conroy said, "before we get down to discussing my client's situation, I suggest you let me have a few moments with her. Okay?"

CHAPTER 29

Saturday, Sept. 21st

"LAY IT OUT for me," Conroy said.

It was the following morning, and the two of them had met for breakfast in a little diner adjacent to Helen's hotel. They'd only spent about an hour at the police station after Conroy's appearance before being allowed to go on their way, with the admonishment that she may have to come back to the area as a witness, assuming Brounton ever got to trial.

After Conroy had spoken briefly with the cops, Grierson and his captain had headed out to confer privately for about five minutes before returning. Coming back, their attitude, especially the captain's, had been a whole lot more deferential. For once, Helen hadn't minded the presence of an expensive, superstar defense lawyer.

All she'd wanted to do was to get away from any prying eyes or ears and fill Conroy in on what Brounton had told her. But as soon as they'd exited the station, she nearly collapsed from exhaustion. Conroy drove her back to the hotel, and they'd made a date for breakfast in the morning.

"The next stop is Oklahoma City," she said while buttering an English muffin.

Conroy stared at her for a minute, his brows drawing

together.

"Excuse me?"

"Oklahoma City. Gray moved there a few years back, chasing some girl, according to Brounton."

"And you're sure that your new best friend is being straight up about this?"

"Come on, Gordon. Don't tell me you haven't had your firm backtracking every inch of Gray's life, looking for some connection between him and Benson. Probably long before you called me in."

The lawyer grinned and chewed a bite of his omelette before answering.

"Of course we did," he said after taking a sip of orange juice. "We even know the name of the girl he went after. But she split a few weeks after, and all Gray did down there was work in a bar for a few months. Then he tucked tail, pardon the expression, and came back here."

"Right." Helen nodded. "For all of a few weeks before heading off to Denver, and we both know what happened from there."

"Okay, so what's the point? Gray left town, got his heart broken, kept on with the same kind of dead end job he's always had, then eventually chucked it all to kill a girl in Denver and get in the slammer. So what's the point?"

Helen took a moment to compose the answer. From the little bit Brounton had said before the cops hustled him away, a theory of the entire case was starting to form. Vague as hell, to be sure. Nebulous, actually, and with far more holes than facts in it. And that was even assuming the lowlife had been on the level with her.

But her brain must have been working overtime

while she'd slept because waking up that morning she'd seen the glimmers of a pattern.

"It's like this," she said. "According to Brounton, and you've got to take that for whatever it's worth, seeing as the guy's a freakin' killer, when Gray came back from Oklahoma he'd changed. The working-class part-time hood, who had nothing much in mind beyond the next drink, fix, or Saturday night lay, had turned into something else."

"What else?"

"That part's still kind of vague. But according to Brounton, Gray had some sort of focus he hadn't had before, had cleaned up his appearance and wasn't doing any drinking or substances at all."

"He'd found God?" Conroy asked.

Helen shook her head. "Not that so much. More like a purpose, some sort of goal. He kept talking about the next level and how he was going to make something of himself. Brounton says he didn't at all talk like the punk, his word, that he'd known before."

"I don't follow this."

"Neither do I exactly," Helen said, "but something seems to have happened to him down in Oklahoma City. Some sort of change or epiphany. And it's that event, whatever it was, that seems to have led to his eventually being incarcerated in Colorado and somehow knowing about Leo Benson's past crimes. At least some of them."

Conroy shook his head. "I know this is getting repetitive as hell to hear, but there's no connection between them."

"I'm assuming Benson has business interests down south?"

"Yes. But I'm telling you we've checked every way

we could, then double and triple checked all over again. Gray never worked for any of the firms and never did any sort of contract work for any of them."

"At least, nothing that's got a paper trail."

Conroy's eyes narrowed as he mulled that one over. "It's possible," he finally admitted.

"I'm guessing it's not out of the range of possibility that not all of the man's financial dealings are on the up and up. To your knowledge, has he ever been involved in any flat-out criminal enterprises?"

Conroy swirled his fork around what was left of his omelette for a minute.

"Confidentially?" he said, looking up at Helen. "Whatever I say doesn't leave this table?"

Now it was Helen's turn to pause. While not wanting to cross the line from her former life any more than she already had, it seemed that every time she told herself that came another hop and skip over said line. Even though her ethics had taken a hell of a twisting the last few years, she still wanted to cling to the belief that there were certain actions or decisions she simply wouldn't take.

On the other hand, the whole Benson/ Gray riddle had taken hold of her, and at the moment even if Benson fired her tomorrow, she would still pursue the puzzle until a resolution popped up.

And yet....

"Let's say this. As long as it's about past crimes, not anything ongoing or in the future, I'll do my best to keep it close. But if it turns out that for some reason I have to come forward, I can't guarantee that I won't."

Conroy nodded. "That's pretty much how I have to look at it in keeping with my law license. The short answer is I can accept that, for now."

Helen figured that the dubious expression on Conroy's face mirrored hers, and that neither of them were entirely happy with the understanding.

"This isn't a very nice business, is it?" Conroy asked.

Helen shook her head before taking a drink of water.

"So why are you in it?" she asked.

The lawyer shrugged. "I did some work piecemeal for Leo over the years, nothing very major. My firm specializes in criminal defense, but for the most part he had in-house lawyers to handle any sort of investigation that would come up."

"So what happened to them?"

Conroy grinned, but without much mirth. "They're still there, but officially they work for the corporation, not for Leo. As soon as he was convicted, the board voted him out of his various positions, leaving him with barely any resources of his own to fall back on."

"Except for his personal fortune."

Conroy nodded. "Which is quite extensive, of course. Probably much more than most people, even his intimates, realize."

"Naturally making bail, even before trial, out of the question."

Conroy's grin had a bit more humor. "For sure. But it was one of my better performances trying to get it approved. Gave it my best Inherit the Wind defense, and got shot down within ten seconds."

Helen nodded and began attacking her Eggs Benedict.

"Mr. Benson has asked about some sort of progress report from you."

191

"When I have something substantive to report, I will. Right at the moment, I have nothing firm to give him."

Conroy's grin changed to a frown, and he drummed his fingers on the table.

"Be sure and remember, Helen, the exact wording of your assignment."

"Meaning?"

"Mr. Benson isn't so interested in you proving Gray innocent of the various murders he's alluding to. If you can do so, fine. But that's not the main thrust of your assignment."

A small cold spot formed in her gut. She knew Conroy was right, had understood the assignment when she'd accepted it, but now felt herself edging even closer to that hated line.

"I know that," she said.

"Just make sure you don't forget. Go to Oklahoma if you need to, but keep in mind the final goal here, and in a way, it's not all that different from what you did in your previous profession."

Helen nodded, that cold spot in her abdomen growing.

"The job isn't to prove Gray didn't do the crimes," she said, "it's to prove that Benson did. In that case," she said, "don't forget I want to see the man before I take this any further."

"When?"

"Why not tomorrow? I'm sure I can get there on time if you can get me a flight today."

"Can't do it," Conroy said. "I actually have a court appearance tomorrow, so I couldn't go with you."

"Then don't come."

Conroy frowned. "I guess I could get one of my associates to—"

"No," Helen insisted. "I want to talk to the man alone."

"Look, I'm the attorney here, and I have to have full knowledge of everything going on. And, please don't take offense at this, but you are just an employee."

"So stop paying me," Helen said.

That one stopped the man in his tracks. He tried to recover, huffing and puffing a bit, before relenting.

"Fine. I'll call the prison and get you cleared. You going home now?"

Helen thought about it for a moment, then shook her head. "I don't really see the point. There's nothing to do there. How about you get me on the earliest flight to Lincoln there is, and I'll just drive in from there."

CHAPTER 30

Monday, Sept. 23th

HELEN'S SECOND MEETING with Leo Benson began a bit smoother than the first.

The security check was as stringent as before, possibly a bit more relaxed due to the guards being familiar with her from the previous visit. Regardless, they took no chances, and it was a good thirty minutes before she once again was sitting across from Benson in one of the small interview rooms.

"You're looking tired," was Benson's opening comment.

Helen instinctively brushed a hand through her hair. "Been busy."

"But not very productive," Benson said, leaning forward and crossing his arms on the table. It was a slight movement, but it served to make him move toward her personal space, if only by a few inches.

Helen had often used the same slight move to put suspects on edge during questioning.

"Depends on your point of view," she replied.

"I'd say that my point of view is the only one that matters, Miss Lipscomb. And I see on the news that that little punk ass has staked his claim to another victim."

Helen nodded. "Nancy Snyder, outside of Boulder. I was kind of busy Friday, but I managed to catch up on the story over the weekend. One of yours?"

Benson turned and glanced over his shoulder at the mirror fronting one wall. Like the last time, like probably any time he had any visitors, there were no doubt prison officials on the other side. Officially, they would say that they were there to protect Helen in case the condemned man got out of control, but she had the same suspicion that Conroy had on the first visit.

Even through the closed door and cement walls, Helen could hear the slightest murmur of life in the prison, almost a white noise effect made up of all the men and women moving around in limited freedom, pacing the confines of their cells, or even using the plumbing.

She got up, walked over to stand directly in front of the mirror, and used the flat of her hand to make a slicing motion across her neck.

"Might as well turn it off," she said to the glass. "I'm working for Gordon Conroy's office, and anything you happen to overhear will be unusable and may, if used, get our client quite a bit of leniency from the courts."

Then she turned back and sat down facing Benson. "So," she said, "one of yours?"

Benson narrowed his eyes. "I hear you had a little bit of trouble in KC. How's the wound?"

Her hand instinctively reached out to massage the rapidly-healing slice across her abdomen. She caught herself, though, and lowered her hand back to her side.

"It got a little tough, but I think it's resolved."

"Kind of ironic, though, wouldn't you say?" Benson asked. "You working for me and crossing paths with another killer?"

Something had appeared behind the old man's eyes, a certain light he seemed to be trying to conceal. Was it possible that a flicker of the true Leo Benson just came through?

"Don't know if I'd say ironic, but it was touch and go there for a while."

"And the woman? This…"

"Toni Orson."

"Yes. Did she have anything to tell you?"

Helen stared at the man, trying to determine where this conversation was heading. She hadn't intended to take the interview in this direction and wondered if for some reason Benson was deliberately keeping her off track.

"No, she didn't. She said she knew all about Gray and was going to tell me the next day, including the name and location of his main running buddy, once I brought her some reward money. Instead, she took off and hooked up with Brounton, the man who killed her."

"Well," Benson shrugged, "at least that saved me some money, right?"

"Back to my question, Mr. Benson."

"Yes?"

"Nancy Snyder?"

Benson drummed his hands on the table for a second. "Let's just say that I was a bit distressed when I heard the news. If life were a poker game, my flush may have just turned into a straight. But before I'm positive, I have a question for you."

"Yes?"

"Was the young woman in Boulder sexually assaulted? They didn't go into that on the news report I heard."

He asked the question in a straightforward, matter-of-fact tone, almost as if asking the time of day. Helen's skin crawled with unease.

"I only know as much as you do. She'd been out in the wild for some time, so it may be a while before they determine that."

"Hmm," Benson muttered.

"I'm heading down to Oklahoma next."

"Why?"

"Because that's where the track is taking me," Helen said. "Gray moved from KC to Oklahoma for a while, then up to Colorado and promptly became a killer. Oklahoma's the middle ground. Something happened to him one of those two places."

Benson stroked his chin for a minute, his features composed into a somewhat overly-dramatic serious mien.

"Did you dig as far as you could into his life in Denver?" he finally asked.

"As much as I could without running afoul of the cops. There's also a federal task force sniffing around up there that I kind of figured you'd want me to stay away from."

"They're probably sniffing even harder after the discovery of another body."

"Probably," Helen said, "but there's something still not tracking here."

"What would that be?" Benson asked.

"Let's pretend for a minute that the word comes back on Snyder that she was molested. That would put a wrench in things, wouldn't it?"

"Why?"

"Because according to your own words in our first meeting, you never molested your victims."

"Maybe I changed it up with experience," Benson

drawled.

Helen leaned back and stared at the man. "If you want me to keep on working for you, I think you'd better—"

"Oh, please," Benson raised his voice as he leaned forward, his handcuff chains rattling on the table.

Almost instantaneously a pounding sound came from the other side of the mirror.

He sank back into his chair and took a few calming breaths.

"They are touchy, aren't they? You'd almost think that they don't have faith in these manacles they've laced me into."

"Maybe they're just being extra cautious."

Benson shrugged as much as he could. "Maybe, but what I was going to say was that I seriously doubt you're going to drop this."

"Oh? And why is that? The money?"

Benson half-lifted his hands in a washing away gesture. "No. Despite your circumstances, I don't believe the money is your main motivation."

Helen stared at him for a moment. "Then what is?"

"The desire to know. I told you, Miss Lipscomb, I've studied your former career. More than once, you took the hard road instead of the easy one. And you did it because you wanted answers."

"You make me sound like someone from a Victorian mystery."

Benson laughed, a dry, somewhat wheezing chuckle. He straightened up as far as he could, leaned back in his chair and placed his arms flat on the table.

"Nancy Snyder was twenty-three-years old and working as a special ed teacher at a middle school in

Boulder. She was engaged, but she and her fiancé were taking a bit of a break, something to do with some racked-up credit card debt. At the time of her—disappearance—she was only living with two cats."

Helen sighed. "And I'm guessing that if I check, I'll find that at least some of that info hasn't been in any media reports."

Benson spread his hands as far as the manacles would permit. "Feel free to check."

"But just because you learned something that's not in the media doesn't mean you knew it ahead of time. After all, the fact that you hired me to help you shows that you still have resources, ways of reaching out."

Benson nodded, a slight grin creasing his face. "See what I mean, Detective? You're not satisfied with an easy answer. And whether you realize it or not, you've got your teeth into this now. For what it's worth, and because you already warned our friends back in the other room, I learned what I knew of Miss Snyder some years back."

"Thus, your card hand reducing in value," Helen remarked.

Benson frowned and nodded.

"How many more, Leo? Come on, it's just you and me now. How many more are out there?"

The convict placed his hands flat on the table, fingers splayed and stared at them.

"Do you really think going to Oklahoma is the best use of your time and my resources?" he asked without looking up.

"Unless you're ready to tell me how Willy Gray connects up to you."

"I've already told you," Benson said, carefully

enunciating each word, "that he doesn't. I don't know how else to say that I simply have never met the man, don't know the man, hell, wouldn't know him if he walked in that door." He lifted his head and nodded across the room.

"Yet somehow he knows your secrets," Helen pointed out.

Benson nodded, back to staring at his hands.

"Then yes, Oklahoma is my next step."

Benson looked up at her, a hooded look in his eyes. "Be careful, Miss Lipscomb. Step lightly as you go. Some answers are more dangerous than others."

Staring at the slight, stooped man, the upper edge of his pot belly just peeking over the tabletop, for the first time Helen felt the fear he could induce in others.

"But as you said," she said, working to keep a tremble out of her voice, "maybe I just need to know the answers."

Benson craned his head and turned to the mirror. "I'd like to go back now," he said, his voice louder than at any moment since he'd entered the room.

As the door opened and the three CO's came in to take him back, Helen stood up to leave.

"Lipscomb," Benson said as the CO's reshackled his wrists.

"Yes?"

"To continue my poker analogy, you're my ace in the hole."

"So?" Helen said.

The officers shuffled him to the door, but he half-turned as they got there.

"Watch your back," he said as they ushered him out. "The last thing I want is to lose my ace."

CHAPTER 31

Tuesday, Sept. 24th

AFTER NEARLY TWO years of muddling around on her own, the idea of having a team at her disposal was appreciated. True, she'd met none of them, save their boss; nonetheless, they were in the background pitching for her. Before heading to Oklahoma City, however, Helen needed more intelligence.

Leaving the prison, she'd driven back to the hotel, the same one she'd used on her first visit to Benson, and placed a call to Conroy. He was still in court, but one of his associates came to the phone and Helen explained what she needed. Then it was just a matter of killing the rest of the day and waiting for a response.

The e-mail, along with another voluminous package of information in the form of a PDF, arrived around ten the next morning. Most of the day was spent going over it, stopping only to down a tuna salad sandwich and iced tea courtesy of room service before calling it a day a little before six. She shut off her laptop, stretched out on the bed, stared at the ceiling, and let her brain rewind through everything she'd read and noted during the day.

Before knowing it, her eyelids were starting to flutter. Jerking awake, she reached out for her cell phone, placed a quick call to Conroy's office to ask for one more task to be done, then said to hell with it and drifted off.

****

Wednesday, Sept. 25th

The next morning, Helen had finished dressing and was contemplating what to do for breakfast when a knock sounded at the door. Her gaze slipped toward the door, then darted over to her suitcase, where her weapon rested beneath the clothes.

She'd paid in cash for the room the day before, and only Conroy and his people knew where she was. When'd she'd returned from the prison, she'd contemplated calling both Carstairs in Denver and Grierson in KC, out of professional courtesy, and updating them on her progress, but realizing there hadn't been much in the way of actual progress had changed her mind.

Conroy had possibly sent someone from his office with something for her, but she'd requested nothing and they surely would have called or texted ahead.

A second knock came, and feeling foolish at her qualms, Helen went over and looked through the peephole.

Two young men stood there, almost clones of each other. Both tall, as far as could be told through the peephole's distortion, around six feet, and wearing light summer suits, one tan and one a light gray. They both had almost military haircuts, and Helen instinctively knew what they were.

She pulled back the safety latch and opened the door.

"Yes?"

"Helen Lipscomb?" the one on the right, he of the tan suit, asked.

"Yes?"

He held up a badge holder to show his ID that proclaimed him Special Agent Roy Jenkins of the F.B.I.

"Yeah?" Helen repeated.

"Someone would like to speak to you," Jenkins said.

"Okay." She held the door open and waved the two men inside, but they stood right where they were.

"Downstairs," the other fed, who hadn't identified himself, said.

"Huh?"

"In the coffee shop downstairs."

The two weren't actually ordering her, but it didn't matter. With a good guess who was waiting downstairs, and figuring she'd have to deal with the man sooner or later, she might as well get it over with.

"Let me get my purse."

****

He resembled the high-school football star who didn't go any further and ended up working at a used car dealership, reliving his glory days in the weekend bars while his muscle eased into fat.

Even without the two guides, Helen could have picked the guy out in an instant. Seated by himself in the hotel's breakfast lounge, nursing a cup of coffee while waiting. His red hair had thinned in places, though not yet to the point where he had to employ a comb-over. His navy blue suit looked a little too heavy for Nebraska in late September, and before too long he'd have to start buying shirts with a half-inch larger collar.

A man who'd been behind a desk, as opposed to out in the field, for a while now.

He stood up as Helen approached the table.

"Miss Lipscomb, thanks for meeting me."

Helen waved her hand in the direction of the two agents, who had taken seats at an adjoining table. "They didn't exactly make me an offer I couldn't refuse," she said, "but it came close."

"Coffee?" the man said, ignoring her jab.

"I'd prefer just quick talk. I assume you're Special Agent Powers?"

"Where'd you get that from?" he asked, his expression slipping for a second before becoming bland again.

"I can't think of anyone else at the fed level who would be interested in me. But how'd you track me down?"

"I missed you in Denver. I was back in town the day after you left. Heard that you'd been nosing around the Brayn case, asking about the others. Is that correct?"

Helen worked to keep her breathing steady in order to not show any alarm. She hadn't done anything illegal, more or less, but any interaction with the FBI could go south in any number of ways. "There's nothing against that. As I explained to Detective Carstairs, I'm employed by a lawyer and working in the normal course of his duties."

Powers took a long drink of his coffee before putting the cup down. "I have no doubt of that, but I'm curious as to what that normal course of duties is. Care to enlighten me?"

"No."

He glanced up, a spark flashing in his eyes. "Excuse me?"

"I said no. I don't want to enlighten you, and at the moment there's no legal reason why I need to do so."

Another long drink, it must be the way the guy

collected his thoughts, and Helen noticed his face and neck getting a little more flushed.

"Cooperation isn't necessarily a bad thing," the fed pointed out.

"As for cooperation, you didn't answer my question. How'd you track me down?"

"What's your business with Leo Benson?"

"None of your business," Helen said.

"Look, lady—"

"No, you look, Agent Powers. Clearly, you've been keeping tabs on me since I left Denver, hell, maybe before. So I'm guessing you know all about what went down in KC and why I showed up here yesterday. Piece it together however you want to, but I'm not obligated to tell you anything."

"You could be hauled in for obstructing a federal investigation."

"What obstruction? Last I heard, Willy Gray's spilling his guts to you every other day. All you have to do is sit back and take notes. Just let him lead you to his bodies."

Powers flushed an even deeper red, and a thin film of sweat appeared on his face.

"Or can it be," she said, "that you don't believe him either. Maybe you think Gray's running a game on you?"

"His intel has been on point so far."

"Uh huh. Which explains why you and your task force…" She jerked a thumb in the direction of the next table where the other two agents still sat. "…are spending your time following me around."

"You could get too far out of line, Lipscomb," Powers said. "Probably wouldn't want that to happen."

Helen stood up and stared down at the fed. "If you

checked me out, then you can probably guess that I don't respond too well to authority figures. So why don't you just consider that I've done you a favor and leave it at that."

"Favor?" Powers looked confused.

"Think about it," Helen said as she walked away.

All in all, she couldn't see it as a negative at all. At the very least, Powers and his people would assume that she'd gone to the prison to visit Benson. He was already on the books as a serial, so pegging him to a few other crimes wouldn't set him back at all. And it would possibly add weight to his claims, when he chose to make them, of other victims he had knowledge of.

So no, she didn't see Powers' task force glomming onto her as much of a problem. At least not so far.

However, if they tracked her down south and interfered with things there, it could make her job more difficult.

And she had a feeling, way deep down inside, that Oklahoma was where the answers lay.

PART IV
Oklahoma

CHAPTER 32

Wednesday, Sept. 25th

THE LINCOLN, NEBRASKA, airport didn't have any direct flights to Oklahoma City, forcing Helen to fly back to Denver and from there head south. Ordinarily, she would have foregone the delay and driven straight through, in probably close to the same amount of time, but she'd had enough of driving cross-country and couldn't imagine anything in Oklahoma that wouldn't wait a day or so. Plus, she needed time to skull over her meeting with the feds.

It had been inevitable, of course, that the task force investigating Gray's "crimes" would look her up sooner or later. She hadn't exactly kept the investigation a secret, and it would have been the height of sloppiness for them not to check out her interest in the matter. And, as she'd realized after meeting with Powers, in the long run connecting her to Gray, and through her Benson, could probably only help her employer's ultimate cause.

Whether it would hamper Helen herself in the short run was another matter.

Debarking at Will Rogers World Airport, she snagged a rental car, actually managing to go straight past checkout and to the parking lot, just as the commercials with that annoying TV actor claimed, pulled up the GPS to orient herself, then checked the time. It was getting close to evening, probably not the best time to bother the people she needed to talk to, but it couldn't hurt to check out the area.

Twenty minutes got her to the general vicinity, the eastern edge of town, and another five had her driving about a quarter mile down a gravel road before pulling up in a plain dirt parking lot outside a bar. The place was named The Last Draw, not really much in the way of originality, and even that early in the evening, the parking lot held something like twenty or thirty vehicles, mainly pickups and jeeps.

The area looked almost too clichéd to hold a run-down, sawdust on the floor establishment. Unlike most taverns she was familiar with, the building reared up two stories and had a peaked roof. The upper part contained, at least from the front, a single quarter-paned window that, from her perspective and in the fading light, looked dusty and unwashed.

Behind the actual building itself lay a broad patch of scrubland, and to the west, on the other side of the road loomed some sort of factory, complete with dull gray buildings and a chain link security fence.

Had this been a weekend night, she would have had a better than even shot at finding the owner inside. Considering nighttime, no doubt, was the establishment's busiest hours, it wouldn't be the best time to bother someone about an employee they'd had for a couple of heartbeats a year or so back.

The packet that Conroy's people had sent included The Last Draw as the only confirmable place of employment for Willy Gray during his time in Oklahoma City. As near as the lawyer's office could narrow down, Gray had only worked at the place for a few months, and even before leaving Nebraska Helen had seen it as a long shot.

Looking the place over, and realizing she was committing the sin of judging a book by its cover, Helen couldn't imagine anyone working there for more than a short span of time. While sitting in her parked car, a few people had left, all men complete with boots and cowboy hats, while several had arrived and gone inside. One fellow, looking in the fading light to be no more than thirty, pulled up in some sort of ultra-jacked-up pickup, complete with large swatches of dried mud on the sides and the requisite cover girl mud flaps adorning the back tires.

Maybe too judgmental, but Helen couldn't quite see the scared, jittery person she'd observed back in Denver fitting in with a bunch like this.

Then again, that could be why the intel showed he hadn't worked there very long.

After getting a feel for the place, noticing that few of the patrons were female, she got out of the rental and made her way across the parking lot and up onto the wraparound front porch. Every third porch board was warped, making Helen glad she'd opted to wear tennis shoes.

A small, hand-written sign stuck in the front door, indicated that every day except Monday the place opened up at noon on the spot. Beyond she could hear the sounds of normal rural barroom revelry.

She realized then that she'd come out here without much in the way of a real plan. A look at Gray's place of employment was helpful, but even more so would be speaking with his former bosses and co-workers. However, the middle of their worknight wasn't the best time to do that, and could easily find them on the defensive.

Helen had no clue as to the level of business acumen of the owners, but assumed that someone would be there by eleven thirty at the latest the next morning. She considered for a second going on in and finding out what she could (she had driven all the way out here, after all), but decided to start fresh tomorrow as an unknown quantity.

Turning away, she headed back to the car. Destination: another night of staring at hotel room walls.

Which lately seemed to pretty much sum up her life.

CHAPTER 33

Thursday, Sept. 26th

THE NEXT MORNING, Helen returned to The Last Draw, timing her arrival to both miss the morning commuter traffic and get there just before noon.

She pulled up to the bar, the dirt parking lot now empty save for an old blue Suburban, rust showing around all four fenderwells and parked up next to the front door.

Exiting the car, Helen made her way to the warped front porch, the sound of cicadas going nuts in the field across the road. Stepping onto the porch, she turned and surveyed the entire area, looking for nothing in particular, merely trying to get the lay of the land in brighter daylight.

The factory that squatted beyond the field, which the night before had seemed to overshadow the area, now looked plain and ordinary in the light of day. Helen had passed an entrance gate about an eighth of a mile down the road, but hadn't been able to catch the name of the place.

Looking around, something about the whole area bothered her. It wasn't just the idea of a drinking establishment all the way out here in the boondocks. Hell, in her day she'd visited, both officially and unofficially, all sorts of businesses situated farther out in the middle of nowhere than this one.

Rather, she felt some indefinable atmosphere of gloom hanging over the area even though she could physically detect nothing to support the feeling.

Turning back to the bar itself, Helen could make out a single faint light inside. Although there seemed no customers around, she squared her shoulders and walked on in.

Helen had spent a lot of time in bars recently. Picking up stray work from bail bondsmen, lawyers and private eyes had sent her into a fair share of establishments. Most of the time, the information she'd gotten was negligible at best, but when you were tracking down someone who'd skipped out on child support or fled the locale after a bail hearing, you had to take what you could get.

Those experiences, however, had taken place in larger cities, and quite often in the more squalid districts. She rarely had the opportunity to visit a place as rural as this, even though it technically fell within a metropolis of over half a million people.

From the doorway she could only see two people in the entire place, a man and woman working, the man washing out glass mugs and the woman wiping down the bar top. Helen guessed they were the owners of the Suburban parked outside, and hoped that one of them was either the owner or manager. In a place this small, they were more than likely one and the same.

"Help you?" the man asked. He was a tall guy, something over six-three, and lanky, probably weighing less than one-eighty. He wore black jeans and a black tee-shirt from which pipestem arms protruded. For some reason, Helen would have expected those arms to be covered with sleeve tats, but they weren't.

"I need to talk to someone," Helen said. "Is the owner or manager around?"

The woman looked up from her work long enough to smile, then went back to wiping the bar top. As far as Helen could tell, she wasn't making it any cleaner.

"I'd be both of those," the man said, extending his hand. "Name's Buck. What can I do for you?"

"If you're looking to buy the place, forget it," the woman said as Helen reached out to shake Buck's hand. "Doesn't matter what you offer, he won't split with this hunk of wood for nothing."

"Actually," Helen said as she sat on a stool and swiveled around to face Buck, "I'm looking for some information."

The man tensed, just slightly, and his eyes shifted from side to side.

"You a cop?" he asked.

"Not hardly. Right at the moment, I'm actually not much of anything, but I'm working for a lawyer."

Out of the corner of her eyes, Helen saw the woman lean closer into the bar, as if deliberately avoiding looking her way.

"A private eye?" Buck asked, and for an instant Helen considered actually going through the ordeal of getting a license. It would make answering such inquiries a whole lot easier.

"Not really," she said. "I'm just nosing around and asking a few questions."

"About?"

She took a deep breath and looked the man squarely in the eye. "I'm trying to track down someone who I think used to work for you."

"What's his name?"

Helen had thought this over ahead of time and had decided to play it as vague as possible. She had no way of knowing how Gray's former boss felt about him, or if he'd heard anything of Gray's troubles, and she wanted the identification to be as organic as possible.

"I'm not sure about his name. But it would have been a little over a year ago. A young kid, just came to town. He would have—"

"You mean Willy?"

Helen's heart fluttered for a minute. It hadn't been Buck who'd spoken, but the woman down the bar. Both she and Buck turned and looked the woman's way.

"Who?" Buck asked.

The waitress had placed the rag under the bar and was wiping her hands on a paper towel.

"You remember, Buck. That kid who showed up here a while back. Said he was from out of state, needed to get on his feet?"

Buck nodded.

"Skinny kid," he said after a few seconds, "eyes kind of empty and confused?"

"That's him." The woman now turned fully to Helen. "My name's Mona. I run the place for the big guy here."

"She's a waitress," Buck protested.

"I'm also the only reason he sees a profit at the end of the year."

"Freakin' small profit, you ask me."

Helen kept her patience in check. The two of them had probably worked together for years, and gone through the same routine, or variations of it, over and over. She wanted to get them to talking more about Gray, but if she got rude they'd probably clam up.

"So he just showed up and asked for a job?" she prodded.

The two of them looked at each other, then Buck nodded. "Yep, I gather he was walking all around the area, applying wherever he could."

Walking around the area? As far as Helen could tell there weren't any other businesses within half a mile or so, except for the plant across the road.

"Was he living close by?"

Another moment of thought, before Buck shook his head. "I don't really know. We didn't really have him fill out anything formal. He said he needed work, would take whatever we wanted to pay under the table."

Helen puzzled that one over. Gray had left KC and somehow ended up here. She remembered noticing a bus depot about half a mile away. It was possible he'd come in on a bus, and this outer stretch of the city was as far as he could get. As far as she knew, he hadn't taken much with him when he left Missouri, and had probably been desperate for any sort of job.

"How long did he work for you?" Helen asked although she already could guess.

Both Buck and Mona puzzled that one for a moment. "A couple of months," Mona finally said, and Buck nodded in agreement.

"Why'd he leave? Was he fired or did he quit?"

"Quit," Buck said. "Kind of surprised me, too. He was making good money, after all, and didn't have to travel for work."

"Huh?"

Buck pointed upwards. "We've got a spare room up there, for nights when someone's too damned wasted to drive away. We let him stay up there and fix it up somewhat. Made for a nice arrangement for the kid."

Mona gave a shake of her head and walked around the corner and out of sight.

"So what made him quit?" Helen asked.

Buck scratched his chin as a thoughtful look came into his eyes. Helen had the idea that he was about to ask for money in exchange for talk. Generally speaking, that wouldn't have been a problem, she was taking up his time after all, but she wanted him to tell the truth, as far as he could remember, not what he thought someone may want to hear.

If only she'd thought as clearly when it came to Toni Orson, the girl may still be alive. Dangling money had no doubt spurred Toni to up the ante with Brounton, which had resulted in her death.

But before he could get around to asking for payment, if in fact he intended to, Mona came back to the front, lugging with her a case of bottled Heineken.

"He never said," she said, hoisting the case onto the bar top. "Came downstairs one night just as we were opening up, said thanks for the help we'd given, but he was off."

A red flag popped up in Helen's mind. "Did you notice anything missing? Any money or anything?"

"What? No, not like that. The whole time Willy worked here, he didn't take nothing. Wasn't the best worker, you understand, but he was basically honest. No, it seemed like he just realized it was time to move on."

Helen ran the pieces in her head, but couldn't come up with any sort of pattern that made sense. Gray had left KC for whatever reason and come to this out of the way place to, what? Lay low, it would seem. And he'd pulled it off. But then why had he taken off again? What had sparked the need to leave?

She talked for a few more minutes with Mona and Buck, but they couldn't shed any more light on Gray's activities. Obviously, he'd kept a low profile, doing nothing too flagrant to attract the attention of the law, but he seemed to have lived a typically nomadic life. So why had he then moved back to Denver, gotten a job at a middle school and proceeded to kill Sami Brayn?

And how did any of it relate to Leo Benson?

A small ache developed behind Helen's eyes, and she shook her head. Time to leave, get out into the sunlight, somehow find a fresh perspective to put all those random pieces into some sort of order.

"Okay, well thanks for your time." She pulled a card out of her pocket and wrote down her cell number. "If by chance you think of anything else, I'd appreciate a call."

Buck took the card and began turning it back and forth, staring down as if it held some secret. Helen waited a moment, didn't get any response, and glanced over at Mona.

The barkeep shook her head and shrugged her shoulders.

Helen turned to leave when Buck called out behind her.

"Just a couple of days before Willy left," Buck said, "there was a girl's body found in the field over there." He waved in the general direction of the area across the road from his building.

"Girl?" Helen turned around, working to keep her breathing normal.

"Well, woman, I guess. You remember how old she was, Mona?"

Mona had moved to the far end of the bar and was pretending to wash glasses. She looked up at Buck's question.

"I don't remember. Twenty or something like that."

"You said her body was found?" Helen asked. "I'm assuming she was murdered?"

Buck and Mona nodded almost in unison. "Strangled," Buck said. "Strangled and left out in that field. Time they found her she'd been nibbled all over the place by animals."

Helen thought quickly. She needed to get as much information out of them as she could without wearing out her welcome. As soon as she got back to the hotel she was going online, but right now wanted as much raw impression as possible from these folks so close to the event.

"She'd gone missing?" she asked.

Again the simultaneous nods from Buck and Mona. "I'm guessing a couple of days before they found her. Young kid, they did all the stuff you can imagine, search parties, TV appeals, all that stuff."

"Well, she wasn't a kid," Helen said.

"True. It was a big deal for a while, then just kind of petered out. You know how those things go."

"And Willy took off the day after she was found?"

Buck and Mona looked at each other, as if concentrating together. Helen was pretty sure Buck didn't keep the most meticulous of records, so their memory was probably as exact as she could get. Still, only a year or so, those memories should be fresh, especially from such an unusual occurrence.

"Not after she was found," Mona finally said. She put a wet glass down in the strainer and focused all her attention on Helen. "It was a couple of days before, but after she went missing. We kind of wondered about it at the time, but figured he just had some reason to go back home."

The three of them talked for a few more minutes, but the two had offered everything they could remember about the murdered woman. It wasn't much, but with the general time frame she figured it wouldn't be too difficult to track down what she needed.

She thanked them and headed out, by this time a moderate number of shift workers stopping in and the place beginning to fill up for lunch. Stepping out into the early afternoon, she blinked a couple of times as her eyes adjusted from the interior gloom of the bar, then hauled out her phone to make a call to Conroy's office.

CHAPTER 34

Friday, Sept. 27th

THE MAIN HEADQUARTERS of the Oklahoma City Police Department lay on Colcord Drive, just to the east of the city's business district, and Helen pulled within sight of it by a little before two o'clock. She'd spent the morning going over another voluminous amount of online material about another murdered girl.

Once inside the building, it only took one look at the directory and a few questions of uniformed personnel to direct her up to the main detective squad room, and from there only a few minutes more before she found herself facing a somewhat hostile plainclothes officer.

"Have a seat." The short, balding man who'd introduced himself as Det. Wilson gestured toward the single chair positioned in front of his desk. As she'd sat, he'd picked up the phone and made a short call before replacing the receiver.

Wilson looked to be somewhere in his mid-fifties, and wore that harried look Helen had often seen on veteran cops. His face could use a shave; his lower gut was threatening to pop a few buttons on his shirt, and his clothes in general could have used a good pressing. If Helen had to, she would have pegged the man as a couple of months away from retirement and loathing every minute of it.

And possibly, judging by his physical appearance, not that much farther away from a stroke.

"My partner will be here in a minute," he said. "She's finishing up processing someone downstairs. From what I understand, you know how that goes."

Helen nodded. "Done it once or twice myself."

"That's how I heard it. Got to tell you, though, when we got a call from Gordon Conroy's office asking for help, we damned near hung up on the guy."

"I understand that reaction as well."

"Actually, for a minute there my partner thought it was a crank. What the hell would someone like Conroy be calling out here in the middle of nowhere for?"

Helen nodded. Back in her time, someone playing a bad joke would have been the first thing she considered as well.

"But then he mentioned Alex Jamison," Wilson said, "so we figured what the hell and decided to give him a couple of minutes."

When Wilson mentioned the name "Jamison" a little tic developed in the corner of his eye.

"We appreciate you doing so," Helen said.

"I'm guessing in your time you had one or two like Jamison."

"One or two," Helen said, knowing all too well that either Wilson or his partner would have, like all the cops she'd met on this case, done their due diligence ahead of time in regard to her history.

Wilson was either doing a poor job of acting like an uninformed yokel, or he was trying to put her at ease.

Either way, Helen watched the tic increase beneath the cop's eye.

No doubt about it. Helen had seen the signs before.

The man had a case he couldn't let go of.

Wilson peered closer at her. "You don't look like most retired cops who go private," he said.

"I'm not exactly retired," she replied. "More like changing careers."

"Still don't look the part."

"How so?" Helen asked, knowing that if he'd checked on her at all, as he'd already indicated, he knew her exact status.

From the corner of her eye, she noticed a young black woman heading their way. She wore a chocolate brown blazer and cream-colored pants and had a holster clipped to her belt.

"Well," Wilson said, "for one you look a little seedier than most. No offense. I mean, you look just about old enough to have gotten out at twenty, depending on when you started. So I'd think—"

"Hank," the woman said as she came abreast of them, "don't ever call a woman seedy."

Wilson turned light red. "I only meant—"

"Naomi Johnson," the woman said, turning away from Wilson and offering her hand in greeting. Helen pegged her age at somewhere close to thirty, fairly young for a detective, let alone a homicide investigator. "Lou Whitmore speaks highly of you."

Helen's heart skipped a beat, and for a moment her vision clouded. "You know Lou?"

"Met him at a VICAP conference in Atlanta a few years ago."

"I figured you'd run down my pedigree, but I hadn't expected anyone to bother Lou."

Johnson nodded. "He says to give him a call when you get a chance."

Helen blinked a couple of times. For a while there, Lou Whitmore had been about the only mainstay in her life. Around the time her old partner, Jack Hollis, had been killed along with several of their colleagues, and the force that she'd devoted her life to had basically dumped her in the gutter, Lou had been the one solid in her life.

But even that connection had frayed as the weeks, then months, went by, and the day came when the big cop had looked around her apartment, the rent two months overdue and some of the furniture sold to meet living expenses, and told her to either get her act together or give it up entirely.

Helen, in not one of her brighter moments, had kicked Lou out, telling him to go fuck himself, and the big guy had shaken his head and acceded to her wishes. Even so, his words had gotten through to her, and shame at the circumstances had finally set in.

It had been in the ensuing weeks and months that she'd begun seeking out and accepting piecemeal investigative work, and slowly, all too slowly, she'd managed to get herself back into something approaching financial equilibrium.

Emotional equilibrium was a whole other matter, though, and sometimes, in the very late parts of the night, she wondered if she'd ever achieve that again.

There had been several times in the intervening year and a half when she'd reached for the phone, intending to give Lou a call, let him know that she was pulling herself together.

The first time, embarrassingly enough, had been when she'd picked up some day work from a small-time insurance agency needing to track down some delinquent payments, and she'd needed some license plate info.

She'd started to call then, but the memory of those last words to him still seared in her mind, and she'd felt a little too opportunistic.

The urge to reach out had never entirely gone away, and she'd seriously considered getting hold of him after Benson and Conroy had offered this job.

Yet she hadn't.

Shame again, knowing all too well that he'd see her as a traitor, a sellout.

The same way she had begun to see herself.

"I'm guessing he vouched for me okay?" she asked Detective Johnson.

The black woman nodded. "Said you were probably the best damned cop he ever worked with."

Helen squeezed her eyes shut for a second.

"This is all nice and everything," Wilson butted in, "but how about we get down to business, huh? We've got a lot to do, Miss Lipscomb. What exactly is it you want from us?"

Johnson sighed, rolled her eyes in Wilson's direction. "Don't let Hank here bother you. Believe it or not, this is him putting on his best manners."

Wilson harrumphed and gestured towards the other end of the squad room. "What say we take this in conference, huh?"

Helen was beginning to think they'd perfected some sort of Hekyll and Jekyll act to keep suspects off balance, but proceeded to follow the two of them to a small glassed-in conference area against the west wall. It held only six chairs; a small refrigerator in the corner; and a six by eight table, bare save for a thick pile of file folders in the middle.

Helen took a seat on one side of the table as Johnson sat opposite her and Wilson closed the door.

"Something to drink?" Naomi asked as she moved toward the fridge.

"Water's fine, thanks."

Johnson gave Wilson a look, but he shook his head.

She took two small bottles of water from the fridge and handed one to Helen.

"Our lieutenant's in court today, otherwise he'd be here as well."

Helen crooked her eyebrows up at that. "How come?"

The two cops looked uncomfortable for a minute before Wilson's shoulders sagged. "The Jamison girl lived in his neighborhood, about five blocks over. He took a kind of personal interest in the case."

"He didn't investigate, did he?" Helen asked. In any department she'd ever known of, command rank didn't take part in field work except in the most supervisory way.

"'Course not," Wilson spoke up. "But he did push us day and night to get it solved. By the time all the leads had fizzled, he'd about worn us down to nothing."

"And then you call from out of state, wanting to talk about it. Why is that?" Johnson said.

"I don't want you guys to get your hopes up," Helen said. "There's a chance, just a chance, that her death ties in to something my firm's working on. So they sent me down to check out a few things."

The two cops wore dubious expressions, and Helen realized that she sounded like every slick legal investigator she'd ever encountered. In her mind's eye, that uncrossable line wavered more and more.

"Is this going to be some sort of one-way arrangement?" Naomi Johnson asked. "Where we show you all our cards and you walk away grinning, maybe using our info to get your client, whoever they are, off the hook?"

"I can assure you, detective," Helen said, the line firming up just a bit, "that the last thing we're interested in is arguing for someone's innocence."

"Doesn't sound like any law firm I ever heard of," Wilson said, genuine interest in his voice. "Exactly what is it you're after?"

"Some work we're doing for a client may have a connection, a faint one possibly, to the Jamison homicide. I thought it wouldn't hurt to sit down and put our heads together, you know, compare notes."

"You want to look through our files?" Wilson asked.

Helen shook her head. "Of course not. But I thought you could maybe give me an overview of the case, and I could see if anything on my end matches up. Then we could—"

"That's awful nice of you." A slight sneer had developed in Johnson's voice. Not enough to be flat out insulting, but there nonetheless. "When you were on the force back in your hometown, would you have gone for something like this? Collaborate with a lawyer's investigator to help them clear their own workload? Exactly how did you all run things back there?"

"Naomi," Wilson said, "hear the woman out. It can't do us any harm to listen to her."

Helen took a deep breath and, realizing she'd been slouching, straightened herself up. Her mind was moving in a couple of different directions.

Johnson was right. In her days on the force, she had

several opportunities to cooperate with private detectives, usually when they had some tangential relation to a case she was working on. And in every case she'd turned the opportunity down flat. Even when the investigator was, as most were, a retired cop, she'd kept her distance. It had been an unwritten rule of the department that the public and private sides of the street never meet.

On the other hand, she'd spent most of the night before reading up on the case of Alex Jamison, and while there'd been absolutely nothing in the public material to definitively point to the young woman being connected with Helen's case, the type of death, plus the proximity to Willy Gray at the time, made it a fairly obvious avenue to pursue.

But something else was causing some consternation. As she watched the two of them playing off each other, almost circling around her in different directions, she couldn't help but think of Jack Hollis and the way she'd interacted with her former partner.

Helen's throat caught. It had been months since she'd consciously thought about Hollis, though he'd never gone far from the back of her mind. Jack had died in the midst of a chaotic, discordant gun battle while trying to take down a killer who'd been targeting various members of their own detective squad, among them the lieutenant himself. In those wild few days afterwards, with his killer dead and the higher-ups holding out Helen as a scapegoat, she'd focused on getting by one hour at a time.

Lou had tried to help, along with George Beacham and a few others, but despite it all, Helen had only had herself to fully rely on.

It had taken weeks before she could get through a day without crying, though only in private, and months without seeing some reminder of her partner everywhere. Now, nearly two years later, she'd managed for some time to thrust Jack into a small corner of her mind. She'd never forget him, but could now finally look back on him with fondness instead of grief.

And now she saw a detective pairing that, in several small ways, reminded her all over again of the work she and Jack had done together.

She shook her head, forcing herself to focus back on the job at hand. She needed to get a look at the file on Alex Jamison, and the only way to get there was through these two.

"Here's the thing. Like I said, there may be a connection between the death of the Jamison girl and a case we're handling for a client. If it turns out there is, I'd like to share any information I can with you. But because of privilege, I can't just give it out without being sure of the connection."

"Are you sure you really understand attorney/client privilege?" Johnson asked her. "No matter what your personal feelings, how would it help your client, whoever they are, to share information with the police?"

Helen hesitated. She couldn't answer that without edging into the nature of her work for Benson.

"All I'm interested in," she finally said, "is helping to bring a perpetrator to justice."

"You expect us to believe that you have a client, in some way connected with our case, and your only interest is in finding out guilt? I find that a little hard to swallow, Miss Lipscomb."

"If you would just—" Helen began before Wilson

cut her off.

"Wait a minute, here." His face had turned a slight shade of red, and his breathing had quickened a bit. "You're coming from out of state and plopping this on us? Are we talking a serial here?"

The air in the conference room had thickened.

"I can't get into any specifics yet. But off the record, yes, it's possible that Alex Jamison was the victim of a serial killer."

"But we haven't had any similar murders," Naomi Johnson pointed out.

"Because whoever the bastard is doesn't live around here. Isn't that right, Lipscomb?"

Helen's mind whirred. She had to choose her words carefully, otherwise the whole thing could blow up on her.

"It's complicated," she finally said, "which is why I'm coming to you."

"Do you know who he was? And just who is your client?" Johnson asked.

"I don't know for sure. That's part of what I'm tracking down. And I can't identify our client because of—"

"Let me guess," Johnson interrupted, "confidentiality. Right?"

Though her expression remained impassive, inside Helen felt like cringing. Somehow, this had gotten completely out of hand, and it didn't take long to figure out why. In the first few minutes, she'd naturally assumed that Johnson would be more sympathetic to the request. Helen had seen her as the more modern, cutting-edge type cop; whereas, she'd viewed Wilson as older and more set in his ways. Yet the two seemed to have reversed those roles.

"Look," she said, reaching for a pad of paper and pen set next to the folders on the table, "I'm at the Doubletree. Here's my room number. Run it by your lieutenant. We're offering to help out your case, and all I'm asking in return is some cooperation. See what he says and, if interested, get back to me. If not, I'm heading out tomorrow at the crack of dawn, and that's that."

"It's early yet," Johnson pointed out. "You could just head on out."

Helen, seeing no advantage in antagonizing the two any further, bit her tongue and glanced at the pile of folders on the table. Were those the files for the Jamison murder? Had the OKC cops more or less intended to cooperate until she came in and somehow screwed the whole thing up?

"Trust me," she said. "You've got a no-lose situation here. Talk it over with your boss and if you're interested, let me know."

The two cops stared at her, showing nothing one way or the other.

Shrugging her shoulders, Helen headed out of the room.

CHAPTER 35

Evening, Friday, Sept. 27th

HELEN WENT BACK to the hotel and spent some time staring at the walls. She'd screwed up big time with Johnson and Wilson and was stumped as to her next move. Out of sheer frustration she grabbed the television remote and flipped on one of the usual suspects of inane afternoon talk shows. In the background, the show's host carried on about the need to love and forgive each other as he tried to keep a mother and daughter separated who'd been sleeping with the same man.

She went back over every word spoken between herself and the Oklahoma detectives. For the life of her, she couldn't see where Johnson's antagonism had come from. Maybe Helen was being a little obtrusive by walking into their station and expecting them to fall all over her, but it isn't every day someone shows up offering to help with a year-old murder case.

Then again, maybe she'd had a weak hand going in and had projected her own unease onto the two cops. When it came right down to it, she had absolutely nothing, other than proximity, to connect Willy Gray with the dead woman in the field. So even if they'd accepted her offer to reciprocate information, what really could she have given them?

It didn't help, of course, that their lieutenant had

been on them extra hard to solve the case, but how could they have expected Helen to know that? And what could she have done about it?

The talk show had morphed into a local news program, and Helen clicked the TV off. She couldn't think of anything, save possibly the weather, going on in Oklahoma City that would interest her.

Then again, she couldn't think of anything else to do except dig back into her laptop and see if she'd missed anything about the Jamison case, and that seemed even less appealing than the TV.

So she ordered a steak from room service and spent a couple of hours surfing cable news channels. After enduring about as much of that as she could, she snapped the TV off once again and stood in the middle of the room, trying to decide how to kill the rest of the night.

Before she'd come to a decision, a knock sounded on her door. Walking over to answer, she happened to cross in front of the mirror over the dresser and paused, almost gasping at the reflection.

Ever since leaving the force, Helen hadn't exactly taken the best care of herself. More than once, back in the early days, she'd neither felt the inclination nor had enough funds to pay much attention to her personal nutrition. But she paused now, finding it hard to believe that the wan, vacant-eyed woman reflected back was in fact herself.

She didn't look anorexic, or as if suffering from cancer, but also didn't look nearly as well cared for as in better days.

And she was in desperate need of a long visit to a salon.

Shrugging, figuring that she'd take better care of

herself once this case was over, she proceeded to the door and glanced through the peephole

Hank Wilson stood there, looking more in need of a shave than ever and with a couple of slim manila folders in his hand.

Helen opened the door. "Detective?"

"Miss Lipscomb." Wilson nodded. "Mind if I come in?"

Helen stood aside and ushered him in. The cop looked both ways down the hallway, probably by instinct more than anything else, and walked in the room.

As Helen shut the door, he walked over and laid the folders on the room's small desk.

"Boss was tied up all afternoon," he said as he threw himself onto the sofa. Helen shrugged and walked over to an easy chair kitty-cornered to it.

"Yeah?"

"Yeah," Wilson replied. "I waited around till after seven before he showed up. Only had a few minutes to update him on the day and didn't get around to your visit this afternoon."

Helen glanced at the file folders resting on the table. "Okay."

Wilson sighed and slumped deeper on the couch.

"Been a hell of a day," he said. "You're showing up was only the cherry on top. Johnson and I had to answer three different calls before one. Reason she was a bit late coming up to see you is she had to process a man we picked up for beating his ten-year-old son into a coma. You have any idea how many violent crimes there are in a town this size?"

"I think I have a pretty good idea."

The cop frowned ruefully and shook his head.

235

"Sorry. Forgot for a minute that you used to be one of us. Do me a favor and don't take it personal, huh?"

Helen nodded. "No problem. So you haven't had a chance to talk to your boss, huh?"

"Right. First thing in the morning, though. For sure."

"So what's in those folders?"

Wilson stretched out and sighed again. "Thing is," he said. "Me, I'm counting down the days. Or at least the weeks. Already got my papers in and ready to pull the pin."

Helen glanced at the table again, then back to her guest.

"One thing I won't miss," Wilson continued, "is trying to keep my desk in order. You know what I mean, right? Even with everything electronic these days, seems like a detective's desk is always a mess. Am I right? Even something as simple as a couple of case summary folders can be misplaced before you know it."

"You want something to drink?" Helen asked, getting the gist.

"Now Johnson, she's a neat freak like you wouldn't believe. If she sees a paperclip laying loose, she goes ballistic."

"She didn't seem to care much for me," Helen said. "Sent me a distinctly unfriendly vibe."

Wilson waved that notion away. "Don't take that too personal either. Nothing you did. Just between you and me, Naomi's on her way. Really going to go places in the department."

"Yeah?" Helen said.

"Yeah. Wouldn't be surprised if she ends up being the homicide boss in three or four years."

"But long after you're gone, right?"

Wilson smiled at her. "That's right."

"Okay," Helen said, wondering why the man was telling her so much.

"Point is," he continued, "she and I've been partners for over a year, so I pretty much have an idea of how she thinks. And the sense I was getting this afternoon is that Naomi's kind of scared of you."

Helen gave him a doubletake. "Scared of me? I just met her."

"Yeah, but she looks at you, sees what happened to you—"

"And is afraid something similar could happen to her," Helen finished.

"That's about it, yeah."

Helen shook her head and, rather than have to face the detective, looked over at the desk.

"So you brought me some reading, thanks."

"Like I said, I think I misplaced some of the basic documents. Nothing confidential or prioritized. I wouldn't be simple enough to lose anything like that. But everything we have that's already been pretty much disseminated to the media, or that's become fairly common knowledge. Oh well, it will turn up eventually."

"Probably will," Helen said.

Wilson gave it a large yawn.

"I talked to Naomi after you left and got her simmered down a bit. Then we went in to see the boss, and if you're still interested in talking he'll see us at nine tomorrow morning. Make sure you're on time, or he'll probably already be tied up. Me, first thing I have to do in the morning is get my desk in order. You know, all the papers in their place, all the files where I can easily find them."

"Okay."

"You may want to show up a little early. Just in case he can see you early. Get you on your way that much quicker."

Helen nodded, and the old cop stood up.

"See you then," he said as he headed, empty handed, towards the door.

After he left, Helen made herself a cup of coffee and sat down to go through the paperwork he'd left behind.

CHAPTER 36

THE TWO FILE folders Wilson had left contained more information than Helen had at first assumed. They clearly did not constitute the entire case paperwork, nor even summarize every move made and tactic employed. But between the two of them, they contained a meticulously written overview of the entire case, though none of it in the form of official paperwork.

As such, Helen assumed the documents were Wilson's own personal records of the case, and as she read through she began to see the older, overweight detective in a different light. Not only was his description and attention to detail, even in an unofficial memo, meticulous but his writing skills, including use of grammar, indicated someone of a lot higher intelligence than he had presented himself that afternoon.

Helen had brewed a pot of coffee, then, with the sun going down and the lights of Oklahoma City coming up outside her window, proceeded to read the document. It soon became obvious, though Helen had already gleaned it from her own survey of local media reports, that Buck and Mona had had their timeframes confused. The girl had been missing for much longer than just a few days, but Helen chalked that up to fuzzy memories on the part of the two.

Alex Jamison had been twenty-one years old in early August of the year before, at the time of her abduction and subsequent murder. A full-time student, she'd lived with her parents in a moderately-priced home in Shawnee, a town about forty miles east of OKC. She'd left home around three o'clock on a Saturday afternoon, telling her parents she was going to meet up with a couple of friends and then head into "The City," as most people in the area referred to the larger metropolis, and begin shopping for dresses for an upcoming wedding for which the girls had been tagged as bridesmaids.

Approximately an hour after Alex left home Susie Jenson, one of the friends she intended to meet, called her parents, wondering how long before Alex was going to show up. Susie and the other friend had been waiting at Susie's house for nearly an hour, and in that time had been calling Alex's cell phone every ten minutes or so, but with no answer. While Alex, according to later interviews, wasn't the most punctual of people, an hour late was a bit of a stretch, even for her.

Mr. and Mrs. Jamison then spent several precious minutes calling Alex's cell themselves, along with everyone else they could think of who may know anything about her whereabouts.

After another hour or so, the Shawnee police were contacted. Because of the girl's age, they couldn't begin a search until seventy-two hours had elapsed.

The hunt for young Alex became a local sensation, including, as Buck and Mona had told Helen the day before, all the modern qualities of such cases: tearful pleas by the parents broadcast on the local news and Facebook, posters stapled to every utility pole and shop window within ten miles, and daily press conferences with the local authorities.

For a brief period, the cops concentrated mainly on

Rick Wagner, Alex's former boyfriend. The two of them had dated through her last two years in college, breaking up about a month before she disappeared. According to several friends, the girl had initiated the break up after seeing some pictures on Instagram of Rick partying with another girl, a local high-schooler. Alex's friends had told the cops that Rick didn't take the parting particularly well, and for weeks had been pestering Alex for a second chance.

Alex's parents had known about the breakup, but hadn't known about the supposed dozens of phone calls and texts Rick had sent her. However, as they quietly admitted, once a kid turns eighteen how much do the parents really know about their activities?

The cops couldn't haul Rick in without some kind of cause, and in the beginning they weren't even officially involved. However, a friend of the family, a deputy with Pottawatomie County, had visited the apartment Rick shared with a couple of friends and had a heart to heart talk with the young man. The deputy's unofficial conclusion, eventually entered into the official record when it became an active missing person's case, cleared the Wagner boy of any involvement.

Two days after Alex disappeared, her car was found abandoned in a strip mall parking lot along the eastern edge of the city, and the OKCPD became actively involved in the case.

While organized search parties combed as much square mileage as possible, Hank Wilson and Naomi Johnson dug into Alex's phone records and discovered that Wagner had indeed been contacting the girl almost nonstop for the prior three weeks. Their suspicions were aroused even further upon discovering that Wagner had been one of the first to volunteer with the search parties, and had in fact been logging in nearly fifteen hours a day since the girl's disappearance.

Former boyfriend, plus constant calling and texting, plus volunteering to search added up to an almost clichéd profile of a prime suspect and, the deputy's opinion notwithstanding, in no time Wilson and Johnson had the young man in an interrogation room downtown.

The Wagner kid cracked fairly easily. Although the memo didn't specifically say so, Helen figured that Wilson, with his gruff, overbearing manner, had done most of the questioning. The "good cop/ bad cop" routine wasn't nearly as common as TV shows and movies depicted, but she could easily visualize Naomi Johnson as the calm, soothing voice of reason contrasting with Wilson's more hard-boiled approach.

However, even though it took less than an hour for the kid to become a blubbering mess (as far as Helen's interpretation of the Wilson's notes went), he kept insisting that he knew nothing of Alex's disappearance. Plus, he'd attended a picnic with his track team the entire day Alex vanished, and despite thorough searches of both his car and home (achieved after shopping through three different judges before they found one to sign the search warrants), no physical evidence, beyond some actual old-fashioned, hand-written love letters Alex had sent Rick over the prior two years, linked him to the dead girl.

Over the next few days, a number of other suspects had come to the fore, only to be ruled out for one reason or another. As these things often do, public interest began to wane; the search parties got shorter and shorter and were composed of fewer and fewer people; and the daily press briefings quickly dropped off altogether.

Helen refilled the coffeepot three times, and the sky outside the window got darker and darker, as she repeatedly read Wilson's notes, searching for anything that would tie the Jamison girl to either Willy Gray or Leo Benson. Other than the proximity of where her body was eventually found to Gray's workplace, Helen had nothing.

The other thing that came through more than once while reading was Wilson's frustration, for lack of a better word, at his partner. If Helen could believe the admittedly one-sided report, Johnson had faded into the background, leaving her older partner to do most of the heavy lifting, at least as far as the official record went.

Sighing, she put the folders down, then grabbed her coffee cup, stood up and headed over to the window. It was now past ten, and the view out the window held a myriad of lights, some sparkling and some steady. It was a fairly clear night, few clouds drifting by in the outdoor sky. At some point while reading, she had turned off all the lights except for the desk lamp she'd been using, which now cast a half reflection of her standing and looking out the window.

Helen's reflection lifted up the cup, took a drink, and lowered it again. Then the reflection stared back at actual Helen, and actual Helen was glad for the diffused, murky nature of the lighting. Softening the edges and muting the colors, her image looked more like her old self, not the wan, drawn-down woman she'd become. She thought back to the dinner with Beacham, trying and failing to get his approval, or at least understanding, of her desire to take on this job. At the time, he must have noticed how worn down she looked, but he hadn't said a word about it.

Naomi Johnson had impressed her as being such a go-getter, a real dynamo, yet the year before she'd taken as low of a profile as possible, at least in paperwork terms, on what could easily rank as one of the major cases of her career.

In retrospect, and taking the cynical view, it seemed a fairly smart way to go. If the Jamison girl remained missing with no resolution to the case, Johnson still came off as a detective on the rise, while her partner slouched around the squad room counting the days until retirement.

And Wilson had probably been correct as to why Johnson had shown such thinly-veiled antagonism toward her. Going back to Wilson's comments, there was no doubt that both the detectives knew Helen's back story. Consequently, Johnson could see a grim reminder of what could be, how Johnson herself could end up if she ever crossed her superiors. As such, she probably picked battles carefully, all while putting forth the public impression of a dynamo detective.

Then, eight days in, Alex Jamison's body was discovered in the field across the street from Buck's bar. She'd been strangled, and the initial determination on scene was that some sort of sexual assault had been attempted, whether successful or not was unknown. The method of strangulation was never conclusively pinned down, though the medical examiner's strong inclination was that some sort of ligature, as opposed to bare hands, had been used. The focus thus moved from a missing person case to a murder, and while the OKCPD had primary jurisdiction because the body was found barely within the city limits, the Pottawotamie sheriff's department took part in the investigation.

All that manpower, and yet nearly a year later no viable suspects and no solid leads. Reading through the folders one more time, Helen could practically feel Wilson's frustration mounting. The impression after reading, although nothing had been spelled out directly, was that the case was verging on going into the cold file.

On the one hand, a year or so was not necessarily enough time to consider a case unsolved, but as far as Helen could tell there had been absolutely nothing in the way of tangible leads, as if Alex Jamison had somehow been abducted into another dimension, then days later her body simply dropped into that field from overhead.

Naturally, the folks at The Last Draw were questioned, but neither Buck, his workers (turns out he had a total of three employees, including the overtalkative Mona), nor any of his customers who had shown up on any of those nights had seen or knew of anything.

At first cringing at the idea of how much manpower and time it must have taken to track down every customer who'd set foot in the bar over a week's time, on second thought, she figured that the Draw probably had the same core clientele most nights, so it probably didn't take all that much effort.

On her last reading of the folders, Helen noticed that Wilson commented on interviewing the night watchmen at Lobard Chemical, the plant facility across the road from Buck's bar.

Helen paused, tapping a fingernail. It took multiple readings for the name of the plant to sink in. Something about the name tantalized her. She wasn't sure what, but figured there was one way to find out.

CHAPTER 37

Saturday, Sept. 28th

HELEN'S CELL BUZZED her awake at five the next morning, and a second or so later the phone in the room rang as well. A sense of caution, combined with the fact that she'd stayed up till past midnight thinking over the Jamison case, had led to leaving a wake-up call with the front desk to complement her own alarm.

Before climbing into the shower, she paused to inspect the belly wound in the mirror. Slowly peeling off the bandage, the cut seemed almost healed. It had turned a little inflamed since her last look. Not really red so much as a little pink around the edges. Considering she'd been spending so much time in hotels of late, she'd considered bringing a swimsuit along but was unsure of how the chlorine in a pool would affect the wound.

After showering, and taking time to carefully soap and rinse the cut, along with a bit of salve and a new bandage, she dressed in faded jeans, plain white sneakers and a tee-shirt picked up at an Eagles concert years before.

Breakfast would have been nice, but it was early enough that that could hold off for a while.

Preparing to leave the room, Helen grabbed up a small notepad with some notes made after reading the night before and, halfway out the door, paused, checked the time again, then turned back and retrieved the two file folders Wilson had left with her. Having no experience with downtown OKC traffic, she didn't want to risk arriving at the station too late for the cop to return the files before either Johnson or his lieutenant arrived.

Even with that slight delay, she was on the road before six, and managed to get to the intended destination just as the sun was rising. Helen eventually turned on a now-familiar dirt road and, following its winding path, ended up parking her car at the outer edge of The Last Draw's parking lot. She climbed out and began walking towards the center of the field in which Alex Jamison's body had been found nearly a year before.

For the most part, she'd ignored the field on her two visits to Buck's establishment, and paid only scant attention to the chemical plant across the way. Now, after the interview with Buck and Mona and after going through Wilson's case notes, this ordinary looking patch of scrubland took on a whole new importance.

Helen wasn't really looking for anything in particular. Obviously, any evidence missed by the investigation teams would have long been done away with by the weather. Instead, she was interested more in a feeling of the place. Because of the timing, common sense dictated that what had transpired in this grassy patch had forced Willy Gray to quit his job without notice and take off.

Why he'd decided to go to Denver, when he'd never lived there before and, as far as the records showed, knew no one remained a question, and somewhere down the line she'd have to find an answer to that. Her main concern of the moment, though, was much more relevant.

Had Gray killed Alex Jamison? On the surface that would be the most obvious conclusion, but the surface look could sometimes mislead. The level of minor violence in Gray's past had never even come close to the level of casual murder, at least not before Denver. The idea that he would show up in a strange place, get a job and begin to settle down, only to jeopardize all that for a random killing, didn't really seem to jibe.

Next scenario. Instead of committing the murder himself, did Gray know Alex's killer or killers? Did he have some connection with them that led him to bolt the area? His leaving after the girl went missing, when she was probably already ensconced in the field, seemed a pretty clear indication of some level of guilty knowledge, but of what exactly if not her murder?

Leo Benson, of course, was completely off the hook for this one. At the time of Alex's killing, he was already sitting on death row in Nebraska and facing a bleak future.

So who the hell killed Alex Jamison? And how did it all tie in with Willy Gray?

A stream of cars began exiting the facility, no doubt the graveyard shift getting off, heading home for rest and relaxation. She saw no similar stream of vehicles entering the place, indicating that the first shift workers weren't due to arrive for a while.

The sound of a car motor, coming from the direction in which she'd come, caught her attention. She turned that way as a dull gray, mid-sized Toyota pulled up and parked next to her rental.

No vehicle could have looked more like a plainclothes car, so even before the driver's door opened, she instinctively guessed the identity of the driver.

Detective Hank Wilson climbed out, looked around for a moment, then waved her over.

Helen tromped back across the field, glad she'd worn sneakers this morning, and joined the cop.

"Fancy meeting you here," she greeted him.

Wilson, who looked to be wearing the same clothes as he had the day before, grunted. "Heading into the shop," he said. "Got to wondering if you'd be out this way, so I made a slight detour and here you are."

Helen glanced back at the sun just hanging over the horizon. "That's some pretty early hours you put in there, detective."

Wilson shrugged. "Stopped punching a clock long ago. 'Sides, figured it wouldn't hurt to head in early, make sure all my paperwork's in order. You know?"

"Sounds like a good idea," Helen said. "I may be even be able to help you with some of that paperwork."

"Never one to turn down a favor. What exactly you looking for out here?"

Helen considered it a rhetorical question, but decided she owed the man enough of a favor to humor him. "Nothing, especially, too much time's gone by. But it never hurts to stand on a crime scene."

"You looking to pick up vibes or something?"

Helen grinned. "Not even close, Wilson. You know better than that. But it doesn't hurt to get the lay of the land, see how everything's set up, in case the knowledge comes in handy somewhere down the line."

Leaning further against his car, Wilson nodded. "You really think what happened to the Jamison kid's somehow related to this mysterious case of yours?"

"It's a possibility," she said. "The name came up, so

I figured it had to be checked out. But I'm still not quite sure how."

Wilson shifted his legs and crossed his arms. "How come?"

"You looked into the family, right? After the boyfriend was cleared?"

"Sure."

"But you eventually closed that line of investigation."

The cop shrugged. "Couldn't find any evidence, couldn't break any of their alibis. So we had to go back to the stranger idea, but that was a dead end too."

Helen puzzled it over for a minute. Glancing to the distance, there were a few vehicles, mainly large pickups, showing up at the plant.

"One thing I didn't see in your paperwork. Was there any final determination on molestation?"

Wilson shook his head. "We found her inside of a week, but even them some critters had gotten to her. Plus, the second night out there was a rainstorm. So, no. No final determination."

"And the first field report mentioned her clothing all torn to shreds. Like completely tattered."

"That's right. Could be that molestation got interrupted. But that's a long shot."

"That's one possibility," Helen said, still considering Willy Gray. "Another is that it was a first attempt, and the perpetrator lost his nerve."

"We considered that. Especially in light of the absence of facial injuries. Almost like he was being gentle with her."

Helen thought about that one, considering it a definite possibility. But she was toying with an explanation she thought even more possible, if not probable, but didn't feel comfortable yet sharing it with Wilson.

More cars were pulling into the factory.

"Lobard Chemical," she said, pointing toward the plant.

"Right. It's not much, but it employs a decent number of people."

"They have any other facilities around the area?" Helen asked, the stray thought from earlier finally taking root in her mind. "Or just this one?"

"Far as I know, there's just the one, and it's a good thing it's located where it is," Wilson said, "or the guy who owns that would be out of business in no time."

As he spoke, he pointed toward Buck's establishment. Helen followed his gesture, her face showing her puzzlement.

"Why so?" she asked.

"'Cause he gets most of his business out of the first shift going home and the second shift coming in."

Helen stared at The Last Draw for a moment, her mind racing.

Something was niggling at her mind, begging for attention, but at the moment she couldn't quite pull the thought into focus.

CHAPTER 38

THEY ARRIVED AT the station separately, and about thirty minutes apart. Helen pulled into the same parking garage she'd used the day before and made her way on foot about half a block to the headquarters.

A civilian would probably have been shocked at the number of people coming and going, not to mention a dozen prisoners handcuffed and sitting on a narrow bench along the far wall, so early in the morning.

A different desk sergeant manned the gates than the day before, a guy with the haircut of an ex-Marine, but a quick call up to the squad room cleared the way for her.

Hank Wilson and Naomi Johnson were sitting at Wilson's desk, their eyes glued on the doorway. They both stood as Helen entered and approached them.

"The boss's got a full day packed again," Johnson said, her tone flat and level, "on a Saturday no less, but he said he could give you a few minutes."

"I appreciate it," Helen said. Johnson grunted and turned to lead the way to the lieutenant's office. Behind her back, Wilson caught Helen's eye and rolled his eyes.

Johnson knocked on the door to the lieutenant's office. A muffled murmur came from inside, and Johnson opened the door. The three of them walked in.

"Boss," Johnson said, gesturing to her left, "this is Helen Lipscomb. Lieutenant Royas." She pointed towards the man sitting behind the desk.

Royas stood up, but not very far. He was barely five seven and carried a squat two-hundred and fifty pounds or so. But it looked, at least in dress shirt and tie, all muscle. His square, full face and deep-set, dark eyes led to the impression of coiled, barely-contained power.

"Lipscomb," he said, extending a hand. "I hear you used to be one of the ranks, more or less."

Helen doubted that he'd just "heard" about her. At the very least she was sure that Johnson, leaning with arms crossed against the far wall, had probably given him an earful.

"So I hear you're interested in digging into the Jamison case," Royas said, motioning for Helen to sit in one of the two chairs in front of his desk. Wilson went over and leaned against the filing cabinet, mirroring Johnson's pose.

"Not really digging into," Helen said. "I'm not trying to step on toes or anything, but there may be a link to something Mr. Conroy is working on. I'm just trying to dot a few i's, so to speak."

"According to what Detective Johnson has told me, and what you've just mentioned, it sounds like you're talking about us having some sort of serial on our hands."

Helen took a deep breath. To an extent, she didn't need the lieutenant's cooperation any more. The information Wilson had surreptitiously provided had filled in a lot of blanks, and as of this morning, it may have finally provided the missing link in the chain she needed to follow.

"Yes, sir," she said, adopting the most deferential tone possible. "I'd say there's a high probability that the Jamison girl was not the victim of a one-off perpetrator."

Royas' eyes hooded over even more, and in the

corner of her eye, Johnson stiffened.

"We considered the possibility, of course," the lieutenant said. "My people went back over the last five years, looking for anything close enough to call a pattern. Ended up with nothing."

"Okay," Helen said in a noncommittal tone. She'd gathered as much from what she'd read the night before but didn't want to say anything that would in any way cause the lieutenant to suspect either of his people of sharing trade secrets. "Did you look statewide, or farther out?"

Now both Royas and Naomi Johnson were giving the stare, and Helen felt herself walking on a very fine ledge.

"Statewide," Johnson said. "Why?"

"You suggesting some kind of roaming nut?" Royas interjected. "There wasn't much in the way of specific MO to latch onto. You have any idea how many stranglings are committed in this country every year?"

"No," Helen said. "Did you find it unusual that the sexual element of the crime was, ambiguous, to say the least?"

"Yes," Johnson said, "but it still didn't give us enough to match with anything."

Helen began to nod in agreement, but before she could complete the motion Wilson spoke up.

"Waitaminnit, boss. She may have something there. Last I heard, the FBI estimates somewhere in the dozens of serials on the loose at any given time."

"And your business involves something along those lines?" Royas asked Helen.

"Yes, sir. I'm not saying for sure, but if the Jamison girl was the victim of a serial killer, maybe one not native to the area, it could be a factor in my investigation."

"Investigation?" Royas' tone deepened, and his entire face tightened. "Let's get something straight right now, Miss Lipscomb. You're not an investigator. We checked, then double-checked. You aren't licensed in any state that we could find, and you for damned sure don't carry a badge any more, and from what I hear probably never will again. Yet you come in here, expecting us to do what? Hand over all our material to you, while you dance around, and expect us to just bow our heads and say thank you?"

Helen's pulse quickened, but she worked to keep her tone as deferential as possible. "No, Lieutenant. That's not what I expect. I know you have the boundaries to observe. I'm just thinking that maybe we could cooperate a little on this."

"Cooperate, huh? Well I've got news for you. Just to show I'm not blowing you off, I've already spoken to the district attorney about this. She and I both agree that it would be detrimental to any possible future prosecution to allow a civilian into this."

Helen couldn't keep from gaping. "Possible prosecution? Way I hear it, your case is going cold on you even as we speak."

Royas frowned even more than before, something Helen wouldn't have thought possible.

"Okay, Miss Lipscomb, here's how it is. I can't do like the sheriff in an old western and tell you to be out of town by sunset, but off the record, I'd suggest you make your stay in our city short and relaxing. In other words, don't try to dig into our case file. Are we clear?"

Wilson and Johnson were both leaning against their respective perches, Wilson expressionless and Johnson with a slight grin on her face. Helen had the feeling the woman detective was struggling to keep a straight face, but couldn't quite manage to do so.

"Are we clear, Miss Lipscomb?" Royas repeated.

Helen glanced one more time at the two detectives before turning back to their boss.

"Crystal, lieutenant," she said before turning and leaving the office.

CHAPTER 39

THE OLD WEST was long gone, and in a day of civil liberties, social protests and cameras in every cell phone, it wasn't exactly like the law could order her out of town. Helen made her way back to the Doubletree, had a late breakfast delivered by room service, and spent an hour or so typing up a report for Conroy. After e-mailing the document to the lawyer's office, she glanced at the clock and pondered how to fill the next four or five hours. She'd already checked on the Lobard Chemical website and, as near as she could determine, they ran their usual work shifts on Saturdays as well.

She figured that Buck's bar would really begin to stir somewhere around four in the afternoon, to be ready for workers from the first shift stopping in for a few brewskies before heading home.

She was also guessing on when the first shift ended, and while it would have been easy to call and get the information, Helen wanted as few people as possible to know about the direction the search was taking. She had no reason to disbelieve anything Buck or Mona had said, but also wanted the chance to talk to regular customers, who had perhaps seen a different side of Willy, to see if anything more could be shaken loose.

She felt a little guilty not confiding in Wilson. During the meeting that morning, she'd deliberately strayed away from asking anything to do with the bar.

Assuming the cops had learned about Buck's new employee who'd gone missing right before the girl's body was found, if they'd pursued anything along that line, it hadn't shown up in the report Wilson had given her.

Willy Gray, of course, was becoming a bit of a name at the moment, but as far as she could tell, the OKC cops hadn't put two and two together on that end, and while respecting Wilson and appreciating him sticking his neck out for her, Helen still felt the need to play things close to the vest.

That line, again. That goddamned uncrossable line that seemed, in her mind, to be shimmering all over the place lately.

On top of that, her conflicting feelings in the matter. Sometime after leaving the meeting with Royas, Helen had suddenly realized a basic line of questioning that she'd neglected to pursue, and wanted to make up for that deficit.

Then, as if she needed any more added to her list, pulling out of the hotel parking lot to head back to The Last Draw, she noticed a yellow VW Beetle whip into traffic a few car lengths behind her. For the next two or three miles, the Beetle seemed to play hide and seek with her, dropping out of sight for a while, then popping into view for a block or two before vanishing again, much as it had the day before.

At first, Helen wondered if she were not becoming a bit paranoid until the VW disappeared for several blocks, only to show up again a couple of blocks ahead of her. At that point, two things became clear. One, she most definitely was being tailed and two, whoever was in the yellow car was about as professional as they could get.

About halfway across town and cutting onto the Interstate, she tracked the tail as being absent for several minutes, and it never showed up again.

Pulling into the bar's dirt parking lot, she hadn't seen a trace of the tail car for about half of the trip. She turned off the engine and sat there, wondering just what it all meant.

Her thoughts were beginning to stray all over the place when her phone beeped. Without taking her eyes off the front of the bar, she pulled it out from the front pocket.

"Yeah?"

"Helen. Where you at? You anywhere close by?"

The caller didn't have to identify himself. She easily recognized Jamie Trixon, a bail bondsman back home. Trixon had been one of her most constant "employers" over the last few years. He'd owned his bail/bond business for over twenty years now, and that, plus the fact he was located in a city with one of the highest crime rates in the country, kept his business booming.

As a result, Trixon had retainers with half a dozen or so legitimate private eyes, but when news had gotten out about Helen's dismissal from the department, he was one of the first people to look her up and offer some day work. Like several others, he'd urged her more than once to get an official license so he could extend a permanent retainer. Even when she refused to do so, he'd still managed to offer several small jobs.

"No, Trix, I'm not exactly local," she said. "I'm actually quite a ways away."

"Like where? Jeff City? Kirksville?"

"Try out of state."

"Damn. So I guess you can't be available tomorrow morning to track someone down for me?"

"'Fraid not. Can't one of your regulars do it?"

Trixon chuckled in her ear. "Hell, girl. They're all backed up with two or three cases each. Business has been brisk lately. Summertime and all that, you know."

Helen did indeed know. The scorching summer months were the worst in terms of violent crime. Soaring temperatures, cloying humidity, and too much time outside all contributed to the problem.

"So how long before you're back this way?" Trixon asked.

Helen paused, mentally running the scenarios. As she did so, the parking lot started to fill up more and several groups of people entered the bar in clumps. If it wasn't peak hour now, it soon would be.

"Helen?" Trixon prodded.

"Sorry, Trix. I'm kind of in the middle of something and my mind wandered. Tell the truth, I'm not sure I'm coming back."

Only upon saying the words did Helen finally admit the truth to herself. A truth she'd been dancing around since the beginning of this case but hadn't wanted to face before.

"No kidding?" Trixon said. "How come?"

An F-150 rolled into the parking lot, casting its headlights, unnecessary this early in the evening, into her car and causing a partial reflection in the rearview mirror. Helen sighed and shook her head at the reflection.

"It's a bit too much to go into right now, Trix, and I'm not saying it's a sure thing. But circumstances are changing a bit."

"Wait a minute," Trixon said. "You saying not coming back to this line of work or not coming back home? You didn't get hurt or something, did you?"

Without thinking, one hand reached across her stomach, tracing the new bandage from the morning.

"No, Trix. I didn't get hurt. There's just been some stuff going on."

A cluster of eight or nine men piled out of the F-150 along with another pickup that had pulled alongside it and headed into Buck's place. There were surely enough people in there to give a chance at picking up some information.

"Got to go, Trix. I'll talk to you down the line."

She hung up, but instead of exiting the car, sat mulling over the conversation she'd just had.

It wasn't entirely a money issue. True, if Benson and Conroy, one or the other, kept to their word, she'd have more than enough to last for a few years without working, but what about after that? And she had to consider her age as well. Pushing forty, if she were going to make some sort of major life change, now was the time to do so.

In the end, she shook her head, unable to make sense of it all, and settled back waiting for the bar to fill.

CHAPTER 40

Saturday, Sept. 28th

BY EIGHT THIRTY, Helen officially classified
The Last Draw as "hopping." She got out of the car,
checked to make sure her gun was readily accessible in
her purse, and headed into the establishment. She didn't
really foresee having to use the weapon, but with the
investigation heating up who knew what could happen.

Her first impression upon entering wasn't much
different than the other day, when Buck and Mona had
been the only two in the place, only that initial
impression was heightened even more by the crowd.

An even mix of males and females, most of them
late thirties to mid-forties, with an occasional sprinkling
of older folks. While technically out in the country in
Oklahoma, Helen saw only a few cowboy hats. Although
most of the people wore denim, practically every sort of
casual blouse or shirt imaginable was represented in that
crowd.

She did a quick look around, but didn't catch sight
of either Buck or Mona. On the one hand, she'd hoped
they'd be around to help break the ice with their regulars;
on the other, she wasn't sure if they'd see her
reappearance as verging on bothersome.

She settled in at the bar and waited until the
bartender, a young black man who looked something like

a track runner, came over.

"What would you like?" he asked, giving a knowing look that he spotted her as a non-local.

Another moment of quick decision. Since leaving the force, moderation was the name of the game, fearing that if she drank too far over the line, she'd never stop. But asking for water or soda water, she'd be sure to stand out even more than she already did, which would screw up any hope of getting people to open up.

The bartender caught the hesitation and must have read her mind. "How about a Coke?" he asked, offering the most genuine smile Helen had seen in some time.

"That'd be great, thanks."

As he grabbed a glass and began filling it, she took another look around. Still no Buck or Mona.

When the young man placed the drink in front of her, she asked about them.

"Buck'll be in later. Saturdays he closes the place."

"What about Mona?"

"She's out back, should be in shortly. Can I tell her who's asking for her?"

"That's okay. I can wait." She put some money down on the counter, picked up her drink, and began walking around.

After about twenty minutes, during which she'd received one complete brush off, three requests to let someone buy her a real drink, and four questions as to how long she was in town for, Helen went back to the bar to get her Coke refreshed.

At least no one bothered to ask if she was a cop or not.

Handing the glass to the bartender, she asked his name.

"It's Sam," he said as he placed her drink down. "I sure hope I'm not the one you've been asking about."

Helen grinned. "Is it that obvious?"

The young man looked around and did a kind of sweeping motion with his hands. "I wasn't listening in or anything, but it's kind of a small place."

Small or not, by now the buzz of conversation, rattling of glasses and clacking of balls at the two pool tables in the back were competing with each other to produce the most discordant noise. That Sam had managed to track anything in all of that was either a testament to his hearing or Helen's lack of conditioning when it came to country night life.

"No," Helen told him. "I wasn't asking about you."

"Okay."

"But if you don't mind, how long have you worked here?"

"A couple of years."

"Really? I'd think this place wouldn't be one for long-term employment. They can't be paying all that well."

The kid shrugged, but before he could answer, a couple down at the other end of the bar yelled out for two beers. He hurried off to take care of them, and, in the process of answering a few more calls, it was several minutes before he returned.

"It's not so bad," he said. "Buck treats people real nice, and I'm studying over at Platt Central. Going to graduate this December. Why are you asking?"

"I was just wondering if you remembered a guy who used to work here. Willy Gray. He was here about—"

"Uh, yeah," Sam said, the pleasantness gone from his tone.

"Yeah?"

"Yeah. Didn't get to know him too well, though. I only work weekends, and he usually had those off."

"He lived upstairs, though, right?"

Sam nodded. "But I still didn't see him all that much."

"A loner?" she prodded. "Hard to get to know?"

Down the bar, a woman in her forties, who even from the distance and in the murky lighting wore way too much spray in her dyed blonde hair, waved in Sam's direction. He waved back, took a step to go to her, then turned back to Helen.

"Too bad Lyndie isn't here anymore," he said. "She could tell you a lot about Willy."

"Lyndie?" Helen queried, but before Sam could answer the front door opened and Buck walked in. His eyes lit right on Helen, and a look of puzzled concern crossed his face.

Sam, hurrying off to serve the blonde woman, didn't notice him.

Buck came over to Helen's side.

"You back, Miss Lipscomb? I wouldn't think my place here would be quite your style."

"Still doing my job, looking for information on Willy. Thought maybe some of your regulars could help."

Buck looked around his establishment. The place by now had become practically shoulder-to-shoulder, and a vaporous blue cloud hung overhead.

"Any luck?" he asked.

Helen smiled. "Not in terms of my job, but I got more than one interesting proposition. By the way, you far enough out here that you don't have to worry about the cops hassling your customers over smoking?"

Now it was Buck's turn to grin. "Actually, we got off lucky. Some do-gooders tried to ram through a law last year, but it didn't take. You can still smoke in bars with no problem."

Helen nodded. She really didn't give a damn about the state's business laws. Instead, she wanted Buck to feel at ease before she hit him with the question she really had.

"As long as I'm here," she said. "What can you tell me about Lyndie?"

CHAPTER 41

"SO TELL ME about Lyndie," Helen said a couple of minutes later.

"Lyndie?"

Just as Buck had arrived, Mona had come in from whatever she was doing out back. Catching sight of Helen, she kind of deflated, as if knowing the night was going downhill from there. Buck didn't look all that happy to see her again either.

Even so, they seemed to adapt the pragmatic attitude of "might as well get it over with." While Helen assumed they didn't know ahead of time what she was going to ask, once they'd sat down in a back booth and she'd sprung the name on them, they didn't seem all that surprised.

"Yes, Lyndie," Helen repeated.

"Girl who used to work for us," Buck said. "So what?"

Helen sighed. "Buck, I'm not here to make trouble for anyone who doesn't deserve it. I was nosing around some more about Willy, and the name Lyndie came up. What can you tell me?"

Buck looked suspicious. "Sam tell you about her?" he asked, jerking his thumb toward the front of the bar.

"Sam your bartender?" Helen asked. On the one hand, no reason to get the young man in any kind of trouble, and playing innocent would be the best way to do that, especially as Buck hadn't actually seen Sam talking to her. Still, once she left, the kid would probably tell them, but that was his problem. As far as that went, once she left she'd never be in this bar again.

"Yeah, Sam the bartender. Were you talking to him before I came in?"

"Only long enough to order a couple of Cokes," Helen said. "And I spent almost half an hour floating around the room. Heard Lyndie's name from three or four people."

Buck and Mona looked at each other, their shoulders slumping in unison.

"Like Buck said," Mona put in, "she was a waitress for us, mainly worked weekends."

"Okay."

"Worked here a couple of years, all told," Mona continued. "About a week or two after Willy showed up, we noticed they were hanging around each other a lot."

"Were they dating?" Helen asked.

"Not so's you could tell," Buck said.

Mona let out a kind of hmmpph.

"You really must be getting old, Buck, if you couldn't tell about those two."

"Now look—" her boss began, but Mona cut him off.

"People that young think they're being all sly and under the table," she said to Helen, "but anyone over thirty could tell exactly what they were up to. Almost anyone, that is," she said, sending a withering eye in her boss's direction.

Buck looked down at the table. "So okay," he said without looking up, "I didn't want her to get in any trouble."

"What trouble?" Helen asked.

Now Buck did look up to face her again. "Come on, miss. It's pretty obvious that you're after Willy for something, and it's pretty obvious to me, and probably Mona here, what that something is."

Helen's breath quickened. "Oh, yeah?"

"Yeah," Buck muttered, and he didn't look nearly as friendly as he had the day before. Helen worked to keep her face as neutral as possible. "What would that be?"

"Do me a favor, lady. Don't try to treat me like an idiot, okay? It's that girl who was found in the field across the way, right? You're trying to connect Willy with that. Now, you want to go bothering his girlfriend too? Don't think so."

Mona cast her eyes down to the table. Helen took a deep breath, giving herself a few seconds to work out an approach.

In the end, she settled on the only plausible way to go: the truth.

"Listen to me, please. Before I walked in here the other day, I'd never heard of the dead girl, Alex Jamison. But I will tell you this. You actually are half right."

"Which means you think Willy did something bad, right?"

Now came the moment of brutal honesty. As far as Helen could tell, the two of them had only had a working relationship with Willy Gray, despite the fact he'd been living above the business. Helen couldn't see inside their heads to tell what they really thought of the man, and there was a good chance a wound was about to tear into them.

But she'd decided to go with the truth, and the truth it had to be.

"A while back, Willy was arrested in Colorado."

"Colorado?" Buck queried.

Helen nodded. "Denver."

"Arrested for what?" Mona asked, though the concern on her face showed she'd already determined the news would be bad.

Still not wanting to hurt these people, Helen hesitated, but only for a second. "Murder. He's admitted to killing a fifteen-year old girl."

Mona reached over and grasped Buck's arm, fingers digging into his flesh. "There's more, isn't there," she asked.

Helen paused again. The various other killings Gray was copping to were public knowledge, but she herself didn't believe that he'd committed them. In another time, she would have downplayed the other killings, but either one of these two could, if they so desired, go online and in no time at all get all the facts.

Sighing, and somewhat hating herself, she took them through the whole story, at least the Gray side of things.

When she was done, Buck was breathing a little heavier than usual and Mona's eyes were glistening.

"Her last name was Black," Buck said, his voice a little hoarse. "Lyndie Black. She was really upset when Willy disappeared, without even so much as a goodbye, and about a month or so later she up and quit on us. Said she'd found a better job, and she was going to move closer to the university and go to nursing school."

"Do you still have the last address you had for her?" Helen asked.

"I think so. Let me go see if—" As he started to get up, Mona reached out to his arm again.

"Let me, Buck," she said. "You never could understand you're filing system."

She scuttled out of the booth and headed toward the back of the bar, her shoulders tight and breathing ragged.

Helen sat there, looking at Buck's distraught face, and wondered what people with ordinary lives were doing on this night.

She was thinking the same thing a few minutes later as she left the bar, walked out into the parking lot and saw a yellow VW sitting parked next to her rental.

With Detective Hank Wilson leaning against the fenderwell.

CHAPTER 42

"COME HERE, OFTEN?" Helen asked as she walked up to the cop.

Wilson grinned and gestured towards the bar. "Find out anything interesting in there?"

"You honestly tail people in that garish of a car?"

"Of course," Wilson said. "This little baby and I have caught more perps than you could imagine." He slapped his hand on the fenderwell. "It's so ridiculous looking that no one can imagine someone's actually using it to follow them."

Helen nodded and looked back at the building behind them. "I didn't really get all that much, if you want to know," she said, at the same time wondering why she was hedging with the OKC cop.

"Didn't think so. You saw it in the folders I gave you. When we found the Jamison kid out here, we naturally questioned everyone who worked or lived anywhere within a couple of miles. More interviews than you can imagine."

"Except there was one person you couldn't find to interview," Helen said.

Wilson thought for a moment, then nodded his head. "That's true. There was a missing worker."

"Guy who'd quit a few days before you found her body," Helen said. "He probably shot to the top of your suspect list."

"Seems kind of obvious, right?"

"He would have mine," Helen said.

"Let's just say that, even though it's been a while, we'd still like to talk to him."

As Wilson spoke, Helen glanced off to the chemical plant on the other side of the field. A long trail of vehicles, mainly pickups, were leaving it now. Whether there'd be a graveyard shift or not, she didn't know. Regardless, the place was lit up like daytime with hot yellow lights showing everywhere. As she looked at the Lobard Chemicals sign atop the plant, something niggled in her brain.

"I said we'd still like to talk to that kid," Wilson repeated. "Have any idea where we could find him?"

Holding up a hand to Wilson, Helen pulled out her cell phone and made a quick call to Conroy's office. Anyone else would think it a long shot, but if she'd learned nothing else the last few weeks it was that the hotshot lawyer always had someone in his office.

Even late on a Saturday night.

Made Helen glad she'd never considered law school.

"What?" Wilson asked, frowning.

She turned half away and held a short, whispered conversation. Then she turned back to the cop, the phone still at her ear.

"I may have found something," she said. "Give me a minute to check it out."

She turned away again and concentrated on the phone, talking into it at a low volume, though not the whisper of a moment before.

"Thanks," she said, after listening for a few seconds. Putting the phone back in her jacket pocket, she faced

Wilson again.

"I found it," she said.

"Found what?"

"What I've been looking for."

CHAPTER 43

WILSON STOOD THERE, staring for a few seconds before saying, "You want to clue me in?"

Helen hesitated.

"Uh huh. That's what I thought. You realize I'm sticking my neck out a couple of dozen miles on this, right? How long you think it's going to be before either Royas or Naomi come along to chop it off?"

"Would Johnson do that?"

"Come on, Lipscomb. You gotta remember how department politics goes. Hell, if anyone knows, you do. I told you, Naomi's headed to the top. You think she's going to let a little thing like her partner's pension and good name get in the way of that?"

Although the words were said in a light tone, Helen could detect the pain behind them. Wilson was right. She knew what it felt like to be hung out to dry.

"I need some information," she finally said.

"Uh uh. Not until I get something in return that—"

"I'll give you something, alright." Her mind felt like it was whipping into overdrive. Not alone because of the piece of information she'd pried out of Conroy's people a few minutes before. More than that, a certain knowledge was beginning to pound in her gut. She had a strong feeling she was close to the answers she'd searched for across three states.

"I'll give you something," she repeated, "but I need

one favor first."

"No way. No more favors. I'm already so far out on a limb with this. I don't even know why I gave you that file. You have any idea what will happen if it comes out that I did?"

The bar door opened up, and four or five good old boys came staggering out. With the opened door, a rush of music and loud talk exited as well. Stepping down off the front porch, the men wavered a bit before four of them headed to different vehicles. The fifth one stood there a moment, then nodding his head affirmatively, headed out of the parking lot and began walking down the dirt road.

Helen felt sympathy for the old cop, for sure. But she had to shake him along a different line. "You gave me the file because it's been almost a year, and you're afraid you'll never track down Alex's killer. That you'll never close it up. But I'm telling you, you can. I'll be able to give you what you need, but you have to trust me. One more piece of info, then I'll dump everything I have in your lap and be out of town within twenty-four hours."

"And what you give me will bust the case?" Wilson still looked doubtful.

Helen considered a slight white lie, but didn't have the heart to do it. Plus, the cop was wavering on her as it was.

"Not immediately, but it will give you the direction to go in. I can tell you this. It's not just a local case."

"You mean some other state?" Wilson asked.

"I mean states. Plural."

Wilson half turned from her, looking across the expanse of unkempt field to the chemical plant, all the various buildings, extensions, pipes and extractors lit up like a galaxy.

"It have something to do with that outfit over there?" he asked.

"Yes, but to put it all together, I need that favor. I could do what I need, and fairly easily. But you can do it a lot quicker."

Wilson sighed, reached into his pocket and pulled out a pocket-sized notebook and pen. "I must be getting senile," he said, "and you're really pushing it, lady. I hope you really got something for me."

Helen smiled. "I need a track on a young woman named Lyndie Black."

"Lynda?" Wilson said as he began writing.

"No. Lyndie. Early twenties, probably just around twenty-one or so. Around a year ago she was heading to nursing school. Did you question her before?"

The cop shrugged. "Probably. Doesn't sound familiar right off, but we talked to so many people around here it's hard to remember."

"If she had anything noteworthy to say, you'd have remembered it."

Wilson shook his head. "You're right. You know, you could have tracked this down on your own."

"Yeah, but you can do it quicker, as I said."

He snapped the notebook shut and put it back in his pocket. "Go back to your hotel and wait to hear from me."

"How long?"

"If we're lucky, probably tomorrow."

"On a weekend?"

Wilson grinned. "The people on staff who do this kind of thing for us don't know what a weekend is. Wait to hear from me. Then it's your turn."

"Fair enough."

Wilson got in his VW, started it up and pulled out, crunching gravel as he went. Helen stood there a few minutes gazing at the Lobard plant, more sure than ever that she'd found the place where Willy Gray and Leo Benson's lives had overlapped.

However, she was just as strongly convinced that she was still missing something, some middle link that so far remained out of reach.

Sighing, she turned to get into her rental car, resolving to do as Wilson had asked and wait for him to get back to her. Whether the chain of cause and effect that surrounded her was short or long, there was no doubt that Lyndie Black formed the next, and hopefully next-to-last, link in that chain.

CHAPTER 44

Sunday, Sept. 29th

WILSON CAME THROUGH by noon the next day. Helen had been stretched out in the room's recliner, idly flipping through cable channels for a couple of hours or so, when the cell phone rang. She hit mute right away and picked it up.

"Hello."

"I've got it," Wilson's voice said, "but I'm half inclined not to give it unless I go out there with you."

"What logical reason would you have for doing so?"

"What do you mean? I'd be a cop following up a lead instead of letting a civilian do so."

"A lead? A former bartender and nursing student whose closest proximity to your case is that they worked across the road from where the body was dumped?"

"It's worth checking out, and I'm not doing anything else today."

"Yes, but you guys have already questioned her. What would be the justification for coming at her again?"

There was a pause before Wilson answered. "New evidence?"

"Wilson," Helen said, "gimme the damned address so I can help you crack your case."

****

It was a modest little apartment complex about a mile out from Oklahoma City University. About twenty buildings, give or take, with what looked like ten units per building, each with its own front door opening onto the grounds. According to Wilson's info, Lyndie Black had indeed left The Last Draw to go to nursing school, and at least as of last semester was still there. Her last known address, a much more reliable detail in these days of cell phones, internet bill payment and social media, was in building ten of this complex.

And if still in school, which Helen assumed would have started about a month ago, and if she were anywhere near a decent nursing student, she'd no doubt be spending Sunday afternoon studying.

An open parking slot right in front of building ten gave Helen easy access. Within a few minutes, she stood outside of Lyndie's apartment—according to Wilson, the young woman lived alone—and knocked on the door. It looked from the outside to be a one-bedroom with a small patio out in front. The drapes were drawn over the living room windows.

After three knocks, there was no answer.

Helen mentally kicked herself for not having Wilson track down the make of car the girl drove, if in fact she had one, because she couldn't tell by a casual glance whether the girl's vehicle was present. She was trying to decide whether to stake the place out or begin canvassing neighbors when a woman's voice sounded out behind her.

"Can I help you?"

Helen turned to see an attractive young woman, early twenties at the most, with black hair and eyes, standing a few feet away. She wore a pair of gray running shorts and a maroon tank top with the slogan "Nurses Rock" splashed across the front.

Helen also noticed a small can of Mace attached to the young woman's wrist by a coiled plastic chain.

"I'm looking for Lyndie Black. Do you know her?"

"Sure." She turned slightly to her left and looked at a black Fusion a few yards away. "Isn't she answering?"

Helen's gut started to tighten. "Is that her car?"

The woman took a step back. "Who are you? Do you know Lyndie or something?"

Helen kept calm, trying to come up with something to ease the woman's obvious concern. If she went out on a limb and identified herself as a cop, the girl would possibly ask to see a badge. That little can of Mace spoke to the fact that this one wasn't easily taken in.

"I'm her aunt," Helen said. "From El Paso. I just got into town and Lyndie was supposed to pick me up at the airport."

Even as she strung out the lie, Helen grimaced, suddenly hoping the other woman wasn't too sharp. Someone really intelligent would ask why the taxi, or Uber driver, or whatever she used to get here, didn't wait. Or may wonder where Helen's luggage was if she'd arrived from out of state.

"Sometimes she's a hard sleeper," the girl finally said. "We're both in the nursing program at school, and believe me, there's more all-nighters pulled than you care to think about."

"I knocked three times. If her car's here, could she be off with someone else, maybe her boyfriend?"

"Could be. But it's pretty late in the day for her to not be back. A few weeks back, I'd say she was probably out on a lake somewhere, but now that school's started…" The girl ran down, and Helen turned back to that door, her guts now screaming at her.

"Hang on just a second," Helen said as she went about the easiest way imaginable to potentially get some answers.

She grasped the knob and, finding the door unlocked, swung it open.

Then she took one look inside that apartment and turned back to the girl behind her.

"Do me a favor," she said, "call the cops."

CHAPTER 45

HELEN WAS SITTING on a curb across from building ten when Wilson pulled up in his VW.

Three patrol units had already arrived, summoned by the 911 call from Lyndie Black's neighbor and fellow student. They'd cordoned off the apartment, driveway, and sidewalk immediately adjacent, and two of the officers had already begun canvassing the nearby apartments. Another one, a woman in her late twenties, was taking down the statement of Lyndie's neighbor.

It suddenly occurred to Helen that she didn't know the young woman's name.

Helen had given the senior officer in charge her version of what she was doing there and how she'd happened to enter the apartment in question. Then he had asked her to stay because sooner or later the detectives would want to talk to her as well.

As soon as the officer walked away, Helen had called Wilson.

Fifteen minutes later, he pulled into a nearby parking slot. Exiting his vehicle, he stood close to Helen without looking at her, fixing his gaze on building ten.

"You got here awfully quick," Helen said in greeting, making sure not to make eye contact with the cop.

"Why be late to the end of my career?" he said as he continued staring at the apartment.

Helen sighed. "Sorry for the flippant tone. I'm doing my best not to start screaming."

He turned and surveyed the movement going on. "I won't be officially assigned to this. It's my day off. But what the hell happened?"

"What happened is I came out here to interview Lyndie Black and found her dead."

Wilson still hadn't turned to look at Helen. One of the uniforms coming out of the apartment noticed him and began walking his way.

"Dead how?" he asked.

"Looked like strangulation, but I didn't spend a lot of time in there. Just enough to verify mortality, then backed my way out to preserve the scene."

"Goddamn," Wilson said. "Lt. Royas is not going to like this."

The officer, a tall, blond-haired man with a slight pot belly, despite looking no more than twenty-five, came up to them.

"Detective," he greeted Wilson, "is this one yours?"

"Probably not. I was just driving by and saw the commotion. Figured I'd stop for a second."

As he spoke, Wilson had turned away from Helen, not letting on that he knew her.

"So who's the deceased?" he asked.

"A young woman. Name of Lynda Black."

Keeping with his air of ignorance, Wilson didn't correct the younger cop's pronunciation.

"How'd she die?"

"Looks like strangulation, sir. But she was beat up pretty bad as well, so won't know for sure until the docs go over her."

"Any idea how long she's been dead?" Wilson

asked.

The senior officer, a black man with a moderate mustache, ambled over. "Doesn't look like all that long, detective. I did a quick check before calling for the ME, but I doubt she's gone through rigor yet."

Wilson harrumphed and walked away from there. As the two officers went on about their duties, he sidled over to Helen.

"Did we get that girl killed?" he asked her.

Never in her life had Helen wanted to lie to herself as much as now. But she really didn't see how that would do any good in the long run.

"I don't know," she said, "but it sure looks like it."

"But how? You didn't even know she existed until last night, and the last time there was any police contact with her was months ago. So what the hell—"

"All I can think is those guys."

"Huh?"

"When we were talking in Last Draw's parking lot last night. At one point four or five guys wandered out of the bar and headed for home."

"Yeah, so?"

"So they weren't together. They went every which way and didn't even say goodbye to each other. Coming out all at once they looked like they were together, but they actually weren't. It wouldn't surprise me if one of them circled around somehow and listened in on us."

Wilson nudged the pavement with the toe of his sneaker for a minute before speaking up.

"You realize that sounds kind of paranoid, don't you?"

Helen nodded. "Yep, but it's the only thing I can think of that makes sense."

"According to that line of thought, the killer would have, what, had to be in the bar while you were in there? How'd he know you were going to be around?"

Helen grimaced. "I didn't say it was all that clear."

"Maybe not, but I need to call Royas and Johnson and clue them in to this. Then you need to come in and, dammit, get all your cards on the table. You'll be lucky if Royas doesn't have the department escort you out of town. And probably me along with you."

"Not a problem," Helen said. "I need to be getting on anyway."

"Why?"

A tan SUV pulled up, parked about fifty feet away from them, and out of it came two middle-aged men with the definite stamp of plainclothes. The two looked questioningly at Wilson.

"Give me a minute, guys," Wilson called out. "This here is your primary witness."

Now one of the men scowled, but they both continued walking into the apartment.

"Let me go talk to them," Wilson said, "to explain what I'm doing here. Then hang around until they're done with you and come on in. I'll try to get Royas and Johnson into the shop today so we can get this squared away."

Helen nodded as Wilson walked away. She'd cooperate in any way she could, do whatever was necessary, to get out of Oklahoma as quickly as possible.

She needed to get back to Denver. Lyndie Black's killer, whoever he was, had made a serious mistake. Clearly, whoever had attacked Lyndie was the same person she'd been pursuing, even though it had only recently become apparent that she was actually chasing someone.

Assuming that Benson was on the level, that there was no connection or crossed paths between himself and Willy Gray, the only logical inference was that someone else was involved, someone else who operated as that link, that connection.,

And Helen had to find that man. But at some point in the last few hours, that link had really screwed up.

He, no doubt, thought that getting rid of Lyndie would impede Helen's investigation, when in fact it quite possibly would have the opposite effect.

Willy Gray was in jail in Colorado, and Benson was tucked away on death row in Nebraska. Therefore, there had to be a third person involved.

And whoever her shadow suspect might be, he quite possibly had just given her the key to unlock the whole damned puzzle.

CHAPTER 46

Death Row, Redding State Correctional Facility

"WHY?" LEO BENSON asked his lawyer.

"Why what?" Gordon Conroy replied.

"Why's Lipscomb care about my business travel? She's been hired to dig into this Gray character. What could when I did or didn't visit any of my businesses matter to her?"

The two of them were sitting in a private room in the prison. Private at least in terms of audio, or so the warden had assured Conroy on more than one occasion. In terms of video, not so much. A small camera in one of the upper corners gave observers a panoramic view of the room, and each time Conroy visited, both he and his client were strictly informed to stay seated at the small table at all times. Any deviation from that and, Constitution or no, future lawyer/ client meetings would be strictly curtailed.

"What I think is going on," Conroy said, "is that she may have found a place and time where you and Gray intersected, where your paths crossed. She's backtracked Gray to some two-bit bar in Oklahoma City, and she intends to go forward from there, try to uncover both how he knows about your activities and why he's acting as he is."

Benson snorted and looked up to the ceiling. "I'm

starting to think hiring Miss Lipscomb was a mistake."

Conroy shrugged. "It's your call, Leo. The whole thing seems kind of convoluted to me. But I think you might want to string it out a little longer, see what she comes up with. Who knows what she'll shake out that may help you down the line?"

"Or she could come up with something that will hurt me. Your initial profile on her suggested that, the loss of her job and reputation to the contrary, she hasn't exactly become available to the highest bidder."

"Like I said, your call."

Benson drummed his fingers on the table for another minute or so, then gave kind of a half nod.

"When you get right down to it," he said, "I don't exactly have anything to lose. What was the name of the plant again?"

"Lobard Chemicals. It seems a fairly small concern, but you are listed as the majority shareholder."

"Fairly small's pretty much an understatement, Gordon. The place has barely turned a profit the last several years. I bought it about, oh, probably a decade or so ago. It was a partnership concern that had fallen into some sort of disarray. I don't quite remember what kind. And we picked it up for pretty much of a steal. They make mainly fertilizers, plus a few of those non-stick materials for pots and pans and such."

"So it's more or less a footnote in the larger network of your companies?"

"More or less."

"Would you know offhand the last time you visited the plant?"

When Benson didn't answer, Conroy prodded him. "Leo?"

Benson sighed and leaned back in his chair. "We've met in here several times, Gordon. Tell me, do you really think they're not listening in?"

Conroy instinctively glanced around the small room. "All I can say is they'd better not be."

"Well, I guess we're about to find out." He leaned forward, placing his elbows on the table and steepling his fingers under his chin. An odd look had come over Benson's face, a look Conroy didn't think he'd ever seen in his client before. His eyes seemed brighter than normal, and a fine sheen of sweat had appeared on his brow.

"What's Gray's connection with Lobard?"

"It seems," Conroy said slowly, "that he showed up in the area a while back and began working and living above a small, run-down bar adjacent to the plant."

Benson nodded, more to himself than to his lawyer. "Truth be told, Gordon, as far as I remember I never personally visited Lobard."

Conroy's mind sped up. He mentally flipped through about a dozen different scenarios as to how this conversation would continue, at the same time double-checking them for any possible trouble for himself.

"Okay."

"So why's she figure that this somehow is connected to me?"

Conroy took about five minutes and explained the basic situation to his client, making sure to emphasize the similarities in the death of Alex Jamison with Benson's other victims.

After he'd finished recounting the events, Benson nodded, and the sheen across his face increased. "Remind me how it works, counselor. I can share details of past crimes with you and you can't do anything about it, right?"

"I wouldn't quite put it that way, Leo. But essentially, yes. Anything you share with me about past crimes is confidential."

"No need to stress it, Gordon. It's not like I'm going to be able to do any crime in the future, am I right?" The businessman cackled, and Conroy felt himself beginning to sweat as well.

"And those fuckin' guards had better not be listening to us." He nearly whispered those last words before leaning in and peering closer at Conroy.

"Yeah, counselor. I did a girl there in Oke City. She waited on me in a restaurant the first morning I was there."

Conroy frowned. "That doesn't make sense, Leo. This woman," he paused to check a pad of notes he had, "Alex Jamison was killed last year. You were already…"

Benson grinned and leaned back, looking looser, more relaxed, though the sweat still shone on him. It suddenly occurred to the lawyer that the man looked almost—orgasmic.

"Sorry about that, counselor. I wasn't very clear. I did a woman the first morning I was in Oklahoma City, but that was something like fifteen years ago. I meant the first day ever that I traveled there."

Conroy leaned back, as if moving out of Benson's proximity could somehow distance him from the man's crimes.

"You're confessing to another murder?" he asked. "One over a decade old?"

"To you, counselor. But only to you. Hell, I don't even remember the broad's name now. Be nice if I did, but there you have it."

"Do you remember the details?" Conroy asked.

Benson nodded again, a slight smile crossing his face. He seemed to have somewhat calmed down physically, but that strange look still danced in his eyes.

Conroy took a breath, figuring his possible moves. "Is there any information you'd like to share with the authorities down there? Lipscomb made a few contacts and we could easily pass on some—"

Benson slammed his hand flat on the table, like a gun going off.

"We're not sharing anything until we get the other thing taken care of," he snarled. "Tell Lipscomb to do her job, damnit, and figure out how that little bastard Gray knows so much about me."

CHAPTER 47

"I SHOULD PUT you both behind bars," Lt. Royas said.

The three of them, the lieutenant, Wilson, and Helen, were sequestered in his office, with the door shut and blinds drawn. Called in unexpectedly on a Sunday, Royas was wearing khakis and a green golfing shirt, but even so, both authority and anger emanated from the man.

"Boss," Wilson asked, "where's Naomi? She should really be here along with—"

"Detective Johnson," Royas broke in with an audible sneer, "is down at the crime scene, trying to explain why the two of you may have to horn in on someone else's case. In other words, she's acting like a professional. Something you could use a lesson or two in, Hank."

That's when Helen knew the extent of Royas' anger at his subordinate. In her experience, bosses never used a detective's first name in front of civilians unless they were really, really pissed.

"Lieutenant…" Wilson tried again, and Helen had to admire the way he was sticking himself out there. Especially so close to retirement, she wondered if she'd have as much guts. "…Miss Lipscomb is doing us a favor here."

"A favor?" If anything, Royas' volume went up a

notch or two, something Helen would not have thought possible a few seconds ago. "And just how do you see that, detective?"

So okay. Maybe he was starting to mollify, if only a bit.

Helen wondered when to jump in. She was responsible for all of this but was also well aware that saying anything the least bit off would make things go even harder for the two of them. She had no doubt that Conroy could eventually get her out of whatever jam developed, but Wilson had his career and pension to think about.

"Yes, boss, a favor. We've been digging for a year now, looking for the Jamison girl's killer. But if Helen's right, the suspect isn't even in our state. In other words, we've spent the last twelve months chasing a phantom."

Royas now turned his harsh glare on Helen. "So where is he? Who is he?"

"I don't know yet," Helen said, "but I've been chasing him for weeks, and I'm getting fairly close."

"Close? You just said he isn't even in town? What the hell do you mean?"

Calmly, at least on the surface, Helen grabbed the back of a chair and slid it out from in front of the lieutenant's desk. She sat down and smoothed her cotton slacks over her thighs. After a second of huffing and puffing, Royas sat down behind his desk and waved for Wilson to grab a seat as well.

When they were all seated and the temperature had gone down a bit in the room, Helen laid out the story.

"Jesus Christ," Royas said when she finished. "If true, that's one hell of a cluster."

"I'm not completely positive on every single detail,"

Helen said, "but that's the basics of the situation."

"If you're right, the guy we've been looking for has been on death row for damned near three years. That doesn't exactly compute, does it?"

"Not entirely," Helen said.

"Oh, yeah. This other killer, the buddy theory."

"I wouldn't go as far as to call it a buddy theory, but the essential idea's correct, yes."

Royas glanced at Wilson for a second before turning back to Helen. "Except that, by your own admission, you don't have any concrete evidence of any of this."

"That's correct."

"So we're supposed to — what?" Royas waved his hands in the air. "Sit around staring at the walls until you snap your fingers and solve our case?"

Helen took a deep breath. Had she been in Royas' chair, she would have felt the same way. "Benson is one of the owners of Lobard, next to where the dead girl was found. Somehow, there's a connection there between him and Gray. It's too much of a coincidence otherwise."

Royas grinned, lightening up for the first time since they'd walked into his office. "Young lady, back in your official life did you ever go to a DA with a case as insubstantial as that?"

"Once or twice," Helen admitted, guessing exactly where the man was headed.

"And of that once or twice, what kind of reaction did your DA give you?"

"Okay." Helen grimaced. "It's thin. But I plan for it to be a lot thicker within a day or so, three at the max."

"Oh? And just how do you plan to do that?"

Now it was Helen's turn to grin, though she had to work some at the effort. "I'm going to track down and bring in the other killer."

"The guy who you have no idea where or who he is?"

"That's right." She made sure to put as much confidence as possible into her tone. "But I will before long. Then you'll have all the evidence you need."

"And you believe he killed not just Jamison but the Black woman this morning? Like covering tracks? You think he's on to you?"

"I think he knows someone's on to him."

"All the way down to eavesdropping on you and Wilson here last night?"

Helen relaxed even more. The lieutenant was back to using Wilson's last name. A good sign.

"Yes, sir. But he's probably already gone from the area. This particular person is highly mobile, to say the least. He probably couldn't have survived long otherwise."

Royas tapped his fingers on the desktop. "So why not just take you out? Matter of opportunity?"

Helen nodded, and she could sense Wilson silently agreeing with her. "There just hasn't been the time or opportunity to get to me. Even last night, there were two of us. Too much for one man, no matter how violent, to take on without a complete sense he'd get away with it. Easier to take out the Black girl."

"But how would he know where to find her? You didn't know until—"

"I'm still working on that. Somehow or other, he managed to anticipate my moves. And there's only one way I can think of he could have done so.

"But you don't have anything yet in the way of actual proof?"

"Correct."

Royas nodded again, by his expression buying into it even more. "And you can guarantee that you can eventually provide us intel on these two cases?" he asked.

"Yes, sir. I only have two more things to do. One, I have to go back to Denver and meet with Gray."

"And the second?"

"I'll know that after I talk with Gray."

CHAPTER 48

Monday, Sept. 30th

ARRANGED BY A phone call before she left Oklahoma, John Carstairs met Helen when arriving at Denver International. As she walked through the terminal, he came up to her and extended his hand.

"Welcome back," he said, casting a glance at her single overlarge tote bag. "You have any luggage?"

"Just this." Helen hefted up the tote. "Not expecting that long of a stay."

"So what's the scoop?" Carstairs asked as they walked. "You already tired of the scenic route along I-70?"

Helen grinned even though the Denver cop's jab didn't begin to dissipate the tension that had developed on the plane. After so many days, or was it weeks, of skipping around the middle part of the country, chasing from one crime scene to another, over the last eighteen hours a bone-deep fatigue had engulfed her, and she could only think of finding some soft, warm beach somewhere and napping for a month.

But she'd taken on a job, and that job wasn't finished yet.

"No time for the scenic route," she replied. "This is going to be a quick in and out."

Carstairs slowed and turned to look at her. "You

need a rental car?"

In the hubbub of a Monday afternoon, people were squeezing all around them, and Helen began to feel a little claustrophobic.

"No rental this time, John. Honestly, I'm hoping to be gone within a day at the most."

"Ready to talk about it?"

Helen sighed, but it was an expression of acceptance rather than irritation. "I am, but can we get out of this zoo and find somewhere nice and warm to drink and talk? How long before you're off duty?"

Carstairs grinned and tilted his eyebrows. "I signed out for the day right before I headed over here. We have as much time to talk as you want."

"Good," Helen said, her voice a shade mournful. "Because it's going to take a while, and I don't have the best of news for you."

****

"So you ready to help us wrap a bow on our modern-day Ted Bundy?" Carstairs asked about twenty minutes later.

They were ensconced in a small booth at the back of a dark bar. As they'd left the airport, Carstairs driving, pelting rain had begun. With the rain just forceful enough to make conversation uncomfortable, by mutual, silent consent, they'd both stayed quiet until they ended up in the bar, with their drinks in front of them.

Out of the window next to their booth, clouds had formed, gathering darkness, and the outside world seemed to disappear, save for the rain pelting against the glass.

Then, without preamble, the Denver cop had jumped to the question of the moment.

"Sorry to break the news to you, John," Helen answered, "but it's not exactly Ted Bundy you've got in your jail. More like Ted Wannabe."

Carstairs raised his eyebrows at that. "Meaning?"

Helen began to answer, but before she did the street lights outside came on in the gloom, and catching her reflection in the window, she paused, leaning toward the glass the slightest bit.

It was hard to tell in the distortion, but her complexion looked a bit better than it had recently, not nearly so sallow and lifeless. There was a light in the eyes that hadn't been there for a while.

"How do you mean 'wannabe'?" Carstairs repeated, and Helen jerked herself back to the task at hand.

"I mean I'm pretty sure he killed your victim, the Brayn girl. But I'm convinced he didn't kill any of the others he's taking credit for."

Carstairs frowned. "But he provided intel, led us to the bodies. Filled in some gaps that were confirmed later. Hell, the feds, mainly that Powers fellow, are patting themselves on the back in the media every hour on the hour. How could a three-time loser like Gray pull all that off if he wasn't the killer?"

"I need to talk to him to put it all together. Can you get me in a room with him?"

Carstairs frowned at that. "That would be an awful lot of strings to pull, Helen. I need something more than just your say so."

"What about his lawyer?" she asked.

"Meaning what?"

"Meaning talk to his lawyer, convince her that I can help clear her client of at least three murders. Could you do that?"

Carstairs frowned in thought for a minute.

"Probably," he finally said. "But the lawyer will no doubt insist on being there."

"Of course. He have the same PD he had before?"

Cartairs nodded.

"Then let's do it. You guys have officially cleared the Brayn case, right?"

"First one up. And from what I hear, from outside the loops, the feds are close to officially clearing two of the other three."

Helen shook her head. "Not yet, they're not. Not quite yet. When can I get in to see him?"

Carstairs remained silent for a minute or two. "Give me a day. I'm going to have to call in a lot of favors for this one, so it'll take some time."

Helen nodded in acceptance. One day, she could live with that.

One day before, hopefully, putting the last of the pieces together.

CHAPTER 49

Tuesday, Oct. 1st

JOHN CARSTAIRS MET her the next day outside the Denver County jail.

Getting up that morning, she'd put on a navy-blue slacks and jacket combo with a maroon blouse, about halfway to the jail realizing that she wore the same type of outfit worn back in her days on the force. Either coincidence or her subconscious trying to say something.

Carstairs noticed the change as well. "What," he said as she came abreast of him, "no sneakers and jeans?"

Helen grinned. "Decided I should look like an adult for once."

"Come on in. Everything's already been cleared, but just so you know, I used up about every favor I had coming to me, now and for the next five years or so. I hope to hell you know what you're doing."

"Marcie Lewis here yet?"

"Yes and no."

Helen stopped in mid-stride, her feet firmly planted on the ground. "What do you mean?"

Carstairs shrugged. "Turns out he fired her last week, first I heard of it. Said he didn't need any public defender to help him confess his sins."

Helen frowned. "I'm not sure about this, John."

"Neither is anyone else. The federal folks are looking at a whole bunch of closed cases suddenly going downhill if the accused doesn't have adequate counsel."

"That part of it won't be a problem," Helen said.

"Oh?"

"Yeah. Unless I'm completely off my game after today, Gray won't be on the hook for anyone besides Sami Brayn."

"You sure of that?"

Helen sighed and rubbed her forehead with her palm. "A hundred percent? No. But I've got almost all the pieces in place. Just need one more to wrap all this hell up."

"And ole' Willy has that piece?"

"He does. I just need to get him to give it to me."

Now it was Carstairs's turn to frown. "You're not thinking of doing anything—"

"Oh, God no, John. I'm just going to talk to him. What did you mean about yes and no on the lawyer?"

"Well, you can imagine how skittish both our DA and the feds got when he bolted his PD. The judge got involved, looked things over and decided there was nothing to stop Gray from doing so, but by the same token he doesn't want to see a whole lot of potentially-solved homicides go down the tubes."

"Did he assign Lewis back to Gray?"

"Yes, but only in an advisory role. Even so, Gray said he doesn't want her around."

"Huh?"

"That's right," Carstairs said "Says he wants to talk to you alone. I kind of twisted his arm to have that include me, said there had to be someone official in there."

"The DA go along with that?"

"Not too nicely. At first, he kicked and screamed and said hell no. Same with Powers and his posse. I finally assured him that this would lead to cracking multiple cases; otherwise, they never would have gone along with it."

"In other words you kind of lied."

Carstairs grinned. "Kind of."

"And Powers agreed to this?"

"More or less."

"Doesn't sound like the man I met a while back," Helen said. "He impressed me as more of a tally marker than anything."

Carstairs shrugged. "Same here, at least on first impression. I haven't worked with him a lot. Once we got Willy nailed down for the Brayn case, my involvement and official interest ended. But we've had a few times we had to get together and dot i's and cross t's, and the more you know him the more professional he is."

"Okay." Helen sighed and looked at her watch. "Let's get this over with."

****

As soon as they led Willy in, Helen felt like standing up and leaving. Her sole contact with Gray had been observing him through a one-way mirror the last time she'd come to Denver. At the time, she'd been focused more on what he was saying than his overall appearance. Of course, as a trained investigator she had noted the unkempt hair, unwashed hands and general unhealthy physique, but all that had been tangential to his story. Now, seeing him again, up close and just a few weeks later, the general decline in his appearance compared to that earlier time shocked her.

His hands, manacled to the table, wouldn't stop shaking. His face had a generally sallow complexion, and his eyes continually skittered back and forth.

The jail jumpsuit he wore looked about two sizes too large.

Once the guards had manacled Gray to the table and left, he turned and nodded at Carstairs.

"They told me you were coming by," Gray said.

"Willy, this is Miss Helen Lipscomb. She's working for a man named Gordon Conroy. He's a criminal lawyer from out of state, and she has a few questions for you."

Up to this point, Helen hadn't said anything.

"I don't need a lawyer," Gray, not even looking at her, told Carstairs. "I thought I've made that clear. I can take care of myself."

"Mr. Conroy doesn't want you to hire him," Helen spoke up. "He's working on a case that's related to yours, and he needs some help."

"Oh, yeah?" A hint of color showed in Gray's face, and he leaned back in his chair as far as the manacles allowed. He smirked, and Helen bet he would have crossed his arms if he could have. "Some big-time lawyer needs my help? Cool. On which of my cases?"

"Only one," Helen said, pulling a picture of Lyndie Black out of her pocket and placing it on the table, squarely between the two of them.

The mirth froze on Gray's face, and even in the two-sizes too big jumpsuit Helen could see his thin muscles tense.

Carstairs, who hadn't known the play ahead of time, stayed silent.

Several long seconds ticked by before Gray spoke up. "What about her?" he asked.

"She was killed last weekend," Helen said.

"No."

"Yes, Mr. Gray. I was coming to talk to her, wanted to talk to her about your time down in Oklahoma, primarily why you left so quickly. But someone beat me to the punch."

Gray shook his head.

"Yes," Helen continued. "Strangled her in her apartment. Also beat the hell out of her beforehand. And I think you know who did it."

"He didn't," Gray muttered, almost imperceptibly.

"He did. And it's up to you whether or not he gets away with it."

Gray looked away from the photo and up to Helen. Staring at him, she knew he was a killer, that he'd abducted and murdered fifteen-year old Sami Brayn right there in Denver, depriving the girl of the life she was supposed to have. But had Helen not known any of that, she would have considered him little more than a lost, confused puppy.

"You want to talk to me?" she prodded.

Gray hugged himself and began rocking slightly back and forth. His eyes focused on Lyndie Black's photo with such intensity that Helen wondered if he were even mentally in the room anymore. She glanced at Carstairs, who gave her a puzzled look in return.

"Willy?" she asked.

The kid began rocking even more noticeably, at the same time shaking his head from side to side, faint tears leaking from his eyes.

"She's gone," Helen said, "and he did it. Give me his name and where to find him."

A muscle twitched in Carstair's jaw, and Helen

could only assume the Denver cop was feeling completely betrayed at this moment. She could empathize, considering her own history, but didn't have time to rectify things.

This was the last chance. If Gray didn't break now, if they didn't pry the truth from him, she doubted they'd ever have another opportunity.

And for Helen Lipscomb the truth meant everything. In the last year and a half of her police career, she'd been involved in two cases where the truth had been murky, obscured, causing her to flail away in darkness. In one, she'd hounded an innocent man while in the other she'd failed to save some of her own colleagues.

No more. She wouldn't be anyone's oblivious patsy any more.

And the key to her salvation sat sobbing right in front of her.

"Willy," she whispered, nudging Lyndie's picture closer to the sobbing man, "don't let him get away with it. Tell me where to find him. Tell me who he is."

"Aargghh!" The tortured scream ripped from Gray's throat as he flung himself face down on the table. The sobs now ratcheted their way up from the bottom of his soul, and when Carstairs made an instinctive forward move, Helen waved him back.

Then she sat back and waited for what would come.

After a long, protracted length of time, Willy shuffled his head up and slumped back in his chair.

Helen reached into her blazer pocket and, totally against jail protocol, pulled out a pocket notebook and pencil. To her side, Carstairs tensed and glanced up to the ceiling.

"Tell me where to find him," Helen said, keeping

her voice as steady as possible.

"You want—" Gray began

"I want to know where to find him."

"I don't know for sure. There's lots of places he stays at."

Carstairs frowned, and his eyes narrowed to slits.

"Give me all of them," Helen said. "I'll sort it out."

Sighing, tears squeezing out of his eyes, Willy Gray bent over the table and stared at Lyndie Black's picture, then picked up the pencil and began writing.

Helen started breathing again. She didn't care if anyone was watching or listening, didn't care that Gray's semi-lawyer, Marcie Lewis, was out of the picture.

She didn't even care what Special Agent Powers would think when he learned about her little stunt.

For the first time since this entire cluster began, she felt she was close to the truth.

CHAPTER 50

"YOU GOT YOUR next moves figured out?" Carstairs asked Helen about half an hour later.

The two of them were sitting in a booth at a local diner a couple of miles from the station. After Willy Gray had written down some information in Helen's notebook, the kid had basically shut down. Several attempts to elicit more information had gone nowhere, and eventually they let him be returned to his cell.

By unspoken, mutual consent neither one had discussed the events of the interview until they'd exited the building and had gotten far enough away to sit down and mull over what had happened. Now, with drinks in front of them, a Coke for Carstairs and a Sprite for Helen, they were ready to talk.

"I think I do," she said, pulling out the notebook and flipped it open to the page Willy had written on. "I would have liked more, but I think he gave me what I need."

"Which you're going to turn over to the feds, right?"

Helen looked up at Carstairs, but couldn't quite read the expression on his face.

"You think he'd take it?" she asked.

The cop sighed and begun toying with his cup, turning it back and forth in small circles.

"I doubt it. They've got their confessed serial. If I were in their position, I wouldn't want to muck things up by going after someone else."

Helen took a sip. Putting the cup down, she stared out the window for a minute.

"Until there were incontrovertible proof," she said, "that they couldn't ignore."

Carstairs nodded but didn't say anything.

Helen continued gazing outside for several more seconds before turning back to the cop. "Then I guess I need to get it for them."

"You have anyone who can help? I'm jurisdictionally restricted to Denver, but I've got some vacation days coming up and—"

Helen made a shushing gesture with her hand. "Don't put yourself out there. I can pick up some help if I need it."

"You sure?"

She nodded. "I've got the addresses Willy gave out. They're scattered around some, but I know people in most of the areas. I'll be able to figure it out."

Carstairs settled back in his seat, his face still grim. "I still don't get it, though."

"Get what?"

The cop gestured towards the still open notebook. "Who the hell is Peter Rogers? That's a name that never came up at all when we investigated Sami's death. And I've never heard the name in connection with any of the others Powers and his people are investigating."

Helen finished off her Sprite and moved the cup to the side of the table. "He's the missing link," she said. "The thing that ties all of them together, and a whole lot more by the time we're done."

"But who is he?"

"I don't know yet. I won't know until I manage to track him down."

Helen's heart constricted a bit. She had an idea as to who the mystery man Peter Rogers actually was. A possible theory engendered by everything she'd done for nearly a month now, everyone she'd talked to, but didn't want to share her half-baked idea with Carstairs.

If correct, she wanted to be in on the final act, foolish as that may be.

"When I get back to the house, I'm going to run him through the system," Carstairs said.

"Go ahead, though Willy didn't give us much more than a name."

"Maybe in a day or so, once he's had time to recover, I can get him to give me more."

Helen shrugged in half assent, though she really didn't buy it. Giving up the name had taken the spotlight away from Willy, and he probably knew it was never coming back on. For months now, he'd been a minor celebrity, the toast of the law enforcement apparatus of several states, and he had to have known that once he gave up Rogers, that would all change. Probably nothing would have prompted him to make such a move except for the hand Helen had played, revealing Lyndie Black's fate to him.

"Even if he does," she said, "something tells me you won't find this guy in anyone's system anywhere."

"It's still worth a shot."

She shrugged again and went back to staring out the window, but she wasn't just idly wasting time.

She was plotting her moves for the next several days.

Part VI
Missouri

CHAPTER 51

Tuesday, October 8th

HELEN STOOD OUTSIDE a seemingly-abandoned apartment building in one of the most run-down parts of Kansas City, the fourth entry on Willy's list. Over the last week, she'd inspected three others, all of which had proven fruitless. This was the last location on the list.

The entire neighborhood had fallen to pieces somewhere around the nineteen eighties and never recovered. Though Helen knew it wasn't possible, all the buildings seemed abandoned, but intuition dictated that once the sun went down, the area would begin to show signs of life, the street people who spent most of their lives living in the shadows.

It felt as though she'd come full circle. The scene before her, with the red Missouri sun setting behind the city, could have stood in for so many other times in her professional life. Poised to enter a potentially-hostile environment, in a sketchy part of town, with no clear intelligence as to who or what awaited inside.

Sure, she'd experienced several such scenarios.

But this one was different.

In the past, she'd had backup, fellow cops all around, maybe even a SWAT team, all of them guarding each other's backs. In the past headquarters, or at least whatever precinct she currently worked out of, would know her location, her plan, and about when to expect to hear back.

In the past, she'd felt secure, or at least as secure as one could in such situations.

This time around, there was no such security. No backup, and no one who knew where she was or what she was about to attempt.

Not that she hadn't tried.

Helen wasn't a movie heroine, and definitely didn't hold some kind of a death wish. The last thing she wanted to do was enter that deserted building alone and attempt to perform a sweep, looking to bring down a serial killer. It would be an insane action.

Yet, the choice was limited. Attempting to contact Powers, she'd called the special number the task force had given her. The sensible thing to do. Believing she'd managed to run the culprit down, at least to within a reasonable area, all she had to do was call up the feds, feed them the info and step back to let the professionals do their job.

She had absolutely no business taking on something others could do so much better. The healing cut on her abdomen was obvious proof of what happened when one tried to showboat into a dangerous situation on their own. The cut itself was really nothing much more than a slight inconvenience, but if she'd been an inch or two closer to Jacob Brounton, the wound would quite possibly have proven fatal.

So yeah, the smartest thing would be to get hold of Powers and drop the whole thing in his lap.

Except Powers hadn't answered.

No one had.

In fact, the number didn't even go to voice mail, leaving Helen with only one conclusion to reach.

The feds had blown her off, cutting her off from them in an attempt to take her out of the game.

It was understandable. In fact, in Powers' place, Helen would probably have done the same. Which only left the problem that she'd tracked down the suspect and, without some sort of action, he was going to get away.

She could call the local cops and convey the message, but that probably wouldn't work any better. She'd have to go through many levels of command before finding someone to take her seriously, and who knew if anyone actually would.

On the other hand, staying out here forever wasn't an option. There was no way for one person to keep watch on four sides of a building for an extended period of time without the suspect slipping away. Physically not possible.

Helen sank back in the driver's seat and thought more furiously than ever in her life. One possibility, call Conroy and see if he had any investigators or operatives anywhere near the scene that he could send out. But the lawyer was over a state away at the moment, and while she'd learned by now that no matter the time someone was in his office, she wasn't all that sure she wanted to run to him for assistance.

The way things had unfolded, could she trust anyone so closely associated with Benson?

Sitting there for God only knows how long, she struggled through every permutation that came to mind. Even more maddening was that there was no proof the dude was in there. The info Gray had given her all pointed that way, but nothing concrete.

The night darkened even more, and traffic in this industrial area became almost nonexistent. Some of the buildings in the neighborhood probably had apartments on their top floors, no doubt rented out to secretive individuals who didn't want to live among normal neighbors, but so far no lights had come on in any of the buildings within eyeshot.

Helen drummed her fingers on the steering wheel, then closed her eyes, looking for a rational way out.

In the end, she couldn't find it and with a sigh climbed out of the car. Walking around to the passenger's side, she dug into her purse for a few minutes, then straightened up.

Deciding to make one last effort, Helen pulled her phone out and made a couple of quick calls. Voice mail, of course, on both, but she shrugged and left messages anyway.

Finally, having delayed as long as possible, she squared her shoulders and, gun in hand, began walking around the building's corner.

A few cars sped by, ordinary people on their way to ordinary lives, as Helen ducked around the building. She'd spent quite a bit of time earlier in the day on her laptop at the hotel, and eventually had managed to pull up original architectural plans for the forty-year old structure. In doing so, she'd managed to come up with the architectural firm's summary of the building's history, and had found in there something that should have surprised her but, by this stage in the game, had only served as one more piece confirming her theory.

The building had been purchased, in 2009, by Central Denver, LLC, a firm out of Colorado that specialized in buying distressed properties, of which there had been quite a few back in the heyday of the Great Recession, and turnkeying them over to new owners. As far as she'd gleaned, no one at the time had been all that interested in why a Colorado firm would want to purchase a property in one of the most rundown areas of Kansas City. The sellers had probably just been tickled pink to get such a white elephant off their hands and to hell with any questions.

But in the case of this property, Central Denver was listed as the last owner of record. From the architect's web site, Helen had scooted over to the Jackson County web site and made a few false turns, before ending up staring at the property tax statement for Central Denver.

Sure enough, right there in the midst of all that mind-numbing paperwork, lurked the property in question.

She had almost stopped there, but she'd been trained by some of the best detectives she'd ever known to never do a job halfway and never, no matter what, assume facts before knowing them, so she kept going.

It took another twenty minutes of digging in all sorts of places before staring at a corporate organization chart for Central Denver, LLC.

And there at the top of the line lay the name she'd expected to see.

Uh huh.

All of which she could have told Powers' task force, or even the local cops, had things worked out differently. But they hadn't, and now here she was, more than likely taking on an unknown killer by herself.

She did one complete circuit of the area, noting doors and ground-floor windows on each of the four sides. Great. Umpteen ways he could escape, if he was even home. And if he was actually in the city, or even the state. If he still had even a portion of the resources she suspected he once had access to, there was really no telling where in the country he was at the moment.

It took all of eight minutes to make a full revolution around the building, ending right back at the doorway across the street where she'd started out.

Decision time now. She grimaced, realizing that she'd actually been procrastinating on a course of action.

She could go in guns blazing and hope for the best.

Sure, break about half a dozen laws within the first three minutes and, if the guy was actually home, get herself blown right out the front door.

Scratch that idea.

Second, she could turn tail, get back to the car, and head to the hotel. Lock herself in and burrow under the covers after ordering a steak and some wine from room service. Then call Gordon Conroy again, give him the intel she'd acquired, tender her resignation, and in the morning head back home. Not seeing the job through to the end but ending it as a complete and utter failure.

Thus, pretty much validating everything her previous bosses had publicly said back when they'd hung her out to dry.

The third option, hanging around for however long it took help to show up, circling the building on a regular basis, and hoping like hell the suspect didn't exit any one of a hundred different ways or directions while out of eyeshot, didn't seem viable either.

Or call 911 and report some sort of violent crime in progress, give the address, and when a patrol car showed up present herself to the officers, and ask them to either check out the building themselves or call in for backup.

Yeah, right. She could figure just about what sort of reaction that would get her.

A sudden urge swept over her to reach out to the other side of the state to old colleagues. Lou Whitmore, for sure. Maybe Richie Lattimer, that young kid who joined the homicide squad after she'd been bounced following the Ron Green fiasco. Someone who was still on the job back home and could intercede with Kansas City officialdom and get someone, anyone, to listen to her.

Same problem, though. In the time it would take to pull that off, her suspect, provided he was even in there, dammit, could be long gone.

And trying to tail someone without being spotted would be almost impossible.

In short, Helen could see no good option.

She pulled out her phone and checked again for messages for any indication that the people she'd called had gotten their messages, but the screen was blank.

So, okay.

The final option, stand twiddling her thumbs until she died of old age, didn't appeal at all, and with that little realization Helen knew what to do.

One, get someone with some authority to listen to her.

Two, in order to pull off that little feat she had to get inside the damned building and find some proof, or at least a reasonable facsimile thereof, and get back out again.

Helen checked the phone once again, even though only a few seconds had passed since the last time.

Still nothing.
Alright then.
Time to go.

CHAPTER 52

SHE DECIDED ON one of the side doors. Back in the day when the building housed actual residents, everything would have been locked up tight. But with the general decline of the neighborhood, any locks that may once have existed had been either broken or destroyed over time by vagrants.

The thought that more than one dangerous person may lurk inside didn't deter Helen. She'd already taken that notion into account when realizing she had no choice but to enter, seek out and find the killer's abode and nail down some evidence that would convince the authorities.

She pulled out her gun and made one last check that the magazine was full and in place. Then she replaced it in her jacket pocket before approaching a battered-in door on the west side.

Some street people lurked around the area, but they gave a wide berth. She figured it was that essential copness that hadn't yet faded that made them keep their distance. It just went to show how much the badge, even if she didn't have it anymore, kept people away. If even two of the vagrants hanging around the corner had ganged up on her, there would have been, at best, a narrow chance of coming out ahead without using her weapon, which she most assuredly did not want to do.

She used a shoulder ram to push open the broken

door, the action causing a slight twisting of her abdomen, which made the wound flare up for an instant. She waited, breathing deep, until the pain subsided.

In the faint light from the street she could see that a pile of trash, including a soiled sleeping bag, had served to block the door. Helen paused, listening intently for the sounds of either people, rats or other vermin, but heard nothing.

Even just inside the door, the faint odor of cooked meth, a stench which, light as it was, set her teeth on edge.

Regardless, the quicker she got to it the faster she could be gone from the area.

She pulled a small flashlight out of her pocket and switched it on.

The inside layout was about what she'd expected. A long, central hallway, a few tattered easy chairs and tables still littering the way; apartment doors on each side; and a central staircase. She flicked her light around, searching for some indication of a doorway to a basement or lower level, but didn't see any.

She frowned. Surely when this place had been an operating apartment house there'd been a basement of some sort. Shrugging, she decided that the basement door must be further down the hall, lost in the gloom that enshrouded the other end.

The floors were laid out with six apartments on each side of the hall, and with six stories that would take an inordinate amount of time to cover the whole building. So, stop and think. Piece it together, and where would her prey most likely be hiding?

The sort of people who made their homes here would by definition be fairly physically wasted. Such a description wouldn't apply to her quarry, of course, but would fit most of the denizens of the area. Therefore, Helen reasoned, they would be unlikely to physically exert themselves more than they absolutely had to.

It would be rather surprising if the majority of the homeless, drug addicts, or street corner prosies who made use of this structure would ever get much past the second or third floors. And if the person she sought wanted to keep his presence as secretive as possible....

A door halfway down the hall, on the right-hand side, creaked open, and something shuffled out. In the gloom, Helen couldn't quite make out if the figure were male or female. As it stood in place, swaying as if from a slight breeze, she peered closer.

The clothes, what could be seen, seemed standard street issue. Shapeless jacket, or some sort of upper covering; a hat hanging askew; and formless, baggy pants. The person stood there for a moment, wavering back and forth in front of her, before coming her way.

She reached into her jacket, grasped her weapon but didn't pull it out. Killing someone, let alone an innocent, was the last thing on her list. If the stranger was merely some poor soul being kicked around by life, they would probably pass by with no problem. If instead it were someone strung out on something, they may see a potential source of income to feed either their habit or their stomachs.

Also, if the figure in front was a man, upon spotting a strange woman he could have something entirely different on his mind.

A low moan escaped the figure, and it continued shuffling in Helen's direction. Gripping her weapon tighter, she still didn't withdraw it.

No reason to escalate things if it could be avoided.

When the person came within a few feet, Helen could clearly see it was a young woman, haggard and unkempt beneath the worn Amy field jacket and faded black jeans. A black knit cap only partially hid straggly, oily hair, and if the woman's face were any indication, she'd been a long time without soap and water.

The woman stopped and stared at her, peering closely. Helen's gun remained hidden, but she didn't let go of it either. Up close, the woman was actually more of a girl, and while the street definitely ages its denizens quickly, Helen guessed the age no more than seventeen.

The girl nodded, then moved on, heading out the door and off to who knew where. As the door opened, a smallish-sized rat skittered through and ran off down the hallway. Helen gasped and instinctively took a step backward, even though the rodent hadn't even come close to her.

Now alone, Helen breathed deeply. The faint squeaks, squeals and rustlings echoed in the building that had seen better days, but she hoped that any other residents of the rooms and halls, either human or animal, would give a wide berth.

Squaring both shoulders, she headed towards the staircase. No matter how unsettling it could get, property canvass had to be done.

Doing so secretly, however, wasn't going to be an option. With her first step on the staircase the riser squeaked, and considering the state of the entire building, she figured she'd be squeaking and squealing all the way up.

So be it, she thought. One way or another, time to end this.

CHAPTER 53

SHE FINALLY TRACKED him down on the sixth floor.

Bypassing the first two floors, it had taken nearly an hour to sweep the third, fourth and fifth. There were a total of twelve empty rooms she encountered, six where people were cooking low-grade meth over hot plates, twenty or so malnourished teens who were probably runaways, and one room with no human occupant but an honest-to-God pit bull, standing two feet tall and colored a motley of black and grays, chained to a window.

So much for her theory of people being too physically wasted to climb all those stairs.

The pit, contrary to popular reputation, stared with beseeching eyes and whined as she elbowed the door open. In the gloom, it didn't particularly look like it was starving, and a red plastic bowl half-filled with water sat close by. Taking a quick whiff, Helen could smell dog, but nothing in the way of waste or piss, so figured there was an owner around somewhere, who just happened to be out at the moment.

In the corner, on the side of the room opposite from the dog, she made out a couple of large pieces of cardboard propped against the wall. Safe to assume the dog belonged to a street-corner panhandler who used it as part of their shtick.

Helen exited the room, the pit still whining behind

her, and made a note to call animal control as soon as she departed the building.

Emptiness painted its picture upon reaching the sixth floor. She stood at the top of the stairway, looking down a hallway similar to the others in the building, and intuitively knew that all the rooms were empty. If asked, she couldn't have told how she knew it, but sensed a deeper level, a more intense vibe, to the silence here on the top floor.

Even so, she had to clear the area, make sure the intuition was right, before calling it a night.

And if there were no trace of her quarry?

What then?

Shrugging, Helen figured she'd have plenty of time to worry about that later. But first, another floor to cover.

The first four rooms loomed as vacant as she'd expected, none of them holding even a trace of furniture. Any chairs, bed or dressers had disappeared over the decades, no doubt cut up by neighborhood vagrants for firewood.

The fifth room contained a soiled air mattress, the stains apparent even in the feeble light of her flashlight. Several used condoms littered the floor around the mattress, and a compact refrigerator and hot plate sat in one corner. Obviously, someone was using this room, and where they were at the moment was anyone's guess, but she saw nothing to specifically indicate the man she sought had been there.

On down the line, empty room after empty room, until the last one at the end of the hall.

And the first she'd come upon that was locked.

It took only a quick twist, fingers light on the knob, to verify the door was locked. Automatically, she jumped back and to the side, just in case someone lurked beyond that door with an unsteady trigger finger. All sorts of reasons for that locked door flashed briefly, but only one that mattered to her.

She had no real evidence that Peter Rogers waited on the other side of that door. And if it was him, he could be asleep, her light grasp of the knob not nearly enough to wake him up. But all the other options had played themselves out, leaving only this last possibility.

In fact, in a weird way Helen had the feeling that everything in her life had come together to lead to this particular here and now.

She couldn't retreat. No way of knowing if or when help would arrive, and no way of predicting what would happen in the meantime.

Same debate issue before entering the building. Analyzing options, scenarios.

If it was him.

If it wasn't, instead, some harmless old coot in there, sleeping off a jag brought on by a bottle of cheap wine and too many memories of what used to be.

For all she knew, some vagrant had taken up residence and propped a two by four under the knob, thus securing the door.

So many possibilities, so many directions to go.

But in the end, Helen really had only the one choice.

Instead of rushing in, she pulled out her phone one last time.

Still no messages from anyone. Sighing, she put the phone away and grasped her weapon a little more firmly and moved to the side of the door. Reaching out, she gave three rapid knocks.

Ten seconds went by, then another ten. Helen

listened but couldn't hear anything on the other side of the panel. She knocked again, louder this time, at the same time straining to hear the sound of a window going up or any other sort of movement.

She began to stretch an arm out to give one final knock before saying the hell with it and kicking the door in, but as she did so a sudden flurry of shots whipped through the panel.

Helen crouched, fearful of losing her hearing with the deafening din, and counted five shots before they stopped. Motes of dust danced in the feeble shafts of light created by the holes in the door.

As crouching to the side wouldn't accomplish anything, she mentally shrugged, took a deep breath and swung around, one leg hiking up and kicking just to the side of the doorknob.

Fortunately, the door was old and rotted enough that it gave easily. In the past, Helen had seen several instances when young, husky patrolmen had difficult times kicking in doors, and even Lou Whitmore, the big, muscular detective back on her old force, sometimes had to give a second or third kick.

But in this decrepit building it only took one solid blow, and the flimsy portal damned near imploded.

Instantly, Helen crouched as low as possible and hurled herself into the apartment, almost instantaneously darting to the left and getting as close to a corner as possible. From there, she scanned the room, looking for the danger point.

Adrenaline kicked in. She scanned the dimly-lit room identical to all the others in the building, gaze finally landing on the suspect.

The shooter stood in the middle of the room.

He seemed around five-eleven, though he was crouched a bit so Helen couldn't accurately guess his height. He wore faded, grimy blue jeans and a white "wife-beater" tee-shirt. His straggly hair hung down half to his shoulders and was cut into something close to bangs down the forehead. In the dark, Helen couldn't make out his hair color or much of his features.

He held a 9mm of some sort in his hand, the barrel half-raised in her direction.

"You came for me," the man said, his voice a kind of raspy croak.

Helen didn't quite know what to say to that, so kept silent. Her own weapon leveled straight in his direction.

"No one ever comes for me," the man said. "I'm the one who hunts them down."

Helen's breath constricted at his use of the word "hunt," but she kept herself still.

"Who are you?" he asked.

She thought that one over, but couldn't see any reason not to answer. "My name's Helen Lipscomb."

The man's head cocked to the side. "You a cop?"

Intense fatigue suddenly hit her, and not just from the last several weeks of running down the man who stood before her. In that moment a complete, all-consuming weariness came over, not just body, but mind and soul as well. She wished that, two years before, when she'd been bounced from the job, she'd emptied her bank account, climbed into her car, and started driving. No destination, no schedule. Just a long, deliberate drive until reaching the end of the road, wherever that may be.

But she hadn't, and now stood here, in a cruddy apartment in a run-down old building, facing a strange man who may have killed who knew how many people.

Her stomach roiled, and teeth clenched to keep from vomiting. She was sick to death of killers, and killing, and just about anything else that had to do with her former life. In a flash resolving that, if she made it out of this deathtrap alive, she would have nothing more to do with crime or criminals ever again.

First, however, she had to get past that big If.

"No, I'm not a cop. Not anymore."

At the same time wondering if she'd ever, really, been one.

"Then what are you here for?" the man asked.

"To take you in."

A short laugh, almost a bark, and he took a few steps forward, his weapon still only half-raised. He stopped in the middle of a beam of light coming from one of the dirty windows, providing Helen a better look at him

"Hello, Mr. Rogers," she said.

The man frowned, cocked his head to the side, then nodded.

"Okay," he said. "So where'd you get the name?"

"Does it matter?" she asked.

Rogers managed to shrug without wavering his aim a bit. "Could have only been two people. Either Benson or my brother. Probably Benson finally got smart to things."

"Actually," Helen said, "you really don't look all that much like Willy."

"Good Lord," the man said, "you mean that little pussy finally got some balls on him?"

"Enough to give you up. He got smart, as you put it. But because of the name I'm guessing not full brothers?"

"Uh uh. Different dads, same mom, and all the looks from the dad's side. How about that?"

Okay, so that began to make sense, but she still needed to fill in a few holes.

"So Willy wasn't a killer?"

Peter Rogers snorted. "Little brother? That simp could barely tie his shoes in the morning. Thought by hanging around with tough guys he'd get tough himself."

"Not like you."

Another nod, stringy hair flipping around his head. "That's right. What the heck. I was the big brother he looked up to, and he wanted to be like me."

More holes filling in, and Helen felt as if she almost had the entire thing right within her grasp.

"But what's it all have to do with Leo Benson?"

Rogers frowned, and his weapon leveled upwards the smallest amount. Slight as the movement was, Helen noticed and tensed even more.

"I don't know who you mean. I'm just—"

"Come on, Rogers. Don't treat me like the idiot you think your brother is. You just said his name a minute ago. Leo Benson. Your partner."

The frown vanished from Rogers's face, replaced by a look of almost serene calm. Helen's nerves kicked into overdrive.

The man had just made some sort of decision.

"I think you know a little too much to stick around," he said.

Something new popped into Helen's mind. The one thing that had been gnawing away ever since this case began. The one thing, technically, that Benson had hired her to find out.

"The jail," she said.

"Huh?" Her verbal swerve caused Rogers's forehead to pucker.

For a moment, something behind her distracted Helen's attention. She thought she heard sounds in the hallway.

She needed to focus, not get distracted.

"The jail in Denver. You're a blood relative, so you got to visit Willy."

Another barking laugh.

"You dense or something? You really think they'd allow that?"

Helen grimaced at her own stupidity. With Gray convicted of one killing and spouting details about several others, all of his phone calls and mail would be rigorously checked by his jailers. Even family conversations would be monitored. Any communications with anyone would have to go through them.

Or almost anyone.

"His lawyer," she said, more to herself than the man facing her.

"Huh?"

"That's how Willy had the info on Benson's, and your killings. What'd you do, pass them on in letters or something? Then the lawyer passed the letters on to Willy?"

"Maybe. You're a pretty smart lady."

But Helen shook her head. That didn't make any sense. Why would Marcie Lewis, even working as Gray's attorney, have willingly...

No. The solution, such as it was, popped into her head. Gray had been in and out of trouble with the cops his whole life. This older brother, when they could somehow get the right records, no doubt the same.

And she knew from past experience that low-level,

hairbag crooks were the best at seeking out and using jail and prison grapevines. In most cases, the two-bit street hustlers she'd known could teach Mafia dons a thing or two about getting word in and out behind prison walls.

Add that natural proclivity with the kind of money and influence Leo Benson could wield, and who knew what sort of things, beyond mere information, could be trundled back and forth behind prison walls.

That could be nailed down later, but for now Helen had to resolve this standoff, and the only way was to somehow distract the man in front of her.

"Why do all of that, Rogers? For what? Benson do something that you had to get back at him for? Or did you just resent what he'd turned you into?"

The puckered forehead smoothed out, and Helen knew the tactic had failed as Rogers began to level his weapon all the way up.

"Wouldn't you like to know," he said as he began firing.

With that first leveling of his arm, Helen had shifted out of the way. A tight corkscrewing motion served to both move her out of the original line of fire at the same time twisting herself into the smallest possible width of target.

His first shot whizzed overhead, but his second came much closer, actually plucking at her jacket sleeve. Becoming almost horizontal, Helen blasted three rounds in Rogers' direction. Hitting the floor, she whipped around, now facing him, body outstretched and arms locked straight in front, hands clasping her own weapon in case she needed to fire again.

But there was no need. Rogers stood still, straight up and staring at the ceiling for several moments as the three holes in his chest began to spew blood.

Then the killer of so many women closed his eyes and fell to the floor.

"Behind you," a familiar voice said. "Don't shoot, okay?"

Helen stood up, weapon down by her side, and turned to look at the still-open doorway of the apartment.

Deputy Sally Briscoe stood there, her own service weapon in hand. Behind her, Helen could see other figures filling the hallway.

"What?" Briscoe said. "You couldn't wait for backup?"

Part VII
Nebraska Death Row

CHAPTER 54

Thursday, Oct. 17th

IT MAY HAVE been the same room as on the previous visits, but Helen wasn't sure. And didn't much care. Most of the meeting rooms at Redding State looked pretty much the same, and with everything she'd gone through in the last few days, whether they'd put her in the exact same room as before to meet with Benson rated pretty low on her scale.

Okay. But if it matters so little why am I spending so much energy thinking about it?

No Gordon Conroy today. Or any of his associates. As on the last visit, she'd managed to get in to see the client all by herself, although she had doubts if he'd want to see her when he heard what she had to say. Didn't matter all that much. No matter how it went, despite whatever reaction he had, she'd already determined that this face to face with Leo Benson would be the last.

Even so, he'd better not stiff me any of what I'm owed.

And where the hell had that come from? Right now, here at the end of the long trail, was money really a concern?

Even so, when you came right down to it, she'd accomplished what he'd wanted her to do.

More or less.

A soft rap on the door sounded, giving Helen a fraction of a second to sit up straight and wipe any hesitation or uncertainty from her expression. Then the door opened, and in came three guards and Benson.

From nowhere, Helen wondered if they were the same guards as before, and it surprised her that the other times she hadn't really noticed their faces. Again, it didn't matter if there was a standard assignment, or if they rotated, but she did wonder. So much for those stellar powers of observation she used to have.

In tandem, they walked up to the table, Benson sat down, and the routine of unshackling then reshackling him to the table ensued. When they were done, two of the guards left the room, but the third stayed behind, a definite breach in the routine.

Helen glanced at the remaining man, somewhere in his mid-fifties with a full head of red hair beginning to go gray.

"I'm supposed to stay here, ma'am," he answered her unspoken question. "Warden's orders."

So far Benson, staring at Helen with a blank expression, had not said a word.

"I'm part of Mr. Benson's legal defense team," Helen replied, "and as such am entitled to have private consultations with him."

The guard frowned. "It was my understanding you're not a lawyer, miss."

Helen almost sighed at how quickly she'd gone from "ma'am" to "miss."

"Doesn't matter if I am or not. I'm duly employed by the legal firm representing Mr. Benson, and he and I have matters to discuss of a legal nature. If you're concerned for my safety, you can observe us from that window in the wall, but you cannot listen in to our conversation at all. If I have to, I'll leave now and be back within twenty-four hours with a court order stipulating just that."

She had no idea why the change in routine, unless somebody out there had been putting two and two together, but it didn't matter. She was quoting basic legal procedure, the same as she'd heard from the other side for years, and both she and the guard knew it.

Finally, he nodded his head and relented. "I'll be observing, ma'am," back to that again. "Let me know if you need anything."

Helen gave him a smile, and he backed out of the door. Leaving her and Benson alone.

"You've been busy," the billionaire said, his first words since entering the room.

"That's pretty much of an understatement. In fact, I've been working my ass off."

The old man frowned. "That kind of language doesn't become you, Detective Lipscomb. I thought you were more professional than that."

He sneered slightly, almost under his breath, on the word "detective." Subtle, but noticeable enough for her to catch.

As he'd no doubt intended.

"Which is why you hired me, right?"

"Pardon?"

"My professionalism. That's why you had Conroy hire me. Only that, right? Not because of my reputation. Not because as far as the law enforcement community's concerned I'm a pariah?"

"I don't follow where this is going," Benson muttered.

Helen slammed her palm down on the table. She put enough shoulder in it that it sounded like a shot in the bare room, and she didn't give a damn what the men on the other side of the glass thought.

"Stop bullshitting me, Mr. Benson. You needed a gopher, a bloodhound, to sic on William Gray. Someone who could backtrack him and prove he didn't kill those girls he claimed to. That was the job, correct?"

"You know damned well it was. And I don't get what your problem—"

"But you didn't want someone really good, someone who would go through any door and wiggle into any crevice. Conroy would have access to any number of competent investigators, but you didn't want to go that route, did you?"

"I'm pretty sure that was all explained at our first meeting."

"Explained, yes. But not all that convincingly."

Benson sighed, attempted to cross his arms, then grimaced at the shackles' restraint. Instead, he leaned forward and placed his forearms flat before him.

"Meaning?"

"Meaning that you wanted a flame out, a loser. Someone who was so disgraced that she wouldn't get the time of day from most law enforcement types. Someone who would maybe figure out a convincing explanation for Gray's knowledge, and I'm sure once they're done digging they'll find you already had one laid out."

"Surely, you don't—"

"But at the same time, you needed someone with enough of a media profile that their activity would garner attention from the press. So, a total loser of a cop who was already known to the media. I must have seemed like the golden child to you."

"How could I—"

"Connections, Mr. Benson. With your money and connections, prison walls don't mean a whole lot, except in terms of actual, personal freedom. So you wanted someone on the outside who could follow the bread crumbs you probably already had laid out, but not someone really good who could get to the actual truth. You didn't want someone who would actually dig up the franchise."

A quick sip of air, and for an instant his composure slipped, his eyes becoming hooded and dark.

"Franchise?"

"Of course. You're a businessman after all, or at least you were before they caught up with you. Isn't it hell when franchisees don't live up to their end of the bargain?"

The slightest rattle of metal as he leaned back in his chair, and Helen had the impression he wanted to do nothing more than cross his arms. He made an instinctive motion in that direction, just as a few minutes ago, and was again thwarted by the handcuffs.

"I don't know what you mean, Miss Lipscomb," he said, but his voice wasn't as sure and confident as it had been a minute before.

"Of course you don't. But I'm sure the federal prosecutors won't mind explaining it all to you."

Under his prison-issued blue denim shirt his shoulders tensed.

"I wrote up my report for Mr. Conroy," Helen continued, "and also sent a copy of it to the FBI and Justice Department. I'm sure you'll be hearing from them shortly."

Benson glared at her but said nothing.

"It's kind of odd," she said. "Most serials, at least the majority that've been captured, eventually fall into bragging about their deeds. The most famous ones spend years, sometimes, taunting authorities with their cleverness. That makes you an exception, Leo. You never did want to be found out, did you?"

"You bitch," he hissed under his breath.

Helen smiled, though her insides had begun constricting, and she hoped the handcuff chains were as sturdy as they looked.

"Here's how I've got it figured," she said. "Feel free to tell me where I'm wrong. I've read up on you, gone over all the corporate literature, at least what you can still find. Something I should have done right from the start. Who knows, maybe I am the incompetent you thought I was."

"I never—"

But Helen, not really caring for anything the man had to say, cut him off again. "You grew up in Arkansas, a ways east of Little Rock. Probably didn't have, as they used to say, a pot to piss in? I've been out that way before, Leo. Tell me, did you live in one of those mobile homes up on concrete blocks?"

Benson placed his arms flat on the table and glared at her.

"You got the urge long ago, probably while still a teenager. Considering you grew up in such a small town, there wouldn't be any records, as such, but I'm sure once the feds start nosing around they'll find someone who thought that even as a kid you were a little off, maybe heard stories about you out in the woods torturing animals. That's usually how freaks like you start out."

His face had turned a couple shades darker, and his eyes had narrowed to slits. The peaceful, commanding countenance of the once-successful businessman had fallen away, and the true monster was showing himself. Helen took a deep breath, hoping her voice wouldn't quaver.

"What do you want?" Benson finally spoke. "More money to keep quiet?"

Helen shook her head. "Even if I was so inclined, it wouldn't do any good. The cat's too far out of the bag, Leo. I've spoken to too many cops the last few weeks, visited too many cities. You've no doubt been watching the news, and getting reports from Conroy, both mine and his own, but even so a lot of it hasn't yet hit, and I wanted to be the one to tell you that it's all coming out.

"You probably had a good old time of it back when you were young and poor, and could wander around attracting no attention, but as you got richer and more well-known, well, that must have constricted your movements a lot. Ironic, isn't it?"

"You're right, detective." The man spoke through gritted teeth, his sneer more pronounced now. "I have been keeping tabs on you. And I don't see anything you've done that puts any sort of weight behind this—franchise—did you call it?"

Helen grinned, though not from humor. She was bone tired, absolutely bedraggled, and the last thing she wanted to do in life was sit in front of this psychopath and play games.

It was time to wrap it up.

"Peter Rogers," she said in a near whisper.

Benson froze, his face drawing into something resembling a death mask, and his eyes began darting around the room.

"Did you really think," Helen asked, "that I was that clueless of an investigator that I wouldn't find the string and manage to unravel it? The Oklahoma City police have warrants out for Rogers, and as far as official paperwork, KC and Denver aren't that far behind, but it doesn't really matter. Seeing as how a week ago I pumped three bullets into the bastard's heart."

Benson seemed to have aged a decade in the last minute.

"For what it's worth, your boy did try to finish the job and kill me. But then, I guess he wasn't really your boy the last few years, was he? Tell me, Leo, did you have any contact at all since he decided to strike out on his own?"

Benson's arms began trembling, and he looked like he wanted to throw up.

"You're so goddamned sick," Helen hissed, "that when you got to be rich and famous you had to keep on going. But you couldn't, could you? Even with all your money, you couldn't kill as freely as you had in the past. And that's the irony. The more resources you possessed, the less you could indulge in your hobby."

Benson stayed silent, continuing to glare at her. His flattened arms nearly trembling in their shackles.

"So you decided to farm it out, to find another, younger guy to take part in the killing, right?"

Benson took several deep breaths and, after a moment, managed to find his voice.

"So what? Even if I did something like that, why would I? To live vicariously through some no-account bum? What do you think? That he handed his trophies over to me? Gave me blow-by-blow accounts of their work? Just where are you getting this from, Lipscomb?"

"I got a little of it from Willy Gray and a little from his brother Peter, then guessed most of the rest. By the time it's all turnkeyed over to the feds and they kick into gear, who knows what else they'll turn up?"

"You still can't—"

"But Rogers messed you up," Helen interrupted. "He went off script."

"Off script?"

"Come on, Benson. If you'd been controlling him, would you have allowed Rogers to leave a victim right on the doorstep of one of your businesses? Across the way from where his brother was working? What'd he do? Fly out to visit baby brother and end up unable to control himself? The Jamison murder was what gave me the connection between you and Gray, a connection you swore up and down never existed, and from there all I had to do was find the link in the middle, and here we are."

Benson glared at her, his lips pressed tightly together. Helen smiled, even though sickened by the entire experience, but she'd come here to pound the nail all the way in, and she didn't intend to leave until she had.

"As for what happened to set your protégé against you, I don't have a clue. But again, I don't need it. That's for the real cops, not the castoffs like me, to uncover. And they will. Just as they'll uncover how you two crossed paths, and how it is that Rogers managed to get word to his brother on the inside. Must have really torn you up when you realized someone else had all that knowledge about the killings someone was doing on your behalf, huh?"

Benson's eyes flashed, and the muscles in his scrawny arms and chest tightened at that last jab. But Helen had to hand it to the sick freak. He was managing to keep in control pretty well.

After a moment, he relaxed a bit and managed to bring forth something close to a smile.

"You're still working for Conroy, right? Technically?" he asked.

Helen knew where he was going. She just didn't care.

She shrugged. "At the moment, but I'm thinking of quitting. You boys are going to be on your own then."

"So whatever I say is still covered by privilege and you can't divulge anything I say. As long as I don't give you foreknowledge of crimes yet to be committed."

Helen was a little iffy on that part, but figured Benson had had more than the normal share of legal knowledge pumped into him over the years. Especially since his arrest.

"Far as I know, that's right," she said.

The billionaire leaned back, and some of the tension seemed to melt away, almost as if he were glad it was coming to an end.

"I always had my doubts about Rogers, thought maybe he was a little too weak for the project. Even so, I didn't think he'd be the one to betray me."

Betray, Helen thought. What an odd choice of words. Benson had sent a young man out to kill for him so that he could continue to get pleasure in his own way. How much misery had he and his acolyte spread over the years?

When she didn't answer, the man's small smile blossomed to almost grotesque proportions, and it occurred to Helen that at the moment Benson looked more like a predator than ever before.

"I could see him starting to get sloppy," Benson continued. "But I never expected him to turn on me as he did. I'll admit that was my hubris. I thought I had him under better control. And of course, I knew absolutely nothing about his brother until the little bastard started talking."

"So what was the hold?" Helen asked. "Beyond the sick opportunity you gave him, you must have had something on Rogers. Something that kept him in line, at least until he saw his kid brother as the way to get back at you. What'd you have on him?"

"Does it really matter? The son of a bitch went off on his own, and now he's dead. After all I'd done for him." Benson sighed and leaned closer to her, which because of his shackles wasn't very far. "Okay, then. If you insist, look at it this way. Everyone, even someone like an embittered, out-of-work ex-cop whose friends have all abandoned her, has something to lose."

"Lose?" Helen worried that his leaning over would cause the guards to come in. She didn't want this moment interrupted.

"Pressure points, detective. Relatives, parents, close friends. It's how I made such a success in business. Find the pressure point, and you'll find your control."

Helen's brain raced, running through everything she'd learned about both Gray and Rogers, going all the way back to her first trip to Denver. In some ways, despite all the turmoil she'd gone through, it felt as if she'd been doing nothing for weeks but gathering reams of info in an attempt to understand something beyond understanding.

"There was a sister," Benson said. "A half-sister, their mom must have really gotten around, who I had someone watching. As long as Rogers did what I wanted, the sister was safe."

Helen cudgeled her mind some more. For the life of her, she hadn't come across anything about a sister. She wondered if Benson hadn't made the whole thing up as another way of screwing with her mind.

"She must be really under the radar."

Benson nodded, seeming almost pleased that she'd figured it out.

"She was, once, but not entirely. An address or phone number dropped into conversation, a couple of private pictures acquired. It doesn't take much. But then a few years ago the bitch had to go and die on me. Leukemia, for Chrissakes. And it didn't help that right about then was when the law caught up to me, and well, you know."

"And you had nothing to hold over him," Helen said.

"Not a thing." Benson shrugged. "Then the bastard started using my kills to get himself some leverage. Almost like he wanted to get back at me, when the truth was I made him more alive than he'd ever been."

"You've got to admire the way he did it, though," Helen said. "Kind of genius, actually."

"If you say so." For the first time since he'd entered the room, Benson's voice turned a little glum.

Helen gave a quick, brief nod, then stood up.

"We're done," she said. "I want nothing more to do with you."

"Don't forget, Lipscomb, you can't divulge anything I'm saying here."

"Wrong, Mr. Benson. In your case, dead wrong."

His face flushed. "You bitch, you said you were still—"

"I lied. Couldn't you tell? Got to say, Leo, for such a shrewd businessman, you're getting awfully sloppy lately."

He started to rise but didn't get far. Shackles forced him to remain rooted in his chair.

"Be careful," Helen said. "You act too aggressive and they'll come busting in here. The fact is, I resigned from your employment this morning. Tendered my resignation personally to Mr. Conroy. Kind of forgot to mention that to the authorities here, so I may get in some small trouble for that. Regardless, I'm no longer working for either you or him. If you somehow got a different impression, well, sorry about that. The only business we have left is to pay my bill in full."

Benson's face flushed and he started to respond, but Helen cut him off.

"Don't worry, though. From this moment on I'm out of it completely. Of course, after I quit I sent a copy of my report to the attorneys general of the various states where your boy was —active. No more secrets, Mr. Benson. It's all out now, and there's no turning back."

As she turned towards the door, Benson began cackling behind her. Helen looked back at him over her shoulder.

"You really think you've won something, you little whore? If anything, you've made it easier for me. Now there's going to be so many cases to unravel that it's going to take a century to get through them all. You think you pulled something over on me? Hell, you've just guaranteed that I'll live out the rest of my natural days, waiting for all the prosecutions to run their course."

"I know that," Helen replied. "I'm not quite the doofus you thought I was. But in your arrogance, you're kind of overlooking one thing."

"Which is?"

"My guess is that all your supposed leverage is just ashes in the wind now. The whole bargaining chip thing didn't work so well for Bundy, and with all this new stuff coming out, my guess is they're going to be anxious to get rid of you as quickly as possible. If anything, you're going to be a public relations bonanza when they finally put you down. Enjoy your trip to the death chamber."

The cackling had stopped, and Benson's face assumed a pale hue, as if Helen were standing there watching his power drain away.

"I've defanged you, you bastard, and there's no coming back."

She turned again, and this time made it all to the way to the door. She made a motion in front of the mirror. The door swung open to reveal three guards standing there waiting for her, Benson spoke one last time.

"Lipscomb," he said.

Helen stood firm, wanting to hear what he said but not wanting to give him the pleasure of seeing her interest.

"Don't imagine," he continued, "that you found everybody."

Squaring herself and standing as straight as possible, Helen exited the room.

CHAPTER 55

AS SOON AS she passed the gates in a rented Corvette—a slight indulgence that she'd decided at the last minute to tack on to the final expense report—Helen felt herself unwinding. The last few weeks had been among the tensest she'd ever experienced, including the time two years before when her fellow detectives back home were being killed all around her. But now she was feeling better.

No doubt, Benson still had several years ahead of him. By herself, Helen had barely enough clout for the FBI or the other agencies involved to buy her a cup of coffee. But her shooting Peter Rogers, plus all of her contacts over the last months with various law enforcement folks, made the story too big to ignore. And she had no doubt that when the various parties received and acted on her report, so much hell would come down on Benson that he'd probably be begging for lethal injection.

It would surely come sooner or later, but more than death itself, his true punishment would be seeing his entire business and financial legacy, everything he'd built up over the years, stripped away from him.

The devil may end up sparing his life, but no way would he even come close to walking away from this.

In a few scant miles she was into the outskirts of town, driving by normal people engaging in normal lives. Pulling up to a red light, Helen tapped her fingers on the steering wheel and wondered how long it would be, if ever, before she felt normal herself.

The light turned, she stepped on the accelerator and was halfway across the intersection when a blue and silver pickup rolled through the intersection, smashing directly into her passenger side door.

EPILOGUE

HELEN'S EYES FLUTTERED open, then closed almost instantly as bright light razored into them. Breathing deeply, pulling herself out of unconsciousness, she slowly eased them open again. After several moments, she managed to take stock of her surroundings.

The light, probably late morning sunlight, filtered through slatted blinds to illuminate what seemed to be a private hospital room. Metal-framed bed, clean white linens, pale gray walls and small end table just to her right. On her left sat two comfortable-looking, brown leather chairs.

One of which was occupied.

Gordon Conroy glanced up from his iPad and smiled at her. He looked almost the same as he had every time she'd seen him, including suit, tie and French cuffs, but focusing closer, Helen did notice about a three-day shadow of beard and red-rimmed eyes.

"Welcome back," he said, laying his tablet to the side and leaning forward. "How do you feel?"

She tried to speak, but nothing came out but a croak. Conroy got up and went over to the night table, pouring a small cup of water for her.

A minute later, Helen's throat was only unbearable.

"Where?" she managed to get out.

"Bryan Medical Center, in Lincoln. You've been

here for a couple of days now."

She struggled, working her mind to bring up shapes and symbols from the past. Eventually, she thought she had a small part of the picture.

"The prison?" she whispered.

Conroy nodded. "You were barely a mile out from it when you hit the edge of town and a truck cut across the light, barreling right into you. That Corvette wasn't exactly the sturdiest thing to be driving. Good thing you wear your seat belt."

Helen tried to smile, but even that slight amount of movement caused fiery red bolts to rush over her body. She tried to get out a question, but obviously failed as the lawyer leaned closer to her.

"Again?" he asked.

Helen took another, longer sip of water, then tried again. "How bad?" she managed to get out.

"Oh." Conroy smiled and sat back down in his chair. "Probably only about a hundredth as bad as you feel. At least, according to the doctor when she came through last night. Thank God for side airbags, you actually got out of it with only a few broken bones and a whole lot of bruises. The doc said you'd probably wake up feeling as if that truck actually ran over you. They've been waiting for you to wake up to run some more tests, but they found no permanent damage and nothing that won't heal itself within a month or so."

Helen frowned, but took a third drink before trying to speak. "The driver?" she said.

"Well, that's the other side of it. He ended up on a slab in the morgue, sorry to be so blunt, with half his face sliced away. Turns out he hit you at just the right angle to flip his little truck and have it ending up with the driver's side smashed into the roof of your car."

Helen took another drink as she tried to process that. "ID?" she finally asked.

Conroy smiled, leaned back and crossed his legs.

"Not at first. No facial and not enough for dental records. Fingerprints came up nada, and so did DNA, suggesting he wasn't ever in the CJ or military systems."

Helen frowned again. Whatever the lawyer wanted to tell her, he was taking his own sweet time.

"Sorry," Conroy said, no doubt noticing her discomfort. "Guess I'm too used to stringing a story out for maximum effect in a courtroom. The guy was showing up as a non-individual every way the cops thought of looking. Until one bright junior detective had a bit of a brainstorm."

"They checked the medical insurance records for Benson's companies, didn't they?"

Conroy's smile was so bright Helen wondered if the man were about to burst.

"I overlooked that you're one hell of a detective yourself, Lipscomb. But you're right. They got a court order for Benson's company records, a court order which I decided not to fight, did a scan, and up popped a young lad named John Werther. Turns out Mr. Werther worked for one of Leo's subsidiaries out west as a quote, operations specialist, unquote."

"Operations specialist."

"Correct."

"Which means exactly what?"

Conroy shrugged. "Probably whatever Leo wanted it to mean. Regardless, after a bit more digging around they confirmed that it was Werther driving the truck that slammed into you."

Helen wanted to recline into her pillow and go back to sleep, but there was too much she still had to know.

"How are you going to get him out of it?" she asked.

"'Scuse me."

"Well, he's your client. And it looks pretty damned clear that somehow he contacted Werther to shadow me and—"

Conroy shook his head as he fought back another grin.

"You don't quite understand, Helen. My firm is no longer employed by Leo Benson. As of yesterday, he's on his own and, if I can speak for a moment as a man and not a lawyer, I hope the son of a bitch rots in hell, right where he belongs."

Now Helen could lean back and drift off. She was safe, and while they'd probably never know exactly how Benson had gone about ordering the hit on her, not to mention how he'd managed to set it into motion even as she left the prison, at the moment it didn't really matter.

"Which only leaves the question as to you," Conroy said.

Helen's eyes snapped open. "Come again?"

"What are your plans now that the job's over with?"

"Tell you the truth, Conroy, I haven't really thought about it. Why?"

"You've got plenty of money now. Enough to last you several months, even a year or two if you're frugal."

"And?"

"And money isn't enough for some people. How are you going to spend your time? Go back to being a half-assed, unofficial private eye?"

"Seemed to work for me."

"The hell it did," and there was a snap in his voice

she hadn't heard before.

"What are you saying, Conroy? And whatever it is make it quick because I've about used up my current jag of consciousness."

"I'm saying you need something more stable than just drifting from job to job until you collect Social Security. Which, actually, you won't have much of since you're not earning real paychecks anymore."

"So?" The healing darkness was pulling her back in, and Helen wasn't even entirely sure her question had been audible.

"So don't you think it's time you got your act together? Sure, you were dealt a bad hand before, but that's in the past. Sooner or later, no matter what the baggage, you've got to start going forward again."

Helen chuckled. "You offering me a job, Conroy? Want me to cash a regular paycheck from you?"

"That's one possibility. Another is to go back to doing what you really want to do."

The darkness relaxed its grip just a bit, and Helen sat up a little straighter in bed.

"And what do I really want?"

"To be a cop," Conroy said. "It's the only real job you've ever had, and it's what you're good at. Fuck those little boys back home. You're good and you know it. And looking back over the last few years, both the Green case and what happened to your squad, it's time to stop beating yourself up for doing your job."

Helen breathed, a deep, long inhalation but said nothing.

"I can't promise anything, of course," Conroy continued, "but, believe it or not, I do have a fair number of friendly contacts in the upper echelons of departments around the country. I also have it on good authority that Kansas City, not to mention Denver, think pretty highly of you right now. Word is that Detective Carstairs is wanting to start a fan club. And even that lieutenant in Oklahoma seems to have come around. Hell, far as that goes more than one state police command knows that you just cleared up a whole lot of headaches for them. Might be something to look into."

Helen finally exhaled. "Even more politics the higher up you get," she said, "and navigating the waters doesn't seem to be my strong suit."

"No." Conroy stood up. "But solving crimes is."

A faint tap sounded at the door, and they both looked over to see a young black woman wearing a doctor's white coat looking in at them.

"Mind if I come in?" she asked.

"I was just leaving," Conroy said. "Helen, this is Dr. Mirren. She's the one that did most of the patching up on you once that truck finished rolling over you. Doctor." He nodded and headed to the door, squeezing past the young medic as she walked in.

In the doorway, Conroy turned back to Helen.

"Give it some thought, but don't worry about getting a job tomorrow. Even though you're not exactly Benson's favorite person at the moment, before I resigned I used my power of attorney to make sure he paid you the original agreed amount, in full. So you're set for quite a while until you get your bearings."

"I may just take a long vacation. The Bahamas, maybe."

Conroy grinned, nodded, and left the room.

Helen leaned back in bed, allowing the doctor to fuss over her, and contemplated the future.

Briefly, she thought of Jack Hollis, her old partner who had given his all two years ago to stop a rampaging cop killer. She wondered what Hollis would think of her current situation, let alone everything that had gone down since the afternoon she'd held him in death.

What would his advice be for her future?

She didn't know. And while sliding back under finally realized that it didn't matter what Jack, or anyone, had to say.

Her future, her very life, was up to her and her alone.

"You look kind of happy for someone who was in such a bad accident," Dr. Mirren said at her side.

"Not happy," Helen mumbled, though she wasn't sure if the doc could even hear her. "Not yet.

"But getting there."

A word about the author...

A high-school teacher, former college instructor and fiction writer, Kevin R. Doyle is the author of numerous short stories, mainly in the horror field. He's also written three crime thrillers, *The Group*, *When You Have to Go There*, and *And the Devil Walks Away* and one horror novel, *The Litter*. Recently, he's begun working on the Sam Quinton private eye series. The first Quinton book, *Squatter's Rights*, was nominated for the 2021 Shamus award as Best First PI Novel. The second book, *Heel Turn*, was released in March of 2021. More information can be found at kevindoylefiction.com.

Thank you for purchasing
this publication of The Wild Rose Press, Inc.

For questions or more information
contact us at
info@thewildrosepress.com.

The Wild Rose Press, Inc.
www.thewildrosepress.com